CURSES & CURES

THE DEANA-DHE DUET
BOOK 2

BEA PAIGE

CURSES and CURES

BEA PAIGE

FOREWORD

IMPORTANT AUTHOR NOTE

Dear Reader,

Thank you for continuing on this journey with Cyn and the Deana-dhe. Book two of their duet is darker than the first but in a different way. At the end of *Debts & Diamonds*, Cyn was taken by the Skull Brotherhood and as such will witness and experience some things that may be triggering to readers.

Please visit the Deana-dhe series page on my website: www.beapaige.co.uk for a full list of those triggers (listed under the blurb for the book). Please also note that ***none*** of the terrible experiences Cyn goes through are between Cyn and the Deana-dhe. Ultimately, this is a story of trauma, and the healing strength of love that she finds with these three men.

Please also note that the name of the main protagonist (and the leader of the Skull Brotherhood) has been changed after I became aware that I'd unknowingly used a name that is problematic and may cause harm or distress. This wasn't something a reader made me aware of, but something I realised that could be offensive after publishing book one. I acted immediately to change it.

If you want to update your version of book one, you can do that on your Amazon account by going to your account settings and hit the 'updated version' for Debts & Diamonds.

Much love,

Bea Paige

CONTENT NOTICE

As an author I think that it's only right to warn you about some of the content within this book that you may find triggering. *Curses & Cures* has dark themes, some that are harrowing.

I urge you therefore to visit the Deana-dhe series page on my website: www.beapaige.co.uk for a full list of those triggers (listed under the blurb for the book).

Please also note that *none* of the terrible experiences Cyn goes through are between Cyn and the Deana-dhe. Ultimately, this is a story of trauma, and the healing strength of love that she finds with these three men.

BOOK PLAYLIST

You can find *Curses & Cures* on my Bea Paige Spotify playlist. I have a couple of favourite tracks. The first is *You Put A Spell On Me* by TikTok sensation Austin Giorgio and *Fields of Gold* by Sting.

Enjoy!

PART I

CURSES

"You give me fever. Drive me insane.
You keep me going in circles with potions and battles, and I can't
escape..."
You Put A Spell On Me - Austin Giorgio

PROLOGUE

C^{yn}

I lied.

Or perhaps it was just an omission of truth.

Either way by now Arden, Lorcan and Carrick would have uncovered my secret and I have to hope that they care about me enough not to punish me for it. But more importantly, not punish the people I love.

My friends, The Masks, have been enemies with the Deana-dhe their whole lives, pitted against each other by the decisions their fathers made.

Malik Brov, who ruled over The Masks with an iron fist, was a cruel and soulless man who sought out and murdered nearly the entire Dálaigh bloodline, including Arden's father, Michael. Years after I left Silver Oaks Institute, I found out that Malik was also responsible for the murder of Nessa Dálaigh, my mother's best friend and Arden's aunt, fuelling the hatred between both families for decades. My own father, Niall O'Farrell, deliberately pitted me against the Deana-dhe by siding with Malik Brov.

Their actions drew a line in the sand between the two families and made me and the Deana-dhe enemies before we'd even met.

No matter how I look at it, my father was just as responsible for Michael's death as Malik Brov was. Just like he was responsible for stoking the flames of hatred between his family and my mother's. His decision to steal my mother and force her to marry him, eventually cost her her life. He may not have pulled the trigger, but he set in motion every single event that led to the moment of her death.

My heart had known this truth all along.

Deep down I've *always* known, even when I'd convinced myself otherwise.

Nevertheless, I sought the help from the Deana-dhe who'd given me the name of the man who actually pulled the trigger, allowing them to later call in a debt. A path that Nessa Dálaigh believed would finally bring peace to all the warring families.

The hatred, the pain, and the endless years of bloodshed have haunted us all like an oppressive fog, binding us together in a bloody cycle of murder and revenge. Families have been shattered, loved ones brutally taken, and deep-seeded resentments remain festering like an open wound.

It's time for it to end.
It's time for us all to heal.
It's time for us to find peace.
Maybe even love.
Or die trying...

1

Arden

Cool air rushes over my skin as I step out of the car, carrying with it the pollution of the city, stinging my eyes and throat as I stride towards Grim's club, Tales. I hate city life. The grime, the smell, the litter, the noise, the fucking people.

Speaking of which.

The steel door creaks open and Beast stands in the doorway, a statement more than a question on his lips. "You're late."

"Traffic," Lorcan replies, stepping around the car and standing next to me.

Lorcan's jaw is tight, his eyes are guarded and alert, and his body is a coiled spring ready to act at the slightest provocation. Despite relaxing his features and forcing his shoulders to drop, he doesn't fool me. He's a master at masking the tension in his face with an expression of utter neutrality but I know better, he's on edge.

We all are.

Nethertheless, we need to live up to our reputation, we need to be the Deana-dhe in this moment even if this man is not our enemy, even if we've come here for help.

"Grim doesn't like to be kept waiting," Beast continues, flicking his gaze between us as he steps to one side and motions for us to enter the club. The guy's so fucking huge there's barely enough room to pass by him. "You appreciate that she hates tardiness, right?"

Despite the lightness to his tone, there's an undercurrent of warning that doesn't go unnoticed.

"And you appreciate that we're not fucking kids who need to be reminded about our manners. There was traffic. We're here now," Carrick retorts, cutting him off.

Beast's nostrils flare, but he lets Carrick's comment go. He knows when to pick a fight, and now isn't that time.

"Let's get to it then," he replies, motioning for us to follow him.

Stepping inside, we enter the antechamber, a locked wire cage enclosed by thick, black, floor to ceiling curtains that obscure our view into the warehouse. Used to disarm criminals of their weapons, the antechamber serves as a holding place to assess potential threats before anyone can enter the club. A camera is fixed in the corner of the room, a tiny red light flashing as our entrance is recorded.

"You know the deal. Weapons are left at the door," Beast reminds us as he folds his arms across his chest, waiting.

"Then I guess I'd better stay here then," Carrick smirks, the vicious scar on his face from the Skull Brotherhood's attack distorting his features into an ugly mask. The wound still hasn't healed properly, the damaged skin around the clumsy stitches Lorcan sewed are puckered and reddened. Not that he cares, Carrick doesn't give a fuck about his looks. Never has.

"Funny," Beast says, raising a brow. "Now put your weapons on the desk. You'll get them back on the way out."

Carrick takes a threatening step towards Beast. "Look–"

"We didn't bring any weapons," I interrupt, sensing Carrick's patience waning. He's never had much of it to begin with, and now that the woman we love is in the hands of the Skull Brotherhood, he has very little left. "We don't need them."

Carrick grinds his teeth, and the look I give him is a warning not to fuck this up. We don't need to start a war here today over Beast's need to keep the woman he loves safe. I understand his insistence even if I don't like it.

"Then you won't mind me checking?" he asks, stepping towards me first.

"Go ahead."

Widening my stance and lifting my arms up, I allow Beast to pat me down. When he's satisfied that I'm not carrying any weapons, he does the same to Lorcan and then Carrick.

"I appreciate your patience. We have rules for a reason,"

Beast says, as he casts his gaze to the camera fixed in the corner of the cage, giving one sharp nod.

Behind him, the door clicks open. Beast reaches for it, tugging it towards him, but before he allows us entry, he says, "Tensions are high, I get it, but remember we're here to help. We're not your enemies. So save your anger for the people who truly deserve it."

"Yourself and Grim might not be our enemies, but The Masks..." Lorcan's voice trails off as I give him a sharp look.

"Are here to help you get Cynthia back," a sweet, female voice says, finishing his sentence.

My head snaps around as I stare at my cousin, the beautiful flame-haired woman who tamed The Masks and befriended Cyn during their stay at Ardelby Castle. The last time I saw her was six months ago in the courtyard of The Masks home when I thought she'd ended their lives.

But just like Cyn, she'd conspired against us to protect The Masks.

It was all a fucking ruse.

"Christy."

"Arden," she replies, a note of warning in her voice as she looks from me then to Lorcan and Carrick. "There will be no violence here today. Only the truth."

"No violence, only the truth," I repeat with a tight nod, internally battling the betrayal I feel despite admiring her strength and loyalty towards the people she loves. It takes courage to stand up against the Deana-dhe, to do what she did in the name of love. I respect that, but I sure fucking hope it was worth it. For all our sakes.

She lets out a controlled breath, then glances at Beast and gives him a gentle smile. "You can let the monsters out of the cage now," she says, a playfulness to her tone that irks me.

"I thought that was your forte?" Lorcan quips, equally light in tone despite the tempered rage in his eyes.

To her credit, Christy doesn't rise to the bait. She simply turns on her heel and walks deeper into the warehouse.

We follow.

"Take a seat," Christy says, pointing to the table situated nearest to the bar, at the head of which Grim sits.

She's relaxed despite the tension permeating the room; Grim is the kind of person who commands respect with her presence. As the owner of Tales fight club, and Christy's older half-sister, Grim is well known in criminal circles. We've crossed paths on numerous occasions over the years. The last time we saw each other was the same night we called in Cyn's debt, and Grim rescued her sister from The Masks.

Or so she had thought.

But just like us, Grim had been lied to. I wonder how she reacted when she found out her sister was fucking the very men who kidnapped her? Not well, I imagine. In fact I'm shocked that she even let them live.

"Gentlemen," Grim says, pointing to the row of seats to her left, the silver chain at her neck glinting in the overhead light. She wears a black leather jacket with studs at the collar, finger-less gloves on her hands and her long brown hair pulled back off her face in a high ponytail. She's a beautiful woman, and deadly.

"Where are they?" Lorcan asks tightly, dragging out a chair and sitting down like the rest of us.

"They're here. I wanted a word first," she replies, resting her hand over Beasts when he stands behind her and squeezes her shoulder.

"Then speak, because time isn't on our side," Carrick orders.

Beast's jaw grits, his fingers tightening on Grim's shoulder at Carrick's demand. She simply pats his hand then leans forward in her seat whilst he glares daggers at us all from behind her.

"You and I both know that this meeting will be tense. I understand your anger better than anyone," she says, glancing at Christy who's quietly watching us all. "The Masks took my sister from me after all. But for better or worse, Jakub, Leon and Konrad are the men Christy loves. They're her family, and in turn that makes them mine too. I protect my family at all costs. Understand?"

Her eyes flick upwards to the three men standing on the walkway high above us, their sniper rifles fixed on our heads. Deathly silence hangs in the air, each of them ready to end our lives with a single shot.

Lorcan leans back in his seat, and nods. "Yes, we understand completely."

The edge to his voice is more a message to me than to anyone else. He thinks I've made the wrong move coming here, trusting these people, and seeking The Masks' help. But he doesn't know what I know. He hasn't seen the sketch I drew the night he sewed up Carrick's face and I left them asleep in his bed, exhausted from the events of that night.

We *will* fail without them.

There is only one way to get Cyn back alive, and that's teaming up with The Masks.

"Despite our history, we're not here to fight," I say, casting a determined look at Carrick and Lorcan who simply clench their jaws and nod.

"Good," Beast interjects, "Because we can't have your blood ruining the furniture. The last time I blew a man's brains out it took the clean-up crew weeks to get this place sparkling. Malik Brov was a dirty bastard in death as much as he was in life. We kept finding little pieces of him for weeks after." He hesitates, then pulls a face. "Come to think of it, we should look into getting a better clean-up crew. Got any suggestions?"

No one answers, but Beast's levity serves as a reminder that it was Grim who gave the command to end our enemy's life. We owe them respect for that, at least.

"You are *not* our enemies," Grim reiterates. "But The Masks are our family now, and Christy is my blood. One wrong move and this is over." It's a final warning to remind us she means business.

I don't doubt her threat.

"They won't go back on their word," Christy says softly, her gaze fixed on mine knowingly.

There's a tug in my chest, the familiar pull of the Dálaighs' gift tightening between us as she stares at me. She isn't just saying that in the hope it will come true, she already knows.

She's *seen* it.

"I have some understanding of The Masks' and Christy's story thanks to Cyn," I explain, recalling Cyn's neat words written across the pages of her recipe book, "And therefore I appreciate what's at stake here, for them as much as us."

"How so?" Christy asks, her curiosity piqued.

"From her recipe book," Lorcan explains. "She detailed your love story within it."

"Really?" She frowns, her gaze slipping from Lorcan's and meeting mine.

"Yes. She documented everything that happened during her stay at Ardelby Castle."

"So then you know about the letters from my mother?"

"I do. I also know that Cyn lied to us to protect your love. I know that she believes that bringing us together now will heal the rifts between the Dálaighs and the Brovs once and for all. I also know that she put herself in danger on the whim of a dead woman."

"My mother, you mean. *Your* aunt," Christy points out. "And it's not a whim. You know that better than anyone."

"I know that Nessa's visions were spot-on, given the truths recounted in Cyn's recipe book. But I also know that won't stop the Skull Brotherhood from hurting her at any and every opportunity. She might be valuable to them, but they treat women no better than animals, and if Nessa knew that and sent Cyn into the fray anyway, then I have no respect for a dead woman, family or not."

Christy glances away briefly as she speaks, her voice wavering and desperate. "Cyn is stronger than you think," she says, her eyes now drilling into mine as she clings onto her conviction.

"We know how strong she is," Carrick grinds out, leaning

forward in his seat. "But Arden's right, Soren will take every opportunity to beat her down, and the second she's no longer useful to him, he'll kill her... Or worse."

"Then rest assured she'll make sure that she remains useful to him until we annihilate them all," a lightly accented, deep male voice says.

Jakub Brov.

My spine stiffens and I force myself to turn my head, eyeing my enemy as he walks out of the shadows with Konrad and Leon on his heels, the expensive tailoring of their suits only outdone by their air of confidence. I'd admire them for it if I didn't fucking despise them.

Beside me Carrick takes a deep breath as if to calm himself, but his fists are clenched and his teeth are gritted tight in anger. He stares at the table for a moment, and I can feel his frustration and uncertainty oozing out of him.

"Carrick," I warn.

But my warning only acts as a trigger for his anger and with a sudden burst of rage, he slams his fist against the table and shouts, "You motherfuckers!"

His words echo throughout the warehouse, and Grim holds her hand up. Within milliseconds a bright red spot dances across Carrick's upper arm then face, the laser sight marking his death with one quick pull of a trigger. Lorcan reaches for him, clamping a hand on his forearm.

"Easy, brother," he says, flicking a look at Grim.

Carrick swallows hard, his own gaze falling to the spot of red light now resting on the table right in front of him. He might be the hothead of the three of us, but he's never shown such outright emotion like this in front of strangers. This is not how we act, and I know it's because he blames himself for Cyn's abduction. He beats himself up daily because he wasn't able to fight them off.

I get it.

I know anger can be a powerful motivator, but sometimes it can overwhelm us and cloud our judgement, but if we're going to get Cyn back then he needs to stay focused and we *must* become united however difficult that may be.

"You can and will do this. We are *not* your enemies," Grim reminds him. "If you want to get Cynthia back, then this is the only way."

"Fuck, fight it out in the ring if you want," Beast bellows, throwing his hands in the air as The Masks take their seats next to Christy, each of them giving her a reassuring touch which she returns with a gentle smile. "Go ahead and waste your time beating each other to a pulp whilst your missus fends off those ugly numbskulls by herself."

"Or put your animosity to one side and *together* take the Skull Brotherhood down," Christy pleads, grasping Jakub's proffered hand and folding her fingers tightly around his.

My eyes settle on their clasped hands, and my skin prickles with decades of animosity. It's as difficult as I thought it would be to be in the same room as a Brov, and I desperately want to

launch myself across the table, bury my nails in his throat and rip it the fuck out.

I hold back, lifting my gaze to meet his instead.

"Your fear is warranted. Soren and the Skull Brotherhood

are ruthless, bloodthirsty murderers," Jakub says evenly, as if I didn't already fucking know. "I understand how you feel."

"You've no fucking idea how we feel," Carrick snarls, a muscle in his jaw jumping as he shifts his attention from Jakub to Leon, who's sitting opposite him.

Rumour has it that Leon's the most dangerous of the three, and I don't doubt that for a second, but Carrick has never lost a fight yet. There's a fearlessness within him, a feral darkness that has never been bested. Maybe Beast's suggestion of a fight in the ring is a good one. I'd like to watch that, but not today.

"Cynthia's our friend and we owe her more than we could ever repay. We want what you want; she needs to be freed from their grasp." Konrad reiterates, turning to Jakub, who nods in agreement.

"And yet you let her step onto this path, leading her straight to the Skull Brotherhood. You *used* her to get more time with Christy knowing it would end up this way," Lorcan accuses.

"No," Leon says, shaking his head. "We didn't know anything about the Skull Brotherhood until you called us. You are responsible for her abduction, you and you alone."

"You what?!" Carrick snaps, guilt and rage forming a twisted expression on his face.

"Except that isn't entirely true, is it Christy?" I ask, focussing back on my cousin.

"You saw something?" Jakub asks her, twisting in his seat to read her expression.

"Not exactly," she replies, heaving out a sigh. "Though I wish I did."

A strand of hair falls across her face and Jakub reaches up

to tuck it back behind her ear. It's a seemingly innocuous act, but it speaks volumes. There's tenderness behind his touch, care. It throws me a little.

"Then what?" he asks her.

Christy glances up at me, and I see the indecision on her face. Eventually she says, "My mother sent Cyn several letters."

"We've already established that," I reply, shifting in my seat as my skin prickles with dread.

"Then you'll also know that my mother saw my future mapped out, and sought the help of Cyn to ensure that The Masks and I were delivered those letters at just the right time, to guide us on the right path towards each other."

"Yes," Lorcan cuts in sharply. "What's your point?"

"My point is that there was one other letter, or rather a portion of a letter from my mother that directly pertained to her relationship with you three."

"Well, what did it say?" Carrick demands.

"I don't know. Cynthia refused to share the details with me," Christy replies with a heavy sigh. "I was hoping perhaps she wrote it down?"

I shake my head. "No."

"Why would she keep that part from us?" Lorcan asks no one in particular. "Why write everything down for us to find, but leave that part out?"

Christy chews on her lip, concern creasing her eyes. "All I know is that she entered into this knowing the risks. She stepped onto the path my mother guided her to with her eyes wide open. She did it out of love. Love for us, her friends, and love for you three, the ones that I believe, deep down, she always knew were her soulmates."

"She said that to you?" I ask, my fucking heart thundering.

"She didn't have to. We both know it's true."

An oppressive silence blankets us as I struggle to absorb the gravity of her words, the air electrified with tension and blame. We could point the finger at each other for Cyn's abduction, but even if we did, it wouldn't change a thing. All we're doing is wasting precious time.

"Well I'm glad we got that cleared up," Beast interjects with a grin, scattering the tension like a bowling ball through Skittles. "Now, who we got to fuck-up to find out where those cunts are hiding?"

"I know exactly where to start," I say, Jakub's piercing gaze falling upon me.

He locks eyes with me. "I'm listening."

And just like that years of animosity between us is put to one side in order to unite for a common purpose: rescuing Cyn.

2

Cyn

I've been imprisoned for just over a week now, spending my days making diamonds for Soren, and my nights pacing the length of the small cell I've been locked in, tracing my finger along the edges of the heavy iron bars that cover the windows.

Another prison.

It seems I've spent my life living in one.

Despite my faith in Arden, Lorcan and Carrick, dread grows like a weed with every passing day, suffocating my hope that they'll find their way to me. Every night, when the sun drops past the horizon of this strange landscape, filled with miles and miles of rolling dunes and sparse vegetation, time seems to come to a standstill.

Tonight, as I stare out of the window with sweat from the heat of the day drying on my bruised skin, the winds stir the dunes in a lazy waltz, wild and free, dancing among the grains of sand in a chaotic rhythm without beginning or end.

Longing beats in my chest as the darkness of night swallows up any light, hoping that the men I love haven't murdered each other in their pursuit of revenge, that they're working together to rescue me, and ultimately save themselves.

With a heavy sigh, I pull out the letter I've kept sewn into the lining of my skirt. Its pages are yellowed with age, and the corners creased from where I've repeatedly folded it. I turn it over, the faint scent of lavender lifting into the air as I hold it up, barely able to make out the neat cursive.

Dear Cynthia,

I don't have much time to explain why you are so very important to me and my daughter, Christy, but I hope that this letter will be enough to convince you to help us both.. To help all our families to heal, including yours...

The words waver in front of me, and I blink back the grogginess from the blow of Soren's fist to my temple earlier today. The bastard has no issues beating women. He does it regularly for kicks, and I'm not the only one he abuses given the state of the blonde woman he keeps by his side at all times. Covered head to foot in bruises, she has met the wrath of Soren on many occasions.

As the leader of the Skull Brotherhood, Soren leads by example. To him, women are nothing more than worthless vessels to use and abuse as he sees fit. They're just a fleshy punching bag, an orifice to suit their base needs.

Worthless bitches.

Unless you have a skill he can profit from.

Then perhaps you're worth stealing, worth starting a war for.

And that's exactly what they've done by stealing me right under the Deana-dhe's noses just like Arden's aunt, Nessa Dálaigh, had predicted.

Casting my gaze to the swirling cursive, I once again read the letter my mother's best friend wrote to me long before I was even aware of her existence. A letter I was given just a few short weeks before I went to live with The Masks and many years after she was murdered.

Your mother and I grew up together. We were the best of friends and I loved her like a sister, but circumstance and hatred between men tore us apart.

When I heard of Aoife's death, we hadn't seen each other in years, not because we didn't want to but because we had no choice. It hadn't surprised me that she died protecting you in a war she couldn't prevent. Her love for you was like the ocean, vast and deep.

She was the most beautiful soul, and I miss her every single day..

"Me too," I choke out, my throat tightening at the thought of my mother.

Tears blur my vision, each drop stinging as they fall down my cheeks, a reminder of all I have lost. I blink back my sorrow in a desperate attempt to keep my tears at bay. Swallowing down the emotion, I continue to read.

I wish, more than anything, that I could've been present in your life. That you and Christy could've grown up together and become friends just like your mother and I had. Alas, it wasn't meant to be, but I hope, more than anything, that you will form a lasting friendship after all of this is over. I hope that old wounds between families can finally heal and that you won't be kept apart like your mother and I were.

In this envelope you will find two letters. The first is for Christy. The second is for the men who call themselves The Masks, your old friends and my daughter's kidnappers.

I'm asking you to give the letter to my daughter exactly two weeks after she arrives at Ardelby Castle. The second letter you must give to The Masks on the night of the show when Christy wears the pink dress...

And that's exactly what I did. I followed Nessa's instructions, handing the letters to Christy and The Masks at the very moment she asked me to. I watched their story unfold, guided by the love of a mother for her daughter.

These letters have been kept safe for fifteen years by your grandmother who, like me and Aoife, was tired of seeing the people she cared about hurt by foolish men. She gave them to you on this night for the same reason I am writing this letter, to stop more bloodshed. She was a good woman, and I'm so terribly sorry for your loss...

As I hold Nessa's letter in my hands, I'm flooded with memories of my grandmother. She'd always been a great source of comfort and knowledge, continuing to teach me the craft of herbology after my mother's murder. Her death, almost two years ago now, had been as difficult to bear as my mother's had been. It still is.

You must be confused, so I hope this letter will go some way to explaining things. By now Arden Dálaigh, my nephew, will have asked you to pay your debt. I know this because I've seen it. Like my daughter I have the ability to see things that are yet to happen.

The Deana-dhe want revenge for my brother's death. They want you to kill The Masks.

You can't do that.

Not just because you are a good person and cannot, under any circumstances, darken your soul with murder. Not just because these men and my daughter's future are inexplicably entwined. But because I'm trying to prevent history from repeating itself.

There's been too many deaths, too much heartache, and if I can do one thing before I leave this world, it's to fix this mess our fathers and their fathers before them have inflicted on us all. Your parents' families have been at war for years, as have my family: the Dálaighs and the Brovs. Men have caused these wars, all of this pain, and it's time for the women to take back control and end the violence once and for all. It's what your mother wanted, what I wanted, but fate conspired against us. Your mother died trying to stop a war, and in a few years, I will die in the crossfire of another.

It wasn't our time to fix it, but it will be yours. Yours and Christy's.

This time the stars have aligned better than I could ever have hoped for. There's a chance that peace can be found and lives saved if you help my daughter to fulfil her destiny, and trust me to help you to fulfil yours.

Tonight you must leave your home and revisit your old friends. Go to Ardelby Castle and find your place there. Tell them whatever you need to in order for them to allow you to stay.

You must wait until my daughter arrives and help her to fulfil her destiny. Guide her as best you can without telling her what you know. Not until the time is right. You'll know when the time comes for honesty. Whether I like it or not, she was meant for The Masks as they were meant for her. The Dálaigh's and the Brov's war will end with their love, it has to, otherwise all of this will be for nothing...

At the time I'd read her letter with incredulity, and if it hadn't been my grandmother's dying wish to follow the path Nessa had encouraged me to step on, I may never have ended up here. But my grandmother's faith in a woman long since dead, and her unwavering love for my mother, persuaded me to go to Ardelby Castle and await Christy's arrival. When everything began to play out just like Nessa had predicted, it was easier to do everything she'd asked.

She will fight against it, and there is a point in Christy's future that I can't see beyond, but I'm hoping that with your help it won't be the end of her journey, just the beginning. That is why you must deliver these letters. It's imperative that you do.

I chew on the inside of my cheek remembering the difficulties Christy went through with The Masks. There had been so many times that I wanted to tell her everything, to confess what I knew. But I had to be a silent witness to their turmoil, hoping and praying it would all be worth it in the end. I'm glad that I got to witness their love blossom, that something beautiful and everlasting came out of something so filled with heartache and pain.

Then there is the not so small matter of the debt you need to repay. Your paths will cross with the Deana-dhe again on the night where everyone wears a mask. On this night, you must help Christy to convince everyone that The Masks are dead.

I have every faith in your abilities to pull this off. You are gifted in the art of alchemy, just like your mother had been before you. You know what you must do.

Give The Masks the chance to prove themselves worthy of my daughter. Love can only blossom when it's given the space to do so.

They need time.

But time is something they do not have. Grim loves Christy, and she will not rest until The Masks are dead. Neither will the Deana-dhe.

So find a way to make this happen.

Do this, and you will help two families finally lay their pasts to rest.

Which leads me to your future...

I spent over a year living with my childhood friends before the Deana-dhe arrived to call-in my debt. By the time they came to claim me, I'd already witnessed The Masks and Christy fall in love. With Nessa's foresight, together Christy and I had fulfilled the first part of her request, fooling everyone into believing she had killed The Masks with poison and allowing them the gift of time just like Nessa had wanted.

These past six months that I've spent with the Deana-dhe gave my friends time to strengthen their bond and it gave me time to forge my own path with Arden, Lorcan and Carrick.

I hope I've done enough.

With trembling fingers, I turn over the page and read the second part of the letter, the part I haven't shared with Christy or the Deana-dhe.

It pains me to say what I must, but if I didn't give you complete honesty it would make me no better than Malik Brov who was selfish as much as he was cruel...

I can't lie to you. I can't share everything that I've seen for Christy and not share this.

So I will tell you all that I know and give you the gift of choice.

I've seen two paths for you, both of which are equally possible.

One path leads to a life of happiness, albeit without the true love of your soulmates. It's a good life Cynthia, and if you choose this path, you will be safe. You can practise your craft and heal many, many people, but the Deana-dhe will die.

The other path leads to danger, pain and trauma at the hands of the men with skulls for faces. Your strength will be tested, and you will lose something precious to you, but the Deana-dhe will live.

You have a choice, Cynthia.

Right now that choice may seem easy. You still hold resentment towards the Deana-dhe, hatred even. But I think we both know that deep down your feelings towards them are far more complicated than that. If you're anything like your mother, I believe that I already know which path you'll choose.

You're a healer, it's in your nature to do good, to sacrifice your own happiness and safety for the people you love, and even for those you don't. However, I'm asking you to think very carefully about this decision.

Are the Deana-dhe truly worth your sacrifice? Are you willing to lose a part of yourself in order for them to live?

If so, you must leave with the Deana-dhe the same night you help Christy convince them of The Masks' deaths. If you don't, if you choose a life of safety and seek protection from Christy's sister, the Deana-dhe will die a few short weeks later, caught in the crossfire of another battle between the O'Briens and the O'Farrells, stirred back to life when Grim takes you back to live with your mother's family.

The choice is ultimately yours.

Choose wisely, dear one.

All my love,

Nessa.

I stare at the letter one last time, tracing my finger along the familiar curves of Nessa's handwriting. For a long time I teetered between what my head was begging me to do and what my heart knew was inevitable.

My heart won out.

Swallowing hard, a wave of sadness washes over me as I rip the letter into tiny pieces, and watch the last remnants of my past fall to the floor in a rain of confetti. Then with a heavy heart, I gather up the pieces and walk to the window. Reaching through a gap in the bars, I open my palm, allowing the cool air of the desert night to take my last secret and scatter it to the wind.

3

C *arrick*

"It's just as well you're rich," Beast comments, leaning back in the cream leather recliner on The Masks' private jet as we fly over France, his long legs stretched out in front of him. "Rescuing women ain't cheap."

"Cynthia's not the type of woman who needs a man to rescue her," Jakub says.

Turning my attention away from the view out of the window, I meet Jakub's gaze wondering what point he's trying to make. We know Cyn's capable of looking after herself. She's resourceful, smart, mentally and emotionally strong. Fuck, do I know that, but this is the Skull Brotherhood we're talking about. No amount of strength, physical, emotional, or otherwise will help her escape. She is valuable to them, and because of that will be kept on a tight leash. Of course she needs us. She fucking needed me to prevent them from taking her in the first place, and I failed her.

I fucking failed her.

Me. Not Arden. Not Lorcan. *But me.*

"So what you're saying is that we're flying to Tarifa in the southernmost point of Spain to meet this Vasko fella who may or may not have information on Cyn's whereabouts, but you don't think she actually needs our help?" Beast interjects with a boatload of sarcasm.

"No, of course that's not what I meant," Jakub retorts, cutting a look to Beast. "I just meant that Cynthia has experience dealing with cruel men. She'll do whatever it takes to survive until we can get her out of there."

"And your point?" I ask, feeling the tension mounting like a tangible weight.

It's been getting heavier and heavier the longer we've been in each other's company, and in this confined space it's getting harder to ignore. We all know that this truce is a farce, built on nothing but sand. There's no strength to it, no steady foundation. One wrong move, and we're sinking beneath the weight of our pasts and years of mistrust and hate. The only thing keeping all of our heads above the tide is the thought of getting Cyn back.

"What's the matter, Carrick, guilty conscience?" Leon asks, cutting me a knowing look.

Opposite me Lorcan's jaw clenches. He shakes his head,

warning me not to rise to the bait, but it's too late. My anger has been smouldering ever since Cyn was taken from me, and Leon's just poured petrol over the fire.

"You're a useless prick," I grind out through gritted teeth, feeling this feral kind of rage bubbling inside my chest, not because I hate him, but because he's right. I do have a guilty conscience. It's eating away at me like some sick, twisted little demon, gnawing at my bones, feasting on my insides, tearing at my motherfucking heart.

It's *my* fault.

"No more than you, it would seem," he throws back.

"You cunt," I grind out.

"Enough, Leon," Jakub says with a steady calm that irritates me.

He's trying to prevent a fight, but doesn't he fucking get it?

I *need* one.

Shifting forward in my seat, I glare at The Masks, allowing myself to settle into this feeling, letting it envelop me. I enjoy the way it scorches over my skin and muffles intrusive thoughts. Drawing on the anger, I allow it to block out everything else but the need to smash their faces in. It gives me something else to focus on instead of those bastard's taking Cyn.

"Look at the three of you pretending your shit doesn't stink," I spit, relishing the words that fuel the hatred inside of me for them, for myself. "You might not have hurt Cyn, but you abused Christy and The Numbers. So don't act like you're good men. You can't rid yourself of your past or the things you've done."

"Carrick, don't do this," Arden warns me, his hand resting on my thigh. "This isn't your fight."

I let out a bitter laugh, turning on him. "We're brothers. If it's not my fight, whose is it?"

"You know that's not what I meant."

"We should've settled this bullshit the second they walked into Tales."

"Whether you like it or not, whether I like it or not, we need them. *Enough*," Arden replies, his eyes flickering with an emotion I can't quite read. A sense of dread fills my stomach. He's keeping something from us.

"Arden–" I begin, but Beast snorts.

"If you'd started shit at Tales it wouldn't have gone in your favour, mate," Beast points out unhelpfully. I shoot him a glare, and he shrugs. "Just telling you how it is."

"Grim's mercenaries aren't here now. It's just us," I retort, my teeth clenching.

"Don't!" Arden's fingers curl into my thigh. He knows me too well, understands where this is heading, and in my own sense of grief and guilt at having Cyn taken from me, I let my anger bubble dangerously.

"I'd listen to Arden, mate," Beast pipes up, watching our exchange.

I ignore him.

"You forget we're the keepers of secrets, we exchange truths and lies like fucking currency," I spit, turning my attention back to The Masks. "We're millionaires when it comes to you motherfuckers. We know what you are, and we *know* what went down at Ardelby Castle. Cyn detailed *every-*

thing," I continue, relishing the shocked looks on The Masks' faces.

"And *we* know that you tied Cynthia to a tree when you were teenagers," Konrad adds, quiet until now.

I stare at his face, at the scar that cuts across his features that's not so dissimilar to mine and hate that he knows something so personal about Cyn and our past.

"She's our friend," Konrad continues, holding my gaze. "You think she kept something like that a secret from us?"

Truthfully, yes. I did not expect Cyn to have that kind of intimate friendship with The Masks, where she opened up enough to share the things in her past that hurt her the most. It fucking kills me that they had that relationship and we didn't. It pisses me off that we wasted so much time hating on her when we should've embraced her, protected her. *Loved* her.

"You did what?" Beast asks, his nose wrinkling as he cuts the three of us a disgusted look.

"Then you let your peers rip her clothes from her body," Konrad continues, refusing to let this go. "And encouraged them to write names over every inch of her skin just because her father happened to be friends with ours. Perhaps the men we *were* are not so different, huh?"

Beast scowls. "That's fucked-up."

"No more fucked-up than the Masks keeping Christy prisoner. Do you even know what happened to her whilst she was at the castle?" I accuse, unable, or perhaps unwilling, to back down. My own guilt making me turn on Beast. I realise that I'm being a cunt, but I can't seem to stop myself. "What we did to Cyn when we were kids was nothing in comparison to what those arseholes did to Christy as adults. These men Grim calls family are no better than the Skull Brotherhood."

"Then you're all fucking wankers," Beast says, turning his disappointment and anger onto The Masks now. "I know Grim has already laid down the law when it comes to how you treat Christy, but I'm just gonna say this now so that we're all on the same page. You mistreat that beautiful woman ever again and I will strip the skin from your bones and use your innards as a fucking necklace. Got it?"

A muscle in Jakub's jaw flexes. "I would expect nothing less, but you don't need to worry, Christy is everything to us and we would rather flay the skin off our own bodies than hurt her again. She saved us. She made us whole again. We *love* her."

"Good," Beast nods, before focusing his attention back on the three of us. "And you three need to get your shit together, especially you," he says pointedly looking at me. "Cyn sounds like a first-class woman. So here's a piece of advise, when you get her back, don't fuck it up."

"Don't patronise me!" I snap, pushing to my feet and stepping into the aisle.

"Then stop acting like a prick," Beast retorts, rising from his seat too, meeting me toe-to-toe. "You hate The Masks, we get it. They don't much like you three either. Just fucking deal with it."

"You've no business telling me to do a damn thing, *Beast*," I goad, feeling myself lose all sense of control as my nostrils flare and my fists curl.

Fuck this shit. Fuck all of it.

I want to cause some damage, and I don't give a fuck if that means having it out with Beast. I need to fucking vent. I need to rid myself of some of this pain. I need to hurt something.

I. Need. To. Hurt.

Let him beat me for being a cruel, heartless bastard. I *want* to feel his fist slam into my face for refusing to see that she was always ours. I *want* my stitches to split open and run with blood for allowing those cunts to take her from me.

I *need* to be punished.

"Don't tempt me," Beast snaps.

"Carrick. You're done here," Arden warns, his fingers gripping my upper arm as he tries to intervene.

I shake him off, too far gone now.

"Have you forgotten what you owe us?" I ask Beast, my voice low as I remind him that we already have history.

Not too long ago Grim and Beast sought the assistance of the Deana-dhe for their friends the Breakers, and then later to find Christy. As such, they each owe us a debt just like the majority of the criminal underground do. That makes him in our pocket, not the other way around, and he has no business talking to me this way.

"And here's me thinking that was squared away given I'm here helping you, you ungrateful cunt," Beast retorts, his own fury revealing itself.

"You need to watch your fucking mouth!" I shout.

Out of the corner of my eye, I see The Masks get to their feet. I also sense Lorcan moving to my rear, protecting my back just like he's always done. The tension is so thick, I can almost taste the bloodshed on my tongue.

"Or what?" Beast counters. "You'd rather try and kill me and The Masks because you can't handle the fucking truth?"

"No, that is *not* what we want," Arden cuts in, forcefully pushing me back against Lorcan who wraps his arms around my waist and holds me firm against him.

"Let me go, Lorcan!"

"No," he replies, his thick arms like steel bands around my waist.

"Let me go," I pant, ready to turn on my brother just so I can have it out with Beast, so I can feel his wrath and pay for my sins.

"This is not what you need," Lorcan whispers against my ear. "Think of Cyn, goddamn it."

The mention of her name is a trigger, the memory of those bastards taking her from me is the bullet that rips open my fucking chest, leaving a gaping hole.

"FUCK THIS!" I roar, struggling in his arms, all sense of reason leaving me.

"Carrick stop!" he pleads, holding me tighter, refusing to let go.

"Let me go, Lorcan!"

"Shh, Carrick. It's okay. It's okay," he whispers against my ear, holding me firm as I fight to get out of his arms. We almost stumble sideways into the seats, but Lorcan keeps us both upright. Keeping me steady when all I want is to be unstable.

"It's not fucking okay! They've got her Lorcan. They've got Cyn!"

"I know, Carrick. I know," he breathes against my cheek.

The scratch of his stubble coarse against my skin, rubbing against my still tender scar. "But we *will* get her back."

"They'll break her. They'll fucking break her before we do!" I cry, the sharp sting of anguish gutting me. I know she's strong. I know she is. But those men. They're sadistic bastards. They'll hurt her and fucking *mean* it.

"No," Jakub says. "They won't."

"You don't fucking know that!" I counter, my heart slamming against my ribcage.

My motherfucking heart hurts. IT HURTS.

I want to rage at the world.

I want to claw at my skin.

I want to rip open my ribcage, pull my beating heart from my chest and crush it in my hands.

I want to go back to that night when those bastards took her from me and kill them all.

I want to kill them all.

But more than that, I want Cyn.

I want her gentle touch and her beautiful smile. I want her angry tongue and her stinging bite. I want her words of wisdom and sharp wit. I want her pretty pussy and her sexy mouth.

I want her sweet, sweet voice.

I want her.

"I WANT CYN!" I shout, fucking pain like nothing I've felt before buckling my knees. The weight of my guilt a fucking mountain on my shoulders. It crushes me, makes me weak.

Lorcan hauls me upright. "Arden!" he urges, the fear in his voice palpable.

"You need to sort him out. Get his head straight," Beast

grumbles, shock and pity in his eyes. I know what he's thinking. This isn't how the Deana-dhe act. This isn't who we are, but I can't seem to stop. I'm not a legend at this moment. I'm not untouchable or fearless. I'm not a god.

I'm just a man who's torn apart by guilt.

I'm a man who *needs* to hurt in order to survive the pain.

"Just let me go!" I snarl, rabid now, rage spiking my blood with adrenaline as I feed off of it.

Lorcan yanks me backwards away from them all, half carrying me, half dragging me to the rear of the plane.

"He needs to get his shit together. He's no good to us, *to Cynthia*, like that," Beast adds, snaking a hand through his hair.

"FUUUUUUCK!" I yell, wanting to crawl out of my skin, knowing he's right.

I'm no good for her.

And that only makes everything worse.

I want to hurt and maim. I want to draw blood. I want to tear everyone and everything apart, including myself.

I can't take this anymore.

It's my fault.

It's *my* fault.

My breaths are ragged, my guilt a noose around my neck as memories of that night assault me.

"It's my fucking fault she's gone. Leon's right. I'm a fucking useless prick. I didn't fucking save her from them," I choke out, reliving that night when they took her. It comes back full force, knocking the wind out of me, and the rage is replaced with despair and self-hatred.

"You couldn't have fought them off on your own," Lorcan says, easing his hold a little.

"I can't stop picturing the fear in her eyes. She was supposed to be safe with me! She was supposed to be safe!"

"There were too many," Arden adds, approaching us both. "This isn't on you."

"They punched her in the face," I continue, unable to stop myself now that I've started. Like a bottle of uncorked champagne the words froth and fizz, tumbling from my lips in angry little bursts. "They dragged her from the room by her fucking hair, but not before they groped at her breasts and punched her in the face. They fucking abused her right in front of me and I couldn't do a fucking thing about it!"

"Fuck," Beast mutters, the sympathy in his voice like a pair of scissors to the frayed threads of my emotion.

"I can't stop hearing her screams for me to help!" I yell, banging my fist against my chest, wanting to hurt. Needing to hurt. "I fought for her so hard but it wasn't enough. I wasn't enough!"

"Carrick, please stop torturing yourself," Lorcan says, pressing his lips against my cheek, nuzzling his nose in my hair, trying to comfort me. But I don't want his kindness, or his empathy. I don't want to feel loved.

I want *pain.*

"I need to hurt something," I say, choking on the words, breaking apart as memories of that night flay me. "I *need* to hurt."

Arden meets Lorcan's eyes, a silent conversation passing

between them before he looks over his shoulder towards Jakub. "Is that a private room back there?" he asks, pointing behind us.

"Yes," Jakub confirms with a sharp nod of his head.

"We're going to use it," he states. "And you will leave us in peace until we land, no matter what you hear. Is that understood?"

"Of course," Jakub agrees without argument. "Do what you need to do."

There's an empathetic tone to his voice that sets my teeth on edge. I don't want his sympathy.

I don't fucking want it. Not from him. Not from anyone.

Arden turns his attention to Beast next. "The debt you and Grim owe is squashed. We appreciate your help. Now if you'll excuse us."

Beast blows out a sharp breath before meeting my gaze. "I understand what you're feeling, mate. I get it. No hard feelings, okay?"

I don't reply. I can't.

4

C^{yn}

The early morning sun filters through the gaps in the iron bars of my cell, heating the walls enough to bake off the last remnants of chill from the drop in temperature overnight.

Unfurling my stiff body from a night of restless sleep, my aching joints creak in protest as I roll my shoulders and stretch to the ceiling, basking in the warm sunlight that spills through the window. My body responds with achingly sluggish movements, but eventually I ease out all the kinks, preparing my mind and body for another long day making diamonds under the watchful eye of Soren's soldiers.

The only time I'm free from their shadow is at night when

I'm locked away for seven hours with nothing but a meal of plain couscous and a few pieces of meat, if I'm lucky. It's my one meal of the day, and I eat every morsel knowing that I'll need every scrap of energy to survive my time here. They ration water throughout the day, and I feel constantly thirsty, only giving me enough water not to be dangerously dehydrated but never enough to fully quench my thirst. Licking my dry lips, I long for the cool, salty air of the Deana-dhe's island. If I close my eyes, I can almost feel the ocean breeze on my face, smell the stormy sea as it batters against the rugged shoreline. I can even feel their lips against my bare skin, their touch a different bruising than that inflicted by Soren's hand.

"Where are you?" I whisper, pressing my fingers to my lips, remembering how they'd kissed me,

how they'd pressed needy fingers against my flesh and desperate tongues against my skin. I'd come, not under the influence of diamonds, but by their skilled hands.

I knew then that I was wholly and completely theirs.

The sound of footsteps echoing down the tiled hallway outside my cell jolts me back to reality, and I scramble to the corner of the room, knowing that I should empty my bladder now or risk having to do so in front of one of Soren's men.

Striding over to the bucket, which hasn't been emptied since I arrived here, my stomach churns at the scent. Being forced to eat and defecate in the same room is a degrading experience that I refuse to think too deeply about.

I sigh and resign myself to using it once again. Gathering up my skirt, I push my knickers past my knees, and use the wall to balance, emptying what little I have in my bladder, pulling up my knickers just before a key slides into the lock. The fact that I've nothing to wipe myself with is another intrusive thought I push to one side. Poor personal hygiene is the least of my worries right now.

"You will survive this," I murmur to myself, a mantra I repeat every time I feel despair creep in.

Blowing out a shaky breath, I step into the centre of the room and wait for the guard to step inside my cell.

It's Half-skull, a nickname I've given the guard who accompanies me everywhere around the complex. Not a very imaginative name, but apt given he has half of his face tattooed with a skull. I might not know his real name, but I've paid enough attention to understand that the less your face is tattooed the lower the ranking you have within the Skull Brotherhood. Half-skull is higher in ranking than many other Skulls I've seen.

"Soren wants to speak with you," Half-skull says, his lip furling up at the stench of shit and piss, his emotionless gaze meeting mine.

I nod, following him out into the hallway. Since arriving here, I've barely spoken a word, not because I've reverted to the mental space that stole my voice as a child, but because I don't want to share my voice with men who don't deserve it.

The less I say, the stronger I feel.

We walk past the other cells, the air corded with the scent of sweat and fear. The bowels of this complex are where the women the Skulls abuse regularly are kept prisoner. Most nights I hear muffled crying from the neighbouring cells, and I wish more than anything that I had access to my herbs and flowers so that I could help ease their physical and emotional pain. But I don't, and all I can do is hope that they can survive until we're all set free.

"You'll be dealing with an issue Soren has this morning instead of your usual job," Half-skull says as we take a right at the end of the hallway and climb up a set of stone steps to the ground floor of the complex.

I dip my head in acknowledgement only because if I don't at least do that, he'll have no reservations about hitting me until I respond, and I'd rather start the day without another swollen eye-socket to contend with.

Like every morning, we pass through the now familiar building towards the east wing. I'm not versed in architectural structures, but the building has a Moroccan vibe with horse-shoe arches, coloured mosaic tiles and carved stucco across the walls and ceilings. In another life, under different circumstances, I'd find the building beautiful.

From the little I can gather from overheard conversations and my own vague knowledge, I am somewhere in the Sahara Desert, miles from the nearest town. It's the perfect location to avoid any sort of authority, and allows for many nefarious activities to take place without fear of being caught, or at least have enough warning to prepare for an ambush.

Which is great for the Skull Brotherhood, and terrible for me.

My throat tightens, knowing that even if the Deana-dhe find out where the Skull Brotherhood are keeping me, they'll have no way to approach the complex without being seen.

"Hey, witch, want to sit on my broom?" a gravelly voice shouts as we pass by the courtyard that's central to the building and appears to act as a thoroughfare for the members of the brotherhood to access other parts of the complex.

Half-skull chuckles, greeting his inferior Quarter-skull with a smirk that would look handsome if his eyes weren't utterly soulless.

"You know she's off limits," Half-Skull says, tossing a look over his shoulder at me, a hungry look in his eyes that makes me want to wrap my arms around myself and cower from his attention.

I don't do that, of course.

Instead, I stare him down, refusing to let either man see how much they intimidate me. Growing up with The Masks as friends, the Deana-dhe as my childhood enemies, and my father as a tyrant, has helped toughen me up. Weakness isn't an option. Fear is better left to the early hours of the morning where despair lives.

"We'll see how long that lasts," Half-skull says, licking his lips as he studies me. "Soren is tired of his current bitch. I'm pretty sure you'll be next on his list to break."

I grit my teeth. *Over my dead body.*

"Careful now, witch, a look like that can get you stripped and served as a delicious meal for the entire Brotherhood to share on celebration night," Quarter-skull adds, stepping closer and running his calloused fingers over my cheek to intimidate me. "Insolence turns us on. There's nothing more entertaining than breaking a woman. Keep this up and see what happens."

I force myself to meet his gaze, allowing every ounce of disgust to seep into my eyes, vowing to myself that I will never cower to these monsters, no matter what they threaten me with.

He laughs, lust flaring in his eyes. "Oh, I can't fucking wait."

"We should go," Half-skull interjects, his thick fingers wrapping around my upper arm in a bruising grip. "We've kept Soren waiting long enough."

Quarter-skull steps backwards, his eyes narrowing in displeasure as he cuts a look to his superior. "Damon said we had some new bitches brought in yesterday."

"That's right. They're being prepared for celebration night," Half-Skull confirms. "Off-limits too."

"Fuck, I could've used some downtime with a new piece of ass," Quarter-skull complains, swiping a tattooed hand over his shorn head.

"The brunette in cell three has had it easy for a few days. Why don't you go pay her a visit and ease some of the stress?" Half-skull suggests with a sinister smirk as he yanks me along the hallway, dragging me away from one monster, only to be given to another.

As soon as we enter Soren's private apartment, Half-skull throws me down onto the cold stone floor, my knees hitting the tiles with a crack. Pain ricochets up my thighs and lower back, and a tiny growl rips from my lips. I swallow the curse words, not willing to earn a beating for the honour of hearing my voice.

"She's here, sir," Half-skull says, stepping into my peripheral vision as I push up from the floor to a kneeling position, refusing to remain bowing and scraping like a beaten dog.

It's not the first time I've been inside Soren's apartment, but every time I'm forced to enter, I'm shocked by the human bones that line the walls in some kind of macabre art display. I can't even bear to think of how they came to be here, and there's no way to be certain without examining the pelvic bones more closely, but my gut tells me these are the remains of his past slaves. All women. All victims of his abuse.

Footsteps approaching from a corridor off the central room alert me to Soren's arrival. He appears before me, his naked body draped in a sheer black robe. It's hard to tell his age given he's covered head to toe tattoos, but I would think he was in his mid-forties. He has an air of self-assurance that comes with age, as well as arrogance and cruelty.

"Leave," Soren says, barely acknowledging Half-skull as he stops in front of me.

Even his dick is blackened from ink, disappearing into the stark white of his skeletal hip bones. Most people would find him terrifying, and whilst I am not immune to his countenance, I don't see a monstrous creature. I see a human man disguising himself with fakery.

I see a man who can bleed.

And he *will* bleed.

"Is there anything else you need, sir?" Half-skull asks.

"Check on Damon and our new arrivals. Make sure they're kept separate from the others. Those who aren't suitable for our buyer will be given to the men at our night of celebration. They must not be tainted before then. Anyone caught sniffing around will be dealt with by me personally."

"Of course," Half-skull replies before turning on his heels and leaving the room.

Silence descends as Soren observes me. He's thoughtful,

quiet, the oppressive arrogance and aggression he usually arms himself with a little muted today.

"Follow me," he eventually demands, twisting on his feet and striding back the way he entered the room.

Without hesitation, I do as he asks. I learned early on that patience is not a concept Soren understands, and disobedience is akin to petrol thrown into a naked flame. For now, I will follow his orders until the time comes when I no longer have to. Survival is my priority until I can have my revenge. When we reach a door at the end of the hallway, he unlocks it and pushes it open, gesturing for me to enter.

The room's floor is cool and smooth with polished ceramic tiles, and the walls are painted a deep umber. It's richly decorated with decadent velvet furniture and a huge wooden, four-poster bed enclosed by thick curtains. When I imagined Soren's most inner lair, this was not it.

Motioning for me to sit on a navy winged-back chair in the far corner of the room, he takes a seat opposite. On the low walnut coffee table between us is a carafe filled with orange juice, the sweet, tangy scent making my mouth water.

"Drink," Soren says as he pours us both a glass and slides it across the table towards me.

I take it cautiously, not wanting to let my guard down. For all I know, he's laced it with something to weaken me, make me vulnerable.

He narrows his eyes at me when I don't follow his orders. "You think I've poisoned it?"

My shoulders rise a fraction of an inch in reply. I wouldn't put it past him.

He laughs, raising his glass to his mouth and knocking it back in one long gulp, smacking his lips at the taste. "There. Now drink."

I lower my gaze, my eyes dropping to the glass and the scented liquid that makes my stomach grumble as much as my mouth water. Lifting it to my lips like an offering, I take a sip, forcing myself not to swallow it down in one long gulp. The liquid is sweet, with notes of honey and spice, and a hint of tartness that invigorates the palate. I want to savour it because who knows when I'll be offered such an offering again.

"Your reward for the work you have done so far," he says, resting his inked fingers on his tattooed thighs, watching me as I drink.

My eyes graze over his flaccid cock, flicking away quickly. He laughs darkly.

"If I hadn't already fucked, I'd be tempted," he says, grasping his dick and giving it a tug. "But a night under the influence of your drug has already satisfied my desires."

My nostrils flare at the threat, but that's the only outward sign that his intimidation has affected me. If he tries to touch me, I'll deny making him any more diamonds, and if he persists, a broken piece of glass should be enough to sever his slug-like cock.

Of course, there's no guarantee such an act would kill him, and it would most definitely condemn me to death, but at least I'd die knowing I've made the king of the Skulls a eunuch. He deserves no less.

My thoughts are disturbed by a pitiful moan coming from beyond the heavy draped curtains enclosing his bed. The sound sets my teeth on edge, and goosebumps scatter across my skin.

"That's why I brought you here," Soren says, shifting forward in his seat, his green eyes flashing.

"My bitch is sick, and I hear you're a healer as much as a witch capable of making mind-altering drugs."

Scowling, I meet his gaze. "The *woman* who accompanies you everywhere you go?" I ask, my silence broken by my need to help *her*, not him.

"Yes."

"And you want me to help her?"

"My unborn child is the only reason you are here and she's not carrion for the vultures. Don't mistake my request as anything other than keeping that bitch alive until my son is born. After that, I'll have no use for her."

A spike of rage jabs my stomach, but I swallow every word of anger I want to say and replace it with something else. "Then I'd better examine her."

He nods, getting to his feet. I place my glass back on the table and follow him to the bed, debating whether I should take this opportunity alone with him to end his life, or at least try to. With a shake of my head, I flick that thought away. I might be feeling brave, but I'm not foolish. Besides, whether he realises it or not, Soren has changed my need for revenge to my need to heal the sick. I will do nothing to prevent myself from helping this woman.

Drawing back the curtains, the faintly stale air of sex, dried blood and alcohol assails my nostrils. On the bed lies his slave, curled up into a foetal position. She shivers despite the sweat glistening on her skin, which is covered in a patchwork of fresh bruises and old scars.

Bile burns my throat at her injuries and the pain she's had to endure to survive such abuse, but I force myself to cut off my deepest emotions, allowing only my natural instincts and knowledge to seep to the surface.

"She's been like this since the early hours of this morning," Soren says, without an ounce of empathy in his voice. If anything, he's annoyed.

Kneeling on the mattress, I move closer towards her, gingerly touching her shoulder. Her eyes fly open and she wails, a sound so heart-wrenching my own stutters inside my chest. I've barely touched her, but she's reacting as if I've taken a hammer to her body.

"My God, what have you done to her?" I seethe, unable to help myself.

The anger in my voice is unmistakable, and Soren narrows his eyes on me.

"Can you help her or not?" He retorts coldly.

My mind races as I look at the broken figure before me. She needs more than just a healer; she needs a haven where she can be away from the man who did this to her—but that is not something I can provide right now. Taking a deep breath, I turn towards Soren and answer calmly, "Only if I'm given the time to examine her properly and provided with everything I need to help her. This won't be a quick fix."

Soren stares at me for a long moment before giving a curt nod. "The first batch of diamonds has already been sold and will be collected by our buyers. I want her fit for our celebration night in a few days. You have that time to get her fit," he says.

"A few days?" I ask incredulously. "That's barely enough time to do anything useful. I am a healer, not a miracle worker."

"She was never fully alive at the best of times. Just get her back to her usual state of apathy," he says coldly, glancing at the woman as she groans, delirious from pain.

Apathy? A scream of rage rises up my throat and I have to forcefully swallow it down.

"If you want to save the life of this woman and your unborn child, I urge you to reconsider. She needs time."

Soren rounds the bed, grasping my arm and yanking me from the mattress. His grip is vice-like as he flips me around to face him and snarls, "And if you want to live, I suggest you find a cure for what ails her within the timeframe given."

"If she dies, you have no heir," I counter, refusing to be intimidated. "And if I die, you have no supply of diamonds."

He tightens his jaw, annoyance flashing in his gaze as he lets me go. "Then you treat her during the day until she is better, and at night you make diamonds."

I nod, not caring that leaves zero time for me to rest. My need to take care of this woman, to heal her, overrides my own well-being. I can take naps when she's sleeping. I can do this.

"I'll need some ingredients. Arnica, camphor, alcohol, echinacea..."

My voice trails off as he holds up his hand and jerks his chin towards a notepad and pen lying on the side table next to the bed.

"Make a list. I will send one of my men to get everything you require," he says.

"And that's possible? We're in the middle of nowhere."

"It's possible," he says, refusing to elaborate further. "I will also send a man to help get her back to her cell."

"No," I reply.

"No?"

"She needs a proper bed, fresh air, somewhere to get clean, and a toilet rather than a bucket to shit in," I bite out.

Glaring at me, I expect him to refuse my request, but to my surprise, he nods sharply.

"Fine," he replies, then he turns on his heel and strides from the room.

Alone with the woman, I take a deep breath, feeling the swell of rage cling to my throat and crawl down my spine as I examine her battered and bruised body that's barely strong enough to carry a fragile life. My anger rises with each bump and bruise that I find, with every burn and cut, hoping desperately that she will survive to see justice served.

"My name's Cyn," I say softly, feeling her forehead with the back of my hand.

My jaw clenches at her hot but clammy skin, and in that moment when her eyes blink open and she stares up at me, I make a silent vow to protect her and her unborn child, even if it means risking my own life.

"I'm here to help."

A sob rises from her throat as her arms tighten around her belly. Everything about her is so fragile, so worn down, and yet still she lives. Somehow her unborn child clings to life with everything it has.

"My baby," she whispers.

"I will do everything I can to keep you and your baby safe. I promise," I say, stroking her hair, hoping that they return soon with what I need so that I can try to help this woman. Tears pool in the crook of her eye, spilling over the bridge of her nose as she twists her head to face me.

"I want him dead," she whispers, the tiniest hint of fight lighting up her deep blue eyes. "I want to kill him."

"Then I'll make sure that I get you better so that you can," I reply fiercely, meaning every word.

5

L orcan

Carrick's head drops between his shoulders as he sits on the edge of the bed and stares at the floor, Arden standing in front of him. Seeing them like this, so broken like this... Fuck, it hurts.

Ever since Cyn was taken we've been orbiting around each other, each of us lost to our own guilt. Busy calling in debts in our attempt to find Cyn, we haven't talked about what happened that night, or how we feel. We've been on autopilot, hoping, fucking praying, we get to her soon.

And now here we are.

"Lock the door," Arden orders without taking his eyes off Carrick.

I see the stress that he holds in his shoulders, and it's as heavy as the weight Carrick feels right now, as *I* feel. None of us are handling it well, Carrick was just the first of us to let his mask slip. Fucking ironic given our company.

"Do you want me to leave?" I ask, as I traverse the bed to get to the door.

I know what's about to happen. It's not the first time they've used pain and physical release as a form of comfort. This is how they've always handled their emotions when shit gets too heavy, but I've never been a part of it. Not because I hadn't wanted to but because this was their thing, what they did for each other, and I respected that. Sure we've shared women before, shared each other, but this is different.

This is more than just sexual gratification.

I've never *needed* to be a part of it... until now.

Arden reaches out and grabs my arm. "No. I want you here too. I *need* you here, Lorcan," he adds. "Please, stay."

"Of course," I reply, placing my hand over his before striding to the door and locking it.

Beyond I can hear the muffled sound of The Masks and Beast talking, and the steady thrum of the engines as we fly 40,000 feet above ground. It won't be long until we land in southern Spain, but I sure as fuck hope it's long enough to get our heads on straight. Beast was right when he said Carrick was no good to Cyn in this state. None of us are. If we're to get her back, we have to be the Deana-dhe. We cannot allow ourselves to wallow in our guilt a second longer.

We can't be weak.

We need to be fierce.

We need to be strong like Cyn's always been.

With my back pressed against the door, a little uncertain what to do next, I wait, watching as Arden strokes Carrick's hair. His gentleness surprises me because I know what Carrick needs the most right now is pain. He goaded The Masks and Beast because he wanted a reaction, he wanted a fight, and with it oblivion.

Pain has always been Carrick's way of letting go of stress and dealing with overwhelming emotions, and it's Cyn he has to thank for uncovering that. Even back when we were kids she understood him better than he understood himself. Better even, than we did.

"Carrick, look at me," Arden demands. When he doesn't comply, Arden's fingers curl into his hair, tightening around the strands. "I said look at me."

"Fuck," I mutter, my throat tightening at the devastation painting Carrick's features as Arden forces his head back. The scar might carve across his face in a brutal reminder of how the Skull Brotherhood bested him, but it's the pain in his eyes that has my stomach churning with sympathy.

"This isn't on you," Arden says firmly.

"It's my fault," he says.

"No."

"It's my fault," he argues, his fists curling at his sides.

"You fought for her," Arden reminds him.

"Not hard enough."

"You fought for her. You were injured. There were too many."

"NOT HARD ENOUGH!" he shouts back, slamming his chest with his fist over and over again until Arden yanks him roughly upward, letting go of his hair and gripping his chin roughly.

"Listen to me. You are not to blame."

"If not me then who, Arden? Who's fault is it?" Carrick argues.

"Mine!" Arden shouts back, his own guilt uncorking. "It's *my* fault. I'm the one responsible. I should've known Soren would want her, of course he would. She's clever, she's beautiful, she's gifted. Why the fuck wouldn't he? I brought her back to the island to make diamonds for Soren under the guise of wanting money. I ignored how I felt about her because I was a chicken-shit. I pretended I hated her, that I didn't fucking adore the way she could still my fucking heart with one withering look, or that her gentle touch didn't send blood roaring to my cock. I refused to believe that she was ours, until it was too late," he pants, chest heaving as his grip on Carrick's chin tightens. "So, no, Carrick, this isn't on you."

"But they fucking took her from *me*!" he shouts, reaching up and grasping the back of Arden's head, dragging him closer until their foreheads touch.

"They took her from *us*!" Arden cries, his voice cracking as their breaths mingle.

And then, like two stars colliding, their lips slam against each other in a brutal kiss, guilt lighting their pain like a match. Sorrow draws them together, and without the woman we all love here to ease the ache in their hearts, all they have is each other to burn up in.

My cock jerks as I watch them grasping at each other, seeking solace in one another, and it fires something inside of me.

Something surprising.

Anger.

Not at them fucking each other's faces with their tongues. I don't care about that.

I'm angry at them, at myself, because we wasted time.

We pushed Cyn away when we should've been holding her close. We spent years hating her when we should've spent years loving her. We were fucking cruel to her when we should've worshipped at her feet. Soren wouldn't have known she'd existed if we'd admitted to ourselves years ago that she was ours. We would've protected her fiercely with every last breath.

This isn't just on one of us. It's on all of us.

And I'm angry. I'm fucking furious. At them both. At myself for not fighting harder. For not making them see earlier. We only had a few weeks together before Soren took her and that's on us. No one else.

Striding over to them, I grab them both by the back of the head, my fingers clamping in their hair, pulling them apart. They stumble back from each other with bruised lips, heaving chests and wide eyes.

"Get on the damn bed!" I yell, shaking with fury, wanting to punish them both.

I'm shaking with lust, with love, and with overwhelming guilt, as I shove them both in the chest, forcing them backwards. Carrick blinks up at me, his black eyes suffused with pain. Next to him, fury burns in Arden's amber gaze. Not at me, not at Carrick, but himself.

Because he knows. He thinks the same as I do.

"All I can think about is Cyn. I can't fucking breathe knowing that she's in their grasp. I've barely slept since she was taken. I go over and over what we did to her as kids," I yell, my own regret, a flurry of words burning my lips. "Konrad was right. We were no better than they were. All of this. Everything that's happened is because I didn't speak up when I should've. I knew she was ours back then. I fucking knew it. But I let you *both* convince me otherwise."

"Lorcan," Arden begins, the colour draining from his face.

"No!" I snap, flicking my gaze to Carrick. "I let you hurt her, and I didn't speak up."

"You're right," Carrick mutters, shoulders dropping. "We're all to blame."

"None of this would've happened if we'd loved her right from the start. None of it. Soren saw an opening and he took it. Do you honestly think if we'd made her ours years ago that this would've happened? Because I *know* it wouldn't have," I pant. "And the worst thing of all is that she forgave us for our shitty fucking behaviour a long time ago. Cyn knew she belonged to us and we were too fucking stupid to see it. Imagine how she felt after that night we made love to her in the chapel, because–make no mistake–we *did* make love. We took her virginity and then we turned our backs on her. Just imagine how that must've hurt her."

Gripping my stomach, I double over, winded by the knowledge. I could let this feeling break me, but that won't help Cyn and I refuse to let her down again. Sucking in a few deep breaths I force myself upright.

"It kills me to know that she found her voice with The Masks. Fuck, how it kills me. But do you know what? We never deserved to hear it first, and we were lucky she shared it with us even if it was just to protect her friends."

"You're right," Arden agrees, cutting me an exhausted look.

"My immediate reaction to finding out that she lied to us in order to protect Christy and The Masks was anger. I was angry because I believed *we* deserved her love and affection, her loyalty, but I was wrong. We didn't deserve it. We haven't even *earned* it yet."

"So what do we do about it? Because I can't live with guilt. It's killing me," Carrick says brokenly as he lays back on the bed and covers his face with his arm.

"We deal with this here and now by any means possible. We get our shit together like Beast suggested, then we find Soren and the Skull Brotherhood and we fucking kill them all."

"Then what?" Arden asks, blowing out a shaky breath.

"Then we *earn* Cyn's love," I say. "If that means getting on our knees and begging for forgiveness every fucking day for the rest of our lives, then we do it. If that means giving her exactly what she needs, what she wants, we'll do it. Agreed?"

Arden swallows hard then nods. "You know I will."

"Carrick?" I ask, but still he covers his face, determined to punish himself.

Well he doesn't need to, because I'm about to do that for him. Climbing onto the bed, I straddle his hips then I reach up and forcefully pull his arms apart, pinning them down by his side.

"I asked you a damn question, Carrick."

When he doesn't answer immediately, I stare down at him, but he keeps his head turned away, showing me his still healing scar. It's a visual reminder of everything that went down that night, because not only did they take Cyn from us, they almost took Carrick from us too, and they still can if he doesn't snap out of this.

"Are you ready to earn Cyn's love?" I persist, giving him something to hold on to. Some fucking hope because within that question there's no doubt we'll get her back in order to earn her love.

Still he refuses. Stubborn to the end.

"Hold him down," I demand, taking the lead.

"He'll fight at first. He always does," Arden warns me.

"And you?" I ask as he crawls up the bed and positions himself behind Carrick's head.

Arden locks eyes with me. "I'll take whatever you give, and I will return it in kind. We hurt. We find relief. We get stronger. Then we take down those motherfuckers."

"Yes," I agree.

Grabbing Carrick's arms, Arden pulls them up above his head, holding them down. Then he locks eyes with me and says, "Draw blood. He needs to feel it."

I nod, dropping my gaze to Carrick who's staring up at me now. He's my best friend, my brother, and I fucking love him. Just like I love Arden. Just like I love Cyn.

"When this is over, no more guilt, no more blame. We focus on finding Cyn, getting her back in our arms, safe."

"Safe," he mutters.

And with that, I pull down the collar of Carrick's t-shirt, lean over and press my open mouth against his collarbone, biting down hard. He jerks beneath me, his cock hardening as he holds onto the cry of pain trapped inside his chest. His blood, metallic and warm, oozes over my tongue as I lick at the wound, my cock jerking from the friction as he bucks beneath me.

"Again!" Arden demands, as Carrick's chest heaves and he snarls at me, teeth gnashing, feral as a wolf.

Gripping the hem of his t-shirt, I shove up his top, bunching it beneath his chin then lower my mouth to his pec and bite him just above his right nipple. This time, he can't stop the cry of pain as it rips out of his throat.

"You motherfucker!" he roars, fighting beneath me.

I look up at Arden who still pins his arms. "Again!"

Arden's powerful command floods my bloodstream as I wrap my hand around Carrick's throat, pinning his head in place, and bite down on Carrick's left pec. This time when I lick at his blood, I suck on his nipple too.

Carrick groans beneath my mouth.

"Have you had enough?" I ask, my breath coming thick and fast. The veins in my hands popping as I squeeze his throat.

"No," he grinds out. "Fucking do it again!"

So I do.

I bite him again and again. I bury my teeth in his skin over and over until he stops fighting and starts groaning instead.

"I need Cyn," he cries, neck arched as he pushes his hips up to meet mine, eyes squeezed shut as he imagines her.

"We all do, brother," I say, releasing my hold on his neck and resting my palms against his chest instead. Beneath my palm I feel the frantic beat of his heart. It matches my own.

"I need her in my arms. I need to fuck her, Lorcan," he says, eyes flying open. "I need to show her how much she means to me. I need to apologise with my lips and my tongue, my hands and my cock. I want to see her splinter apart. I want to hear her scream when I make her come. I want her to know that I love her. That I always fucking did."

"Me too, brother, me too," I reply, my cock thickening at the thought of her naked and surrounded by all three of us, worshipping her, loving her just like we did that night in the chapel.

"And she will be in our arms once more," Arden adds with conviction.

"I remember every single moment of that night we took her virginity," I say, locking eyes with Arden now. "I remember her scent, the way she unfurled beneath our hands and lips like a flower blooming from our touch. I remember how her chest rose and fell, how her body flushed with heat. I remember the way she tasted. I remember how thick and hard I was, how you both were. I remember the feel of her tightening around my dick when she came. I remember the bliss I felt to finally have her in my arms, and knowing it was right. I remember the way she fucking *glowed*."

"Fuck, Lorcan," Arden says as he releases Carrick's arms

and reaches for his dick, rubbing himself over the seam of his trousers. "Fuck!"

"She was taken from me," Carrick cries, shattering with grief beneath me.

"Let it go, brother," I say, dropping my gaze to my best friend's eyes, pleading with him now.

We're both hard, partly due to this feral kind of punishment I've just inflicted on him, but a whole lot more to do with thoughts of Cyn. She's the wildflower in a field of thorns. She's a fucking treasure in this world that's so full of shit. She's the reason why we hurt, why we feel pain, why we want to rip the world apart to find her, why our dicks throb and our breathing is ragged.

"We *will* get her back," Carrick says, forcing himself to believe it as he pushes upwards, his arms circling my back.

"We will repent for our sins against her," I add fiercely.

"Yes!" Carrick hisses, before he rips at the top buttons of my shirt, pulls the lapel aside, and bites down on my shoulder.

I roar in pain, bright stars of white hot light bursting behind my closed eyelids, followed by a rush of pleasure that centres in the base of my spine and spreads outwards to my dick.

"Fuuucccck!" I pant, as Carrick licks at the wound, his lips kissing away the sting.

Behind him Arden shifts closer, his cock freed from the confines of his trousers, hot and heavy in his hand as he looks at me from over Carrick's shoulder.

"When she's in our arms again we will love her until she knows nothing else," he says, heat and lust, love and hope in his gaze.

"Yes. Until our last breath," I agree.

"Until our last breath," Carrick repeats, biting down on my skin as Arden presses his mouth against Carrick's ear and licks it.

"I remember the way her tongue stroked against mine," Arden whispers, stroking his cock, pressing his lips against Carrick's neck and sucking on the skin there. "I remember how her legs spread as I plunged my fingers inside her pussy. How wet she was for us. How receptive to our touch."

"I remember the fierceness of her gaze before she bit me," Carrick adds with a groan, reaching between us as he palms my dick over my trousers. "I remember how fragile yet strong she was beneath my grasp, how I knew deep down, as she buried her teeth into my skin, that she was it for me."

"I remember her scent," I add, reaching down and freeing my cock, gasping as Carrick fists it at the base, his thumb sliding over the tip, spreading precum over the sensitive head.

"I remember that night we broke into her room when she was sleeping, and touched her as though she were made of glass," Carrick adds, groaning as Arden bites down on his shoulder and I free his cock too, enjoying the feel of him, the warmth.

"Fuck I miss her," I say, pressing my eyes shut, loving the feel of Carrick's hand pumping me as we talk about the woman we love.

It's both torturous and joyous. Torturous because she isn't here to hear our words of praise, to know just how much she means to us, and joyous because this is us healing each other so we can be the men she needs us to be. So we can do better, be better, for her.

"I've been in love with her for so fucking long now," Arden admits, a moan parting his lips as he pumps his dick faster and faster, his free hand sliding up Carrick's throat as he squeezes gently. "Fuck, I need to show her just how much I love her," Arden says, his voice cracking.

"Show me," I pant, my balls tightening as Carrick releases his grip on me, spits on his hand, then fists my cock with his now saliva-slicked fingers. My fingers flex then tighten around his own cock as he swells in my hand, thickening at our intimacy, at thoughts of Cyn.

Arden moves around to our side and pushes up onto his knees, his dick bobbing, slick with precum as he reaches for me and crashes his mouth against mine in a kiss that's meant for Cyn, but he shares with me now. He groans into my mouth when I switch hands, grasping his cock with one and Carrick's with the other, pumping them both simultaneously.

"Fuck, I need her," Carrick moans, his mouth pressing against my chest, his tongue sweeping over my nipple as he grips me tighter, squeezing the shaft of my cock, then stroking upwards, the pad of his thumb sliding over the thick vein that curls from the base to the tip.

Our knuckles brush against each other, our dicks bumping as we stroke up and down, bolts of pleasure light up my spine at the raw, torrid need between the three of us made a million times more intense with thoughts of Cyn. As Carrick brings me closer to orgasm and Arden fucks my mouth with his tongue we imagine her.

Our Cyn.

Our sin.

Our *soulmate.*

Arden pulls back, panting. Eyes wild with lust, cheeks flushed with desire, chest heaving from a heart full of want and love, he reaches for Carrick and kisses him desperately.

"Cyn," he mutters, pulling back looking between us both.

"Cyn," I pant.

"Cyn," Carrick cries.

Half drunk with lust, we continue to fist each other, kiss each other, and grind into each other's hands with thoughts of Cyn in our heads, love in our hearts, truth on our tongues and determination in our blood, until we come hard and fast.

Carrick releases first, his thick, thready cum covering my hand and my own dick as he cries out her name once more. Then pinning me with his dark stare, he uses his slickness to pump me harder, faster, until my balls tighten, my head tips back, and my eyes slam shut. I come roaring her name over and over and over again.

My fingers loosen around Arden's dick, my orgasm making my whole body boneless, so Carrick pushes me off of him with a smirk, then positions himself in front of Arden and takes his cock into his mouth, deep-throating him in a slippery, noisy, sensual blowjob until Arden grips Carrick's hair and releases with a cry, pumping his cum down his throat.

Five minutes later, once we've all recovered enough to clean up our mess and straighten ourselves out, there's a tap at the door.

"We're about to descend," Beast says, a smirk in his voice

that's undeniable. "But I'm guessing you three already came into land, am I right?"

We glance at each other, the laughter that follows a healing tonic that's only bested by the knowledge that soon Soren and the Skull Brotherhood will be dead, and Cyn will be in our arms once more.

6

C^{yn}

"You still haven't told me your name," I say, gently swiping a damp cloth over the woman's skin as I clean her wounds with salted water before adding the gel of an aloe vera plant. It has antibacterial and anti-inflammatory properties which should help to heal the wounds inflicted by Soren. She winces at the slight sting, her eyes haunted, shadowed by deep bruises and mottled skin.

"It's Faith," she whispers, a sad smile wobbling her lips.

"Faith? That's a beautiful name, it suits you," I reply, dabbing more gel onto a particularly nasty wound on her right hip that looks suspiciously like a cigar burn.

"I used to think so..."

Her voice trails off as she stares off into space, her attention caught in a memory that removes her from the room Soren moved us to on the far side of the complex, and into a place of disassociation. I don't try to draw Faith back from her safe space, knowing all too well that she needs to find strength in the quiet, more peaceful moments whenever she can. Instead, my fingertips gently graze over her body as I take in the true extent of her injuries.

Bruises varying from a deep purple-black to a sallow yellow blossom across most of her skin. I ask myself, not for the first time, how she, let alone her unborn child, has survived such callous beatings.

At a guess I would've said she's around four months pregnant given the slight curve of her stomach, but I've yet to establish just how far along she actually is. There are no signs of bleeding, so I have to assume the foetus is still alive, which is a blessing.

Since Soren called me to Faith's side eight hours ago, we haven't had much chance to talk. Her mind's need to protect itself from all that she's had to endure and sheer exhaustion preventing us from doing so. I've been using that time to make lotions and creams for Faith's skin, and tonics to ease her pain and strengthen her from the inside out.

Truthfully, the list of ingredients and equipment I had given to Soren was extensive, and I didn't expect him to obtain half of what I'd needed, let alone most of the items, especially not within a few hours of giving it to him. The sheer fact that he could deliver has to mean that we're closer to civilization than

I'd first thought, and wherever that town or city may be it has to be on a decent trade route, which gives me hope that the Deana-dhe will be able to find us.

Faith stirs as I apply arnica cream to the deep purple bruise covering almost the entirety of her right breast, Soren's handprint leaving a distinct impression on her abused skin. Eventually it will fade with time, but the mark he's left on her psyche, that will never fade. Even if we do escape, she will always be burdened with his abuse, will have to shoulder the weight of it and somehow try to heal, to live with the memories. I have admiration for anyone who's suffered at the hands of another and survived. That takes true strength.

"I loved him once," Faith mutters, her sad eyes focussing on me once more as she winces in pain.

"Soren?" I question, placing the arnica cream on the side table.

She shakes her head, her slim fingers grasping mine. "No, not him. The man who sold me into slavery."

"Who was it?"

"His name was Phillipe. I met him in France during a gap year when I was travelling around the world. I thought he loved me. I thought I was his forever, but I was just his next business deal. I didn't know he'd sold me until I woke up in the cargo hold of a ship that was headed for Morocco with half a dozen other women he'd fooled."

"Is that where we are now, in Morocco?"

"Yes," she nods her head, shifting her body, the pain making tears spring to her eyes. She blinks them away, forcing herself to continue. "Tangier Med is the nearest Port to our location.

Soren pays the port authorities to turn a blind eye every time the Skull Brotherhood enters and exits the country, but we're actually nearer Marrakech. Don't you remember the train journey from the port to the city?"

"He knocked me out," I say, tucking that piece of information away, hope blooming in my chest.

Where there is trade there is business and where there is business there are criminals. Most importantly, where there are criminals there are debts owed. Arden, Lorcan and Carrick's reach extends far beyond Ireland and the United Kingdom, so there's a good chance they'll be able to locate us through one of their many contacts. They just have to know where to start looking.

"And the other women in the cargo hold with you...?" I ask.

Faith's eyes shutter closed, like she's trying to hide from the memory. "They're all dead," she whispers. "We survived the journey, spent almost a year together, but one by one they fell victim to the Skulls' evil. I'm the only one who's lived this long."

Tears spill from her lashes like tiny jewels glinting in the late afternoon sunlight, which passes through the sheer cream curtains. It warms our skin but despite the heat she shivers.

"I'm so sorry for everything you've gone through. For all of it," I say, the words scraping against my throat as I take her hand in mine.

"That was three years ago. There were eight of us, and now there is only me," she explains, staring straight ahead as another, more painful memory twists the expression on her face.

"You've been captive that long?" I whisper, unable to truly

comprehend the strength she must have to survive such prolonged abuse and maltreatment.

"The things I've had to do..." she murmurs, as though reading my thoughts.

Faith's eyes swim with more tears, the canopy of her lashes breaking the deep blue into scattered shards. I blink away my own tears, filling my heart with hatred for the men who've caused her so much pain, and using that to fuel my determination to keep this woman alive, to make sure she gets to fulfil her wish.

Soren is a dead man.

Blowing out a shaky breath, I gently squeeze her shoulder. "You don't have to tell me if you don't want to, if it hurts too much."

"I need to," she replies, covering my hand with hers, finding strength in my touch. "I need to let it out, some of it at least."

I nod. "Then I'll listen for as long as you need me to."

"Can you help me to sit up?" she asks, trying to push up on her elbows, every movement painful.

Sliding my arm beneath her back, I get her into a seated position then help her shuffle backwards against the headboard, placing the cushion behind her.

"Is that more comfortable?" I ask as she rests her hands on her gently rounded stomach.

"A little," she replies with a weak smile, her gaze sliding from mine as she takes in her surroundings fully. This room is nowhere near as extravagantly decorated as Soren's bedroom, but it does have a sturdy wooden bed, thick mattress, and a bathroom with running water, so it's a darn sight better than what we've been used to.

"I'm surprised Soren didn't send me back to the cells," she replies.

"He was going to," I explain, "But I managed to persuade him not to. You need access to running water, a toilet, and a decent bed. You need light, fresh air, and I need a place to work that isn't a health risk."

"How did you do that?" she asks, shifting slightly, her expression registering the pain. "Soren couldn't care less about the condition of our cells. He loves knowing we're treated worse than dogs. The Skulls call us their bitches after all."

"He wants your baby to live," I say, hating that's the truth, that if it weren't for the baby she carries she'd probably be dead already.

She nods, her hands rubbing gently over her bump. "I've survived up until this moment because I allowed Soren to do whatever he wanted to me. I didn't fight him. Not when he raped me over and over until my insides bled. Not when he beat me unconscious. Not when he tried to break me with his words as much as his fists. I never fought back, until now."

"Because of the baby?"

"Yes."

"How far gone are you?"

"I'm not certain, a few months?"

"And he's been beating you despite the fact you're pregnant," I say, fisting my fingers, wishing I could gut the bastard.

"He didn't know until last night."

"Why didn't you tell him earlier? He could've killed you and the baby."

"At first I wasn't sure if I was pregnant. My periods had become irregular from the trauma and the abuse. Then a week ago I felt something fluttering deep inside of me, like the edge of a butterfly's wing. It was so soft, so fragile, and I knew. I *knew* I was pregnant, that my boobs weren't just sore because of his rough treatment of me, but because my body was preparing to be a mother."

"So what happened last night?"

"I sensed I didn't have much longer, that sooner or later his hands around my throat would tighten until I couldn't breathe anymore. He fucked me, took what he needed and then he began to hit me. I knew I had to fight back. I knew I had to protect my child."

"I'm so sorry, Faith," I reply, my voice strangled with emotion.

"He only stopped trying to beat me to death because I told him I was carrying his son," she continues, the emptiness in her voice finding fire with every word.

"How do you know it's a boy?"

Faith lets out a harsh laugh. "I don't, but I knew he would kill me if I said it was a girl."

Instead of replying, I reach for Faith again, gathering her into my arms as she cries against my chest, her emotions spilling over once again. After a few moments she pulls away, wiping away the tears with shaking hands.

"You'll survive this," I say, fresh determination settling in my blood.

Her eyes meet mine and there is a strength that wasn't there before. I see a woman filled with courage and resilience, one who will do what it takes to protect herself and her unborn child.

"I will," she says with a quiet resolve.

"We'll get out of here, *all* of us."

"But how?" she asks, her eyebrows drawing together, not because she doesn't believe we could, but because she needs to hope that we can. "Soren's men are everywhere. Even if we were somehow able to slip past the Skulls without them noticing, we're miles from anywhere. We'd die from dehydration before we'd ever reach the nearest city. And even if by some miracle we make it there, we still won't be safe. Soren has many people under his control, not just the Skulls."

"Because we're not going anywhere," I say.

"I don't understand?"

"The Skull Brotherhood stole from the wrong people, and the men I care about won't stop until they've found me," I say, letting out a soft, incredulous laugh at the thought of The Masks and the Deana-dhe working together. I *know* they'll do it, but that doesn't make it any less surprising.

Faith gives me an intense look. "You're special, aren't you?"

I shake my head. "No more than you are. No more than any of these women held captive are."

"And yet no one's coming to rescue us," she replies, a hint of sadness seeping into her words.

I take a deep breath and meet Faith's gaze. "That's about to change."

Faith stares into my eyes, searching for something that I cannot name, before she speaks again.

"I believe you," she finally says, her voice low and determined.

"Good, because I need you to live up to your name. I need you to have faith," I say with a wry grin. "I already know you're emotionally and mentally strong, but I need you to get physically strong, then together we can give my men the best chance of succeeding."

"How?"

A devious smile pulls up my lips. "Not all of the ingredients I requested are for you."

7

Arden

"Bienvenidos, bienvenidos," Vasko says with a warm smile as we enter his courtyard garden, surrounded by lush greenery and a pergola covered in grapevines. The evening air is pleasant and I remove my jacket as we follow Vasko towards the seating area. "Please, come and sit. I have tapas and wine, or beer if you'd like?"

"I could use an ice-cold beer," Beast says, settling himself in the wicker chair which groans under his weight.

"Very well. And you?" he asks, turning his attention to the three of us.

"We'll have beer too," I reply for all of us.

"Four beers, coming up," Vasko says as he disappears inside the villa, returning moments later with four bottles of chilled beer that he hands out to each of us.

As I take a bottle my gaze lands on Vasko, whose silver hair shines in the fading sun behind him. He takes a sip from his glass of red wine and clears his throat before speaking again.

"I didn't expect to see you so soon, Arden," he begins, eying me carefully.

"Needs dictate," I reply tightly, recalling our last interaction.

One year ago, Vasko contacted us to get the details on a competitor who sold counterfeit items, hoping to become the biggest supplier of women's luxury handbags in Europe. He wanted to know who was supplying them and where the rival's warehouse was located. We supplied him with the information he required in exchange for a debt. We later heard that the warehouse had been destroyed by a fire. It doesn't take a genius to figure out he was behind it.

"So how's business?" Lorcan asks, reminding him that he owes us a debt, and we're here to call it in.

"Booming," he replies with a wide grin, swirling the wine around his glass, airing the dark red Rioja before taking another sip. "Thanks to you."

"I'm glad we could be of assistance..." I say, allowing my voice to trail off as I study him.

Vasko looks at me expectantly, waiting for me to continue, but I remain silent. We're not here for small talk. We have one goal and that is to find out where Soren's keeping Cyn, and according to Vasko he knows a man who might have some information. It's the sole reason we travelled here, given it's the only lead we've had. Keeping my gaze pinned on Vasko, I wait.

"I was under the impression there'd be more of you," he eventually says.

It's a seemingly innocuous comment but one which raises my hackles nonetheless. "And why would that be?" I fire back quickly, noticing the way Vasko keeps looking nervously over my shoulder.

"Something interesting out there, mate?" Beast asks, catching on.

I know he's thinking the same thing too. Vasko's on edge. There's a tenseness around his shoulders and a look of uncertainty in his eyes. Granted, it's not everyday you're faced with four of the most well known criminals in Europe, but this isn't a healthy fear he's showing, this is a jittery kind of fear. The kind that tells me he's up to something we're not going to like.

Which is just as well that Jakub, Konrad and Leon took a different route to Vasko's villa, parking in a dirt track that leads to the fifteen acres of land backing onto his villa. Vasko might be a small-time criminal trading mainly in fake handbags, but it pays to be cautious.

"You are in search of the Skull Brotherhood," he continues, looking between us. "I assumed by our very brief conversation they had something of value to you."

"That assumption would be correct," I confirm.

"I also know Soren has quite an army," he adds evenly, though I don't like the hint of a smirk playing about his lips.

"And your point?" Beast asks, as Carrick and Lorcan exchange looks, picking up on the sudden rising tension.

"There are only four of you and many of them," Vasko points out, picking up a croquette and taking a bite, his gaze smouldering with arrogance. I don't like it.

"Our allies are following up another lead in France," Lorcan lies, grabbing a piece of bread and dipping it into olive oil, then popping it into his mouth and chewing slowly. "There was no need for us all to come and visit you."

"Ah yes, that seems a sensible option," Vasko muses, patting his mouth with a napkin. "Better to widen the net, hmm?"

"Your contact," Carrick prompts, shifting the conversation back in the right direction. "You said he might have some information about the Skull Brotherhood's whereabouts."

"He does," Vasko replies, passing around the tray of tapas.

I shake my head. I can't stomach food right now. Every day, every hour, every fucking minute that goes by is just more time for Soren to hurt Cyn, just the thought makes me want to puke.

"So where is he?" Beast asks, selecting a green olive stuffed with minced chorizo, and taking a bite. "Because as nice as it is to sit here and eat tapas, we've got to be getting on."

Vasko rests his glass of wine on the table, his fingers gripping the stem. "Señor Medina is nervous to share what he knows. The Skull Brotherhood is feared by many, and as you know their leader, Soren, is vicious."

"I don't care how nervous he is. If he wants to live, then he *will* tell us everything," I reply evenly, forcing myself to remain as calm, and in control as possible. Which is no easy feat when the life of the woman you love is on the line.

"It may take some coaxing to get the information you want from him," he continues, oblivious to my inner turmoil.

"Need I remind you that we travelled all this way because you said you had a lead," I snap, unable to stop the rush of anger rising up my chest. "If coming here turns out to be a wild goose chase then I'll have no issue slitting your throat and feeding your body to those nice, fat pigs on that farm three miles down the road. Understand?"

Vasko flinches at the threat, colour draining from his face. "Excuse me, I meant no disrespect. I just meant that it will be a difficult conversation, he might be hesitant at first."

Beast snorts. "Do you know what I do best?"

Vasko looks between us. "You're a cage fighter, yes?"

"I was. Those days are behind me now," he replies, leaning forward in his seat and taking another long swig of his beer before resting it on the table and cracking his knuckles.

"You're retired?"

"From fighting in the cage? Yes. But don't worry, I'll get the fucker squealing. It's kind of my forte," he says, winking at Vasko before popping a slice of pepperoni in his mouth. "Hmm, fuck that's good."

"He's an old man..." Vasko says, a little horrified. "That kind of persuasion won't be necessary."

"Then he's got nothing to worry about, has he?" Beast adds with a grin that is less than reassuring.

"Wasn't he supposed to be meeting us here," Lorcan intercedes, cutting me a look.

"I asked him to come a little later. Thought it best we talked first, yes?"

"We don't have time to waste," I reply, curtly. "Get him here. Now!"

Vasko flicks his gaze behind me again, and the back of my neck prickles.

"Please, trust me. He's on his way."

"What do you mean by that?" Carrick asks, his voice low and menacing as he reaches for the gun tucked into the back of his trousers.

Vasko gives a small shrug and reaches for his glass of wine. "It's just a figure of speech. I meant nothing by it," he replies, lifting his glass and meeting Beast's gaze. "Shall we raise a toast?"

Beast quirks a brow in challenge. "To what?"

Vasko's lips curl into a slow, confident smile. "To making men squeal."

Milliseconds later the wineglass in Vasko's hand explodes, tiny shards of it lodging into the flesh of his palm and scattering over the rest of us.

"Coño!" he shouts, his hand covered in blood as he reaches under the table and pulls out a gun aiming it directly at my head.

"Motherfucker!" Carrick roars to my left, drawing his gun and pointing it at the traitor, Beast and Lorcan aiming their own guns at Vasko in perfect synchronicity.

"One false move and you're *all* dead," Vasko growls, pressing the cold steel of his gun deeper into my temple, as my own anger flares dangerously.

"You bastard," Lorcan spits, his fury barely contained. "You betrayed us!"

"I'm not in the business of backing a losing horse," Vasko

retorts, his eyes blazing with rage, all the hospitality from a moment ago vanished. The conniving bastard.

"A losing horse? The fuck you on about," Beast asks, flicking his gaze my way, before searching the surrounding area behind me. I'm a sitting duck. Beast knows it too.

"He means he's backing the Skull Brotherhood," I reply, my voice tinged with anger.

"But you owe *us* a debt," Carrick hisses, his disbelief palpable in every word.

"Let's just say that Soren offered me a more lucrative deal."

"And Medina?" I question.

Vasko snorts. "A fabrication of course."

"You've made a huge mistake fucking us over," Lorcan says. "Our debt isn't something you can just walk away from. You will pay up or you will pay with your life. Now drop your fucking weapon and tell us where the Skull Brotherhood are hiding or I will blow your motherfucking brains out."

Vasko laughs. "You're in no position to threaten me. I'm the one with a gun pressed against Arden's head."

"My men will cut you down before you can pull the trigger," I retort calmly, hoping to fuck The Masks have our backs and don't use this as an opportunity to annihilate us once and for all.

Beside me, Carrick keeps his aim steady as Beast shifts slightly on his feet and Lorcan adjusts his aim. We all know that if things escalate then there's going to be a bloodbath, and despite wanting to riddle this man with holes, we have Cyn to think of. Right now Vasko is our only link to her whereabouts, and we need him alive. Which puts me in a very precarious position.

"Who do you think fired that bullet?" Vasko asks, a sneer pulling up his lip. "*I'm* not alone." His threat is backed up by the sound of distant gunfire and men shouting.

"The Masks," Beast hisses under his breath, turning his attention towards the treeline surrounding the villa. "If those motherfuckers wind up dead, I won't need to worry about Grim's anger because Christy will kill me."

"By the sound of it, you're men are already dead," Vasko says with a cruel laugh, "And you will be too if you don't drop your weapons."

"Whatever deal Soren has offered you we'll offer something better," I say, changing tactics. "Just lower your weapon and name your price."

"The Deana-dhe might deal in debts, but the last I heard, human trafficking isn't your thing. So unless you can supply me with a steady stream of tight, virginal cunts, I'm not interested."

"You dirty fucking bastard," Beast growls. "A turncoat and a deviant."

Vasko laughs. "You think I care about what names you call me? I may be both of those things, but I'm not a fool. You, however, walked right into this trap. Soren knew you'd come after him. He also knew I owed you a debt and that eventually you'd make that call, asking for information. He was right. All I had to do was dangle a carrot and you'd come running."

"Yeah, but here's the thing," Beast says, chuckling as he lowers his gun. "You ain't really thought this through all that well, mate."

"Beast?" I question, but he just throws me a wink and keeps talking.

"Whilst you've been banging on about how clever you are, I realised something important," he says, grinning more widely now. "We ain't dead, and the glass *you* were holding shattered."

"And?" Vasko retorts, his confidence wavering.

"And that tells me either your marksmen are a crapshoot, or one of our guys was sending us a warning. They know we need you alive, but you sure as fuck don't need us still standing. So my question is, why are we?"

Vasko's face visibly pales because Beast's correct in his assumption. By rights we should all be dead by now, the fact we're not means The Masks got to his men first. Still, it doesn't change the fact that he's got a gun pointed to my head.

I should be more worried.

I'm not.

I may not have seen this coming, but I know that today isn't the day I die.

Meeting Lorcan's gaze, I give him a small smile and it's enough for him to lower his gun too.

His gaze drifts behind us before focusing back on Vasko. "It's over."

"It isn't over until I say it is!" Vasko shouts, and in that millisecond before his finger squeezes the trigger, the sound of a bullet ripping through his skull rings out in the air around us, his brains and blood spattering over the table and our faces.

Vasko's limp body collapses, the gun still clasped in his hand.

"Arden!" Carrick shouts, grabbing me and twisting me to

face him. Given the expression on his face, he was clearly expecting me to have a similar fate.

"I'm okay," I reply.

"Thank fuck!" he replies, grasping my head between his hands and pressing his forehead against mine.

"Would you look at that? It's gotta be the luck of the Irish," Beast says, snorting with laughter as Carrick lets me go and throws him a dirty look. "What did you do, bribe a leprechaun to keep you safe? You lucky shit."

I let out a tight laugh. "Christy isn't the only Dálaigh left who has the gift. I knew I wasn't dying today."

Beast's whistles. "No shit?"

"Yeah," I reply, scraping a hand through my blood splattered hair and looking at Vasko's slumped body. "Fuck."

"But you didn't see that coming?" Beast asks with a smirk. "Because it would've helped us a ton."

Carrick slams his fist against the table, rattling the china and beer bottles. "We needed him alive!"

"We'll figure this out," Lorcan says, resting a hand on Carrick's arm. "We've got this, remember? She's coming home."

Carrick tightens then flexes his fingers, releasing the tension. "She's coming home," he repeats.

"Who fired the shot?" I ask, flicking off a piece of Vasko's skull from my jacket and rolling my shoulders, trying to ease some of the tension there. I might have known I wasn't dying today, but the adrenaline still gets pumping nevertheless.

"I did."

We turn to find Jakub walking towards us from the tree line, his clothes dishevelled, his right cheek swollen, and his lip split.

"Looks like you've been busy," Beast says. "Where are the other two?"

"You've just killed our only link to Soren!" Carrick interrupts angrily, taking a step towards Jakub. "What are we supposed to do now?"

"We finish what we came here to do," Jakub replies, stepping to one side as Leon and Konrad approach, hauling a man between them, his feet dragging across the gravel, his head lolling between his shoulders. Long, blood-matted hair covering his face.

"One of Vasko's men?" Beast asks, grabbing a napkin from the table that isn't covered in the dead man's blood, and cleaning his face.

Konrad shakes his head as they drop the unconscious man on the ground right next to Vasko's dead body. "Not exactly."

"But he is someone who'll tell us what we need to know," Leon adds, swiping the back of his hand over his own bloody cheek before crouching beside the man and grabbing a handful of his hair. Yanking his head back, he twists the man's head to the side, showing us the portion of a skull tattooed onto his battered face.

"Yeah, I think he'll do," I agree.

8

Cyn

I wake up with a start, heart pounding in my chest as a nightmare lingers in the recesses of my mind, its claws digging deep furrows into my thoughts. I try to blink back the tears pooling in my eyes, but tears stream down my face, mixing with the sweat that's sliding over my skin. My chest is heavy, and I feel a vise-like grip around my abdomen, as if someone is squeezing me as hard as they can.

"Oh God, no!" I pant, fear crawling up my throat at this phantom attacker.

Beside me sleeps Faith, her hair is a dirty blonde halo around her head, her jaw slack and lips parted as she breathes softly, unaffected by the nightmare that has left me in a cold sweat, with tears streaming down my face.

Keeping my gaze fixed on her chest, I watch as it rises and falls, dragging in my own shaky breaths to match hers, until eventually the heavy weight of my nightmare lifts off my chest and the crippling tightness in my stomach abates. I'm so fixated on breathing in time with her that I don't notice her eyes blinking open.

"Are you okay, Cyn?" Faith mumbles groggily, moonlight from the window pouring over her in a silver blanket.

I nod my head but don't respond, still unable to muster any words. Faith tucks a strand of hair behind her ear before she reaches over and places a hand on my shoulder. Her silent comfort gives me exactly what I need, and I take several deep breaths as I attempt to steady myself. The nightmare slowly fades into the background until all that's left is the warmth of Faith's hand and her comforting presence.

"I'm okay," I say shakily, wiping my cheeks with the flat of my hand, and forcing my lips into a wobbly smile. Yesterday I praised her strength, yet here I am breaking because of a nightmare.

"What is it?" she asks.

Even in the darkness I can see concern etched in her features as she looks at me with deep understanding and compassion, and the cold fear that gripped me with the night-mare slowly begins to dissipate.

"A nightmare, that's all."

"A nightmare?" She questions, sympathy in her gaze. "Do you want to talk about it?"

"I'd rather not." I give her a weak smile. "Besides, it's over now."

But it's not. It never will be. Seeing my mother's murder in stark colour is about as bad as a nightmare can get. It's been a long time since I've dreamt of that day, and I know the trauma is bubbling to the surface because of everything that's happening right now.

"Is it?" she questions gently, taking my hand in hers.

I nod, forcing strength into my spine. "Please go back to sleep. You need to rest, not stay up comforting me. I'm going to have a wash. It's been a while since I've felt clean and I may as well make use of the running water whilst I can."

"It takes just as much strength and energy to heal the sick as it does to heal from abuse," she says knowingly. "We may have only known each other a short time, but this isn't a one-sided relationship. Of course you're going to be affected too, and I'm here for you."

"Thank you," I murmur.

Releasing my hand, she gives me a soft smile. "You know I dream about a warm bath most days. I miss being able to relax in one," she murmurs, her eyes drifting shut as exhaustion pulls her back under.

My throat tightens, and I vow to myself that one day soon she will get to sink into a warm bath, her body relaxing with the knowledge that Soren and his men are dead. Climbing out of bed, I pad across the tiled floor to the bathroom. There's no shower or bath, just a toilet and sink. But at least we have running water.

Plugging the sink, I fill it up, adding a drop of lavender oil to the water, then strip naked.

The water is freezing, and I use a threadbare towel to wash myself, shivering at the frigid temperature, the coarse material of the towel harsh against my skin. Strip washing in a chipped stone sink is a poor substitute for a hot shower, but I make do, feeling grateful at least to scrub more than a week's grime from my body.

After washing, I pull out the plug then refill the sink again adding a touch more lavender oil. This time I wash my hair, getting as much dirt out of it as possible before squeezing out the excess water. Grabbing another, slightly larger towel, I wrap it around my body, tucking the end between my breasts. Next I clean my clothes, then hang them up to dry on a hook fixed to the wall. In a few hours the sun will rise and with it will come the heat of another scorching day. It won't take long for my clothes to dry, but for now the loose threadbare t-shirt and cotton shorts left for us both to wear will have to do.

Stepping back into the bedroom, the cool night air hits me and I shiver, goosebumps puckering my skin as I pull on the clothes, hating how short the shorts are, and how cropped the t-shirt, though at least it's better than nothing. All of the women Soren keeps prisoner are naked but for a leash about their necks, so these clothes are luxury in comparison.

A cool breeze flutters through the open window and Faith mutters something indistinguishable in her sleep. She's turned on her side facing away from me, the harsh bumps of her spine stark beneath her skin, and for what seems like the thousandth time I curse Soren and his men, wishing my words alone were powerful enough to cast the kind of spell that only exists in fairytales.

With a heavy sigh, I sit back on the bed, and careful not to disturb her, gently pull up the blanket over her thin shoulders. Not only has she been beaten repeatedly, she's also malnourished. Her breasts might've filled out slightly due to the changes in her body, and her stomach rounded a little by the growing foetus inside of her, but she's worryingly underweight. I make a mental note to bargain for more food the next time Soren asks for an update. He can't expect Faith to carry his baby full term if she isn't given enough sustenance to do so.

Not that he'll ever get to meet his child.

I'll make sure of it.

Settling back onto the pillow, I turn my attention to outside the window and to the vast darkness of the desert. The sky is clear tonight, and the stars and moon hang like precious stones on a velvety dress only serving to remind me of why I'm here.

It's been almost two days since Soren asked for my assistance and just as long since I've made diamonds. I have no doubt that very soon he'll send one of his men to escort me to the lab. But I've not been complacent with my time. Earlier today I mixed up an immune boosting tea of ground wild oats mixed with crumbled stinging nettle. The tea has a slightly bitter aftertaste thanks to the nettle, but is full of calcium, iron and magnesium which are essential minerals for a pregnant woman with depleted energy. It was the first thing I encouraged Faith to drink.

But that fortifying tea wasn't the only concoction I brewed whilst she slipped in and out of sleep. I also used the time to create a poison that replicates the symptoms of dysentery. Chronic diarrhoea and sickness might not kill off our captor but it will make them weak, and a weak target is far easier to kill. All I need is an opportunity to drop it into their food, but that's a concern for another day. Right now, my priority is Faith and getting her as fit as I can, that and getting some sleep before one of Soren's men turns up demanding a shift in the lab. Closing my eyes, I breathe deeply, letting the exhaustion take hold of me and allow myself to fall into another restless slumber.

◈

"**G**ET UP!" a deep, male voice orders, the sharp pain of someone pinching my breast startling me awake.

My eyes spring open, my vision blurred as I scramble upright, jolting at the sight of a man towering over me. He's big, with broad shoulders and a thick neck, and under his hideous, unkempt beard I can see a sharp, rectangular face. His eyes are deep set, close together and with a slightly yellow tinge to their whites, but it's the sneer on his thin lips that I dislike most of all, that and the three-quarter skull tattoo covering his face.

"You bastard!" I hiss, rubbing the spot he pinched, feeling equal parts incensed and violated.

"Call me a bastard again and I'll take great pleasure in smacking those bad words right out of your cunting mouth!" he snaps, roughly snatching the blanket from me.

I grind my teeth together in anger, cursing him silently as I stare up at him.

"Yeah, that's what I thought," he goads. "Now get your shit together. You're needed."

He gestures for me to move, his gaze fixed on Faith who has frozen beside me. Fear radiates from her and my heart aches at seeing her react like that. I want to rush to her defence and shout at him for making her feel that way, but I know it won't do any good. Her fear is a natural reaction, one I would never blame her for, but I can and will blame the men responsible for it.

"Hello, pet," he says, his tongue snaking out to wet his cracked lips. "Soren wanted me to report back on your condition. Shall I tell him that you're looking quite the pretty picture. It's amazing what a few hours of sleep without a cock rammed up your arse can do."

I push upright, stepping in front of the man, drawing his attention back to me. "You can tell Soren that it's only been forty-eight hours. That she needs a lot more rest and recuperation."

Three-quarter skull smirks, his lips curling. "You can tell him yourself."

I glare at him. "And what if I don't want to?"

"Then I'll tell him that you refused to come with me and got a beating as a consequence."

"She shouldn't be left alone," I argue.

"Then I'll come back and sit with her. Make sure she's okay," he says with a smirk.

"No. Absolutely not!"

Without any warning Three-quarter Skull lifts his hand and

slaps me across my cheek, sending me stumbling sideways, my head ringing from the power behind it.

"Don't make me repeat myself, because it won't be pretty."

I bring my hand up to my face, my fingers brushing over the harsh, hot sting of his strike. A large part of me wants to go feral and launch myself at him, but he could snap me in two without thinking twice. So I force the rage I feel deep into the pit of my stomach, biting my tongue, fighting the desire to strike back. Instead I put all of my anger and disgust into my stare, making sure he knows that he's nothing more than shit beneath my shoe.

"You know what, fuck it!" he snaps, and in the instant before he curls his fingers into a fist I know I've made a huge mistake.

The impact of his fist against my jaw is like a sledgehammer, sending shockwaves through my skull. I feel the warm trickle of blood on my chin and taste the iron of it on my lips. My vision blurs and the world around me fades to a dull roar. As I stumble backwards, I hear his laughter, a cruel, hollow sound that seems to fill the room. In a daze, I bring my hand to my jaw, feeling the tenderness of the bruises already forming there.

"I've been wanting to do this since you arrived," he says, grabbing a fistful of my hair and yanking my towards him. This time he bites me on my ear, drawing blood.

I let out a blood curdling scream and Three-quarter Skull laughs, shoving me away from him roughly. I fall to the floor, but instinct and rage forces me to stand back up, my whole body trembling.

"Stop!" Faith screams, forcing herself upright, her face

twisted in pain from the sudden movement. Her back bows as she stands, but regardless she moves towards me, her steps unsteady.

"No! Get back in bed," I shout, holding my hands up and urging her with my eyes not to get involved. I wouldn't forgive myself if this bastard hurt her and she lost the baby because she was trying to protect me.

"Well lookie here, aren't we just best buddies. Have you been sucking on each other's tits and getting friendly whilst Soren's been distracted with his new bitches?" Three-quarter Skull asks, smirking.

My hate for this poor excuse for a man burns within me, but I hold my tongue. I'm not going to give him the satisfaction of my response.

"Nothing to say, *witch*?" he taunts.

I clamp my mouth shut, and fold my arms across my chest stubbornly.

"Cynthia, please just go with him," Faith says quietly, her soft voice filled with concern as she hobbles back to bed. "I'll be okay."

I glance over at her. "I won't leave you."

"You will," she insists.

Three-quarter Skull grips my arm, squeezing tightly. "Listen to the bitch."

"Please, Cynthia," Faith begs, collapsing onto the bed.

The pain in her eyes is like a knife twisting in my gut, but if I fight this man I probably won't see tomorrow to help her, and I have to help her. Reluctantly, I nod. "I'll be back as soon as I can, okay?"

"Okay," she whispers, giving me a tremulous smile that breaks my heart.

Her fear is a visceral thing, heavy, choking. I hate to leave her so vulnerable. I hate it, but I do it anyway. Turning my attention back to the brute, I say, "I'm ready."

"No, witch, I don't think you are," he says, squeezing his fingers tighter, so tight that I can feel my bones grind together from the pressure. "Now be a good bitch, and come quietly."

I have no choice but to follow.

9

Carrick

"We haven't got long to get what we need out of this arsehole," I say, striding over to the man and ramming the butt of my pistol into his forehead, he groans, slowly rousing. "Wake up, motherfucker!"

"Have you tortured many men lately?" Beast asks, casually inspecting his nails before eying me. "Because generally speaking, shouting doesn't work. In my experience, chatting to the fuckers like they're your best mate then chopping a bollock off, does. Know what I mean?"

"Then chop a bollock off!" I reply, jabbing the man's head with the gun again.

He winces and blinks open his eyes, squinting up at me and Beast, his gaze going in and out of focus as he looks between us. Cursing in a language I don't recognise, he mutters something in broken English.

"You might want to speak up, Bones, ain't nobody hearing that," Beast says, cocking his head at the arsehole.

"I said, fuck you," he spits.

That earns him a punch to his cheek from Beast that snaps his head to the side and knocks him out once more.

"I thought you were good at this?" I say, gripping the man's hair and shaking his head. "He's out cold again. At this rate he'll be dead from a bleed to the brain before we find out where they're keeping Cyn!"

"He's not dead. I didn't hit him that hard. Just reminding him to be respectful, that's all," Beast retorts, smiling knowingly when the man starts groaning again. "See."

"Just get him to talk, and do it quickly," Arden says, turning his attention from Beast to Jakub. "We need the other car brought up to the villa. As soon as we get what we need from this bastard, we're gone."

"Leon and Konrad will go. I will help with the questioning," he replies.

"I'll go with them," Lorcan says, flicking his gaze to Arden who nods his head in agreement.

"Be safe, brother. There could be more of them out there," I say, my gut twisting at the thought. Lorcan is more than capable of looking after himself, but we rarely do anything alone, and him leaving without us doesn't sit well with me.

"*Always,*" he replies, giving me and Arden one last lingering look before following Leon and Konrad out of the room.

"You know I'm more than capable of getting the information we need, if you want to go with loverboy," Beast says with a wink as he grips the man's face in his huge hand. "I don't need you hanging around and cramping my style."

"We're staying," I reply, brooking no arguments. "Now if you wouldn't mind getting on with it."

Beast smiles. "I like it when you're bossy." Then he pulls out a flick knife from his back pocket, opens it up and stabs it into the man's thigh.

The scream that rips out of the bastard's mouth has my lips curling up in a cruel smile. Violence is second nature to the men in this room. We've grown up swimming in it our whole lives. There have been many, many times I've witnessed this kind of violence, delivered it myself even, and eventually it begins to eat away at the empathy within you until all that's left is a cruel husk of a man with barely a human heart.

The only shred of light and real, *true* happiness that has tempered the darkness has been Lorcan and Arden, and now that I've finally opened up my heart to Cyn, her too.

"Tell me where your cunting leader is hiding!" Beast demands, applying more pressure to the blade, sinking it further into his muscular thigh.

Blood oozes out the side and the man chokes out an incomprehensible string of syllables, his eyes popping with the pain as spittle flies from his mouth. Eventually he finally manages to wheeze out a reply. "Fuck. You."

"No, I'm pretty sure you'll be getting fucked in the arse with this blade if you don't tell us what we want to know," he replies, twisting the blade in his leg.

More screaming. More fucking tears. But still no answer.

"Listen," Beast says, removing the knife and pulling up a chair, blood pumping from the wound "We all know you ain't living to see another day. But I can make your passing quick if you tell us."

"Fuck... You..." he repeats.

Beast slams the knife into his other thigh, this time up to the hilt. The cry that leaves the cunt's mouth is more animal than human.

"Looks like you're the one getting fucked, mate," Beast says conversationally.

The man laughs. He actually fucking laughs as blood coats his teeth and his eyes turn wild.

"He's not going to talk," I say, glancing over at Jakub and Arden who are both watching intently as this all unfolds.

Neither make any move to intervene, clearly trusting Beast to get the job done, but I'm not so certain. When I meet Arden's gaze, he shakes his head, and I know he's warning me not to get involved, to let Beast do what he does best. So, despite my instinct to slice off one of the man's ears and forcefully feed it to him, I don't.

"Look, I'm gonna level with you," Beast says, pulling a packet of cigarettes from his jacket pocket and lighting one. He drags in a long breath, smoke trailing out of his mouth as he speaks. "I've been doing this for a long, long time. I have a one hundred percent success rate. You ain't dying before we find out what we want to know, and I have no issue making this as excruciatingly painful for you whilst I do it. So do yourself a favour and fess up."

Beast leans back in his chair, puffing on the cigarette, and waits. After a minute of silence, Beast launches forward, grabs a handful of the man's hair and yanks his hair back.

"Fuck, fine. Have it your way," he says with a shake of his head, before turning to me. "Carrick, pin his left eye open, would you?"

I get to my feet, and grab the man's face, forcing his eye open. He spits and curses at me, trying in vain to throw us both off.

"Ever wondered what it felt like to have a cigarette put out in your eye?" Beast asks, before taking the cigarette from his mouth and hovering it just above the man's eyeball. "I hear it's fucking painful."

"No! Noooo!" the man screams as Beast lowers the burning ember over his eyeball.

"You gonna talk?" he asks, holding it there.

"Motherfucker," the man spits.

"Wrong answer," Beast smirks, stubbing out the cigarette right into the centre of his eye, the hiss and pop as it burns through his cornea is stomach churning.

"Fuck," I grind out, letting the man's head go and taking a step back as he screams and screams, this stub of the cigarette sticking out of his eye.

"I did warn you," Beast says, leaning back on the knife still impaled in the man's thigh.

The man whimpers and shakes his head, trying to loosen

the stub, but I see some of the fight leaving him as his body registers the pain and he begins to shake violently.

"The key to successful torture is not pushing too hard too quickly. We don't want this fucker's mind to detach from his body and the pain," Beast says, as he pulls out the knife and gives the man a moment. He turns to Arden and Jakub. "I need a piss. Let him stew for a bit. I'll be right back."

Beast returns a couple of minutes later, giving us a wink as he re-enters the room. Crouching down in front of the man, he rests the tip of the blade under his thumb nail, then says, "I can tell you now that cutting off your dick would be far less painful than sliding this knife under your nail," he says knowingly.

"Wanna talk?"

He remains stubbornly quiet.

"Fine," Beast huffs, then rams the blade beneath the man's thumbnail removing it and a good portion of flesh and muscle across his knuckle.

The scream that follows is louder than a fucking freight train passing through a station. I almost cover my ears, not in sympathy but in annoyance. I'm getting a fucking headache.

"Are you gonna tell us what we want to know?" Beast persists.

The bastard shakes his head so Beast does the same thing to his pointer finger, moving to each finger every time the man refuses to reply. By the time he gets to the man's pinky finger he's begging for Beast to stop, to end the torture.

"Enough," Arden says, stepping forward. He crouches beside the man, cupping his chin and forcing him to look up. "The pain will stop if you just tell us where Soren is keeping our woman. But if you don't I will make sure that Beast removes all your toenails in the same way, then I will watch him strip your skin from your body slowly, inch by excruciating inch."

"Okay, *okay*," the man replies, before he starts talking quickly in a language that's unrecognisable to anything I've ever heard before.

"In English," Arden says, his voice soft, deadly.

"Marrakech," he pants.

"That's Morocco, right?" Beast asks.

"Yes," Arden replies, dropping the man's face then rearing upright. Meeting my gaze, he sweeps his eyes from me to Jakub, then says, "Let's go get our girl."

"Don't be fucking stupid," the man laughs hysterically, bloody spittle flying from his mouth. "The Skull Brotherhood will end you."

Arden doesn't bother to respond. Instead, with one sharp jerk of his chin towards Beast, he strides from the room. Jakub and I follow suit, the gurgling sound of a dying man choking on his own blood following us out.

10

C^{yn}

"This isn't the lab," I say, my heart racing as Three-quarter Skull pushes open a heavy wooden door inlaid with gold rivets, revealing a small, dark room with thick, patterned rugs covering the floor. The only light comes from a single gas lamp lit in the far corner of the room.

As I step inside, the smell of absolute terror fills my nostrils and as my eyes adjust to the light. I'm shocked to see half a dozen naked women to my left, shaking with fear and stricken with grief.

I open my mouth to ask him what's going on, but before I can get the words out Soren strides into the room, his lips curling into a smirk as he takes in the frightened women huddled together.

"GET UP!" he roars, bare-chested except for the skeletal tattoos and a pair of loose black slacks covering his legs. The room is so dimly lit that he actually looks like a walking, talking skeleton, the definition of his muscles lost to shade and shadow.

A portion of the women jump to their feet quickly, but a few take their time standing, their fear making it difficult for them to move fast enough.

"Get them into position," Soren orders with a terse wave of his hand.

"Sir," Three-quarter Skull replies, striding over to the women and ushering them to the other side of the room, their cries gutting me as he shoves at them. One woman has a swollen left eye and there's a cut to her lip. She's sobbing hysterically. My fingers curl into fists, my blood boiling with rage as Soren turns his attention back to me.

"Cyn," he says, lips curling as his salacious gaze drinks me in. "You have no idea how much I've been looking forward to seeing you again."

The feeling is definitely not mutual, but I keep those thoughts to myself.

"How's my bitch doing?" he asks, cocking his head to the side as he takes a step closer.

I consider not answering him, but that would lead to a beating and my head's still ringing from Three-quarter Skull's punch to my face.

"Like I said to him," I reply, casting my gaze to his goon,

contempt seeping into my voice no matter how much I try to curb it. "It's barely been forty-eight hours. *Faith* needs time."

A flash of anger passes across Soren's face as he reaches for my chin and pinches it between his thumb and fingers painfully. "You might want to lessen the attitude if you want to remain untouched. Just because I've not allowed any of my men to fuck you until you pass out from the pain, doesn't mean I won't."

Swallowing down the bile rising up my throat at the thought, I school my features, forcing calm into my voice. "Faith needs rest and I need to remain conscious and in good health in order to look after her and continue to make diamonds," I calmly point out.

For a moment Soren's grip tightens on my chin, his fingers digging into my skin so hard I can feel the pinch in my bone. He's desperate to punish me, but I force myself not to give him any outward sign that I'm afraid that he'll live up to his threat.

He leans in closer, lowering his voice. "And my son?"

"Is still alive." *No thanks to you.*

"Excellent," he says, his piercing gaze meeting mine before his hand moves around to the back of my head. My stomach roils as he presses his hips against mine, his erection hard against my stomach.

"Why am I here?" I ask, forcing myself not to react and knee him in the balls like I want to do.

"You're to examine my newest shipment of bitches. I need to know how many, if at all, are intact."

My throat dries out and I can barely respond. "Intact?"

"I need to know if any are virgins," he replies.

"And you can't tell that yourself?"

He smirks. "Would you rather one of my men did the examination?"

"No! I'll do it," I rush out, not wanting any of those bastards near those poor women.

"I thought you might say that," he replies before slamming his lips against mine.

I'm so shocked that for the briefest of moments I don't react. Then my brain catches up with my body, and my hands fly up to his chest as I try in vain to push him away.

He growls into my mouth, yanking me tighter against his body before gripping my face and prying my jaw apart with his fingers, forcing his tongue past my lips.

I gag, hating the vile way he violates me with his tongue. I contemplate biting it off, but the consequences will be too great for me, for these women and for Faith, so I let him defile my mouth and squeeze my tit roughly. I don't fight back, knowing that he wants me too more than anything.

Finally he pulls away, leaving the evil taste of him still lingering on my tongue, and my mouth fills with a rush of saliva as though my body is trying to rid itself of his taste. Forcing myself to swallow, I start to recount the recipe for the poison I've made, drawing strength from the mental process. It's the only thing that keeps me from collapsing into a heap of tears.

"Examine them. Tell me what you find. If their hymen isn't intact, I want to know."

"What will happen to the women who aren't virgins?" I ask.

"They will be given to my men on celebration night," he says.

"Celebration night?" I ask, remembering him mentioning that previously. If I'm correct, that's only a couple of days away.

"Once a year the Skull Brotherhood get to fulfil their deepest, darkest desires. Like The Masks masquerade ball, only a lot more... *enjoyable.*"

The shock must show on my face because he laughs. "You think I don't know who your friends are? You think I don't know about your history with The Masks *and* the Deana-dhe? You're not immune to witnessing darkness or being a part of it, are you, *Cyn*?" he asks, my name rolling off his tongue like a dirty prayer.

I swallow the bile burning the back of my throat, ignoring the way he makes me feel dirty for being friends with them. The Masks had many faults, a great deal of which I despised, but they are not the same as the Skull Brotherhood. Arden, Lorcan and Carrick even less so.

"And the virgins?" I whisper.

"Already sold to a man who likes to break in the untouched. They will ship out tomorrow. I've heard he likes his virgins stiff, and I don't mean from fear."

"You mean?" I choke out, hoping that what he's insinuating isn't true.

"There are plenty of people out there with very undesirable tastes..." he allows his voice to trail off as I try to mentally comprehend what he's saying.

"You'd let that happen?"

"These women are nothing to me. I have no conscience, *witch*. Haven't you noticed the bones in my private quarters. Who do you think they belonged to?"

This time I can't stop the puke from rising up my throat and erupting from my mouth. I turn my head away, the contents of my stomach splattering across the tiled floor.

His laughter at my reaction has an odd affect on me. I'm not scared. I'm *angry*.

Swiping the back of my hand over my mouth, I glare at him. "You *bast–*"

Before I can even finish, Soren's fist makes contact with the side of my head. The weight of his fist like a rock against my cheek. I nearly lose my balance as I struggle to regain my composure, the buzz in my ear loud, the pain almost over-whelming.

"You fuck me off one more time and it won't be one of my men taking your cunt until you bleed, but *me*," he says, before turning his back on me and walking across the room without another word.

I'm left quaking with anger and a residual fear that's not for me but these women, for Faith. But I shut it down quickly before it has time to incapacitate me. Instead, I force my spine straight and my shoulders back.

Fuck him.

Fuck. Him.

"On the floor!" Soren orders.

Most of the women lie down immediately, fear making them submissive, but one has a spark of fire in her eyes, and she glares at Soren. I want to tell her to do as she's told, to not take courage from my reaction to the bastard, but before I can do anything Three-quarter Skull grabs her by the arm and shoves her forcefully to the floor.

"Get on the floor where you belong, bitch!" he growls.

She falls hard, the sound of a bone breaking ricochets around the room as she puts out her hand to brace her fall. Crying out, she holds up her hand, the middle finger on her left hand bent at an awkward angle. Just like that, the fire in her eyes dims.

"*Witch*, get over here. Now!" Soren orders, waving at me impatiently before turning his attention to Three-quarter Skull. "A word."

They move to the far side of the room, talking together as I swallow the anxiety rising up my chest and drop to the floor in front of the woman with the broken finger. She's clutching her hand to her chest, tears falling silently down her face.

"I'll be gentle, okay?" I reassure her, resting my hand on her knee, my fingers trembling, feeling sick at what I'm being forced to do.

"I'm not a virgin," she whispers, her eyes filling with tears.

My stomach churns, knowing what that means for her. She'll be at the mercy of the Skull Brotherhood at their night of celebration. It doesn't bear thinking about. Then again, neither is being sold to a sexual deviant who has requested virgins to fuck and murder for his own sick pleasure.

Forcing myself not to panic, I look from the woman in front of me to the rest, whispering under my breath. "I can buy you time. That's all I can do," I say, hoping that they understand I'm trying to help them.

"They'll hurt you if you lie," the woman in front of me whispers back.

"It's a chance I'm willing to take," I hush out, placing myself between the woman's legs and pretending to examine her whilst Soren is distracted behind me.

If I say that they're not virgins at least they won't be sent to their deaths tomorrow. It will give me time to spike the Skull Brotherhood's food, and in turn give us all a fighting chance until The Masks and the Deana-dhe come. And they will come. I *have* to believe that.

Moving on to the next woman, I give her a tight smile, my hands shaking as I skate my fingers over her centre, barely touching her, but having to make it look as though I am. She blinks up at me, her deep brown eyes pooling with tears at the invasion of her personal space.

"I'm so sorry," I mouth, my hands trembling.

Behind me the conversation between Soren and Three-quarter Skull finishes. I move quickly to the next woman. She seems younger than the first two, no more than twenty at a guess. Her mouth trembles and her gaze whips from my face to somewhere behind me.

"Well?" Soren asks.

"So far all three have broken hymens," I say, looking over my shoulder and meeting his gaze with as much confidence as I can muster.

He *has* to believe me.

"Move on to the next," he orders.

Stopping in front of the next woman, a petite lady with pretty blue eyes and a blonde pixie cut, I silently apologise. She locks eyes with me and gently nods her head, giving me permission to examine her. With Soren standing behind me, I can't pretend this time.

"I'll be gentle," I say softly, gently parting her outer labia, and finding her entrance.

She tenses around me, biting on her bottom lip as I slide my finger inside of her, pressing against her hymen. She's intact. She's a virgin.

"Well?" Soren demands.

Withdrawing my finger, I look up at him. "Broken."

"Fuck!" he exclaims. "And the other two?"

I move onto the next woman, she's the one with the split lip and swollen eye. She shuffles backwards away from me, fear making her run. Before I'm even able to reassure her, Three-quarter Skull has gripped her hair and is yanking her back towards me.

"Stop it!" I yell, grabbing his meaty arm, trying to pull him off of her.

Without a second thought, he twists around and throws a punch, sending me sprawling backwards. The woman he's got a hold off starts screaming as blood pours from my nose. I reach up to touch it, hissing in pain. It feels bruised, sore, but hopefully not broken.

"Shut her the fuck up!" Soren roars at Three-quarter Skull before grabbing me by the hair and dragging me to the last woman who's shaking so violently her teeth chatter.

"Check her," he orders, shoving me towards her.

"What about–"

"Virgin," Three-quarter Skull says as he pulls his fingers from between the sobbing woman's legs and shoves them in his mouth. "Hmmm," he hums.

"Oh God, no," I cry, wanting to save her from her fate. "You can't do this!"

"I said check her!" Soren roars, forcing me forward with a hard shove.

Stumbling, I drop to my knees before the last woman. She appears to be the oldest here, but still no older than her late twenties. I meet her gaze, and the deep blue of her eyes swim with tears.

"It's okay," she whispers. "Just do it."

I reach between her woman's legs, entering her as gently as I can. She's not a virgin.

"Her hymen is broken," I say, my mouth pressing together as I remove my hands and gently grip her knee, apologising with my touch.

She gives me a weak smile, tears trembling on her lashes.

"One out of six," Soren says, yanking me to my feet and gesturing towards the terrified woman who still struggles in Three-quarter Skull's hold. "Get her prepared for shipment tomorrow."

"Don't do this," I plead, rounding on Soren.

Soren tips his head back and laughs. "You think begging will work on me?"

"Give her to your men. Don't sign her death warrant, please."

That really makes him laugh, and an ice-cold feeling settles in my blood as he smiles at me. "You think that'll be any better?"

I swallow hard, hoping, praying that Arden, Lorcan and Carrick will be here soon. I just need to steal more time. "I won't make any more diamonds if you hurt any of them. I refuse," I say, changing tactics.

"You will, because if you don't, I will slit all of their throats right now and I will make you wear their blood as a reminder of your poor choices. Am I understood?"

A few of the women begin to cry, and I force myself to breathe, to get control of my wildly erratic emotions. "At least let me give her something before she goes. Something that will help..." I say, my voice cracking as I stare at the woman, feeling utterly helpless.

"Why should I? You're being insolent."

"Because I'm keeping your son alive," I reply, my voice dropping.

For a moment he stares at me, no doubt trying to decide if I deserve more of a beating. In the end, he waves his hand and says, "Fine. Make her a potion, *witch*. I will ensure it gets to her before she leaves."

Three-quarter Skull clears his throat. "And the rest, where do you want them?"

Soren grins as he sidesteps me. "I want them taken to the cells. Get the other bitches to prepare them for celebration night. They're not to be touched by anyone until then. I want my men starving before I feed them. Understood?"

"Understood." Three-quarter Skull gestures for the women to follow him out.

"Thank God," I whisper, my shoulders visibly relaxing. It's not much to hold on to, but it's something at least. Soren hears me, sees the relief on my face. He gives me a vicious look that has me wishing that I never uttered a word.

"Wait! I've had a change of heart," Soren says, smiling wickedly. "One of you lucky ladies won't have to wait until the celebration night next week to feel the heavy weight of my cock in your cunt because one of you is going to get very fucked tonight."

And just like that fear becomes a lit match striking every woman in turn. I watch the flame leap from one to the next, forcing their heads to drop and their shoulders to curl inwards like brittle autumnal leaves on a bonfire. It breaks my heart to see them like this, so utterly afraid, so powerless.

"So who's it going to be?" he asks, cruelty lacing his words with poison.

My chest tightens with anxiety as Soren inspects each woman, yanking them out of the line and forcing them to look into his eyes, searching for something. I'm not sure if it's submission or a spark of fire, but either way a grotesque smile spreads across his face, only adding to the dark gleam in his eyes. Power radiates around him like a poisonous gas, making it difficult to breathe.

The vile bastard.

One by one he moves between them until he reaches the one remaining virgin, the one I lied about. "You want to wake up from this bad dream, don't you, pet?" he asks, grasping her breast as tears cascade down her cheeks.

"Please don't," she whimpers as he bruises her skin with his hateful touch.

"No," I whisper. "Stop."

If he hears me, he doesn't react, he simply keeps on abusing the woman before me. Enjoying her fear, getting high on his own perverted power trip.

"Don't touch her," I say, more loudly this time.

"What was that you said?" Soren asks, turning to face me, his fleshless features morphing into something from my nightmares as his arm drops and he studies me.

Forcing my chin up, I glare at him. "I said don't touch her."

He tips his head back and laughs. An evil belly laugh that makes my skin crawl. "I can and I will."

"She's meant for the celebration," I stutter out, trying to think of something, anything, to make him stop. Not to protect me because I lied about her not being a virgin, but to protect her.

"You told me I can't touch *my* bitch because of her condition, which means I need to find pleasure elsewhere."

He turns his back to me, and forcefully yanks his chosen victim against his chest, grinding his hips against hers. She sobs as he grasps her hair and yanks her head to the side, sucking on her neck. Her gaze pleads with mine, and I know he'll break her, just like he tried to break Faith, just like he broke all the women before her.

"Stop it," I say forcefully, the command slipping past my lips in an angry rush. Fury fires in my blood and I hang on to it with all my might. If I'm angry, I'm not scared, and if I'm not scared I can save this woman. I can save us all.

"Stop? I've only just begun," he replies, an evil glint in his eye as he cups her between the legs.

"Don't!" I rush forward, grabbing his arm, yanking it away

from the woman who sobs, shivering uncontrollably now. She doubles over, hugging herself, backing away.

"You dare to interrupt me? Who the fuck do you think you are?" he snarls, rounding on me as he reaches for my throat, squeezing tight.

"I can offer something better," I choke out as his palm presses on my windpipe, cutting off my air supply.

"My bitch?" he asks.

I shake my head.

"What then?" he asks, licking his lips as he loosens his hold on my throat.

Dragging in a painful breath, I force myself to be strong, to look him dead in the eye and offer him something I know he won't refuse.

"Me."

Lorcan

Twenty-four hours after leaving Vasko's villa we arrive in the vibrant bustle of Marrakech after a gruelling crossing on a ferry, and a very hot and sweaty six hour train journey from Port Tangier Med. It's ten in the morning and the city is a sharp contrast to the Spanish countryside we left behind. The atmosphere in the souk is electric and alive, the streets thronging with locals and tourists alike. Everywhere we look, colour and chaos fill the air; from the bright silks of the marketplace to the smells of spices and incense that cling to the walls of the city, and the colourful language as people sell their wares.

The sun's heat brings a flush to my skin, though the stinging discomfort of sunburn fades in comparison to the chasm opening up inside my chest. It's an abyss of frustration and rage, and whilst I might not be Arden who can see things in the future, my gut is telling me that Cyn's time is running out. It's been almost two weeks since they took her. Two fucking weeks. They could've done untold damage in that time.

"This is taking too long," I say, frustration making a fist of my fingers as I watch Arden and Beast talk to a man selling herbs and spices at a stall opposite me.

So far, no one has given us an exact location, though plenty have said they've seen members of the Skull Brotherhood pass through the souk. The last stall owner we spoke to said that he heard a rumour of a man with almost a full skull tattooed across his face seen buying herbs and flowers from this part of the souk, and so here we are.

"We couldn't fly into the country on The Masks plane, you know that. The ferry from Spain was our only option. Less conspicuous that way. Thank fuck we could call in the debt with Karim, we wouldn't have gotten into the country without him."

Karim is to the Moroccan people what Robin Hood was to the people of Sherwood. Of all the criminals we've ever come across over the years, he's one of the better ones. An honourable man who wants to rid his country of all evil and corruption, starting with the Skull Brotherhood who've brazenly taken up residence in his home. When we told him why we needed his help, he didn't hesitate.

I swipe a hand through my sweat-soaked hair. "Yeah, I know that, but every hour that passes–"

"She's alive, Lorcan. We're *almost* there," Carrick interjects firmly, before slugging back almost a whole bottle of water. He crouches down and reaches inside his rucksack, passing a bottle to me. "Drink. We don't need you passing out from heat stroke."

I take the bottle from him, twisting off the cap and taking a long pull. I've barely been in the sun, keeping to the shade and wearing a baseball cap to protect my face, but even so I feel the sting of sunburn on the back of my neck and hands despite slathering myself in lotion. It fucking sucks having a skin condition that's sensitive to the sun. But that's the least of my worries right now as Arden stalks towards us with Beast hot on his heels, his face a mask of anger.

"Anything?" I ask.

"We have the exact location," he replies, grabbing my bottle of water and downing it in one go.

"Then why are we still standing here!" I say, a surge of energy rushing through my veins.

Arden shakes his head, whilst Beast swipes at the sweat dripping from his forehead.

"Fuck this heat," Beast says, his face almost as red as mine. "I feel like a pig roasting on a spit."

"Just call Jakub, tell him we've found her and let's get this done," Carrick insists.

"I'm in agreement with Carrick. Can we just go kill the cunts so I can get back home to rainy England? This fucking heat ain't for me," Beasts moans.

"That's the issue. Getting into their place without being spotted," Arden sighs, the dark circles around his eyes a deep purple against his sallow skin.

He needs rest. Sleep. He needs Cyn.

"Why's that?" Beast asks, pinching the collar of his t-shirt and fanning it against his skin.

"Weren't you listening to what he said?" Arden asks, his patience waning.

"I may or may not have spaced out a bit during some of the conversation," he replies, pulling a face. "I told you I don't like the heat, turns my brain to fucking mush."

Arden huffs out a breath. "Soren's stronghold is another eight hour drive away, just outside of Zagora and several kilometres into the Sahara Desert."

"Eight hours!" I exclaim, my stomach churning at more precious time lost. "Fuck."

"Not only that, it's surrounded by dunes and nothing more. We can't get in or out without being spotted," Arden adds, swiping a hand over his face.

I draw in a deep breath, trying to quell the rising panic. Despite now having the exact location of the Skull Brotherhood's lair, we can't just rush the place given it's in the middle of the fucking desert. They'll pick us off one by one.

"So what now?" Carrick asks, shifting on his feet as he picks up his rucksack and swings it onto his back.

"Call Jakub, update him on what we've found out," Arden says, looking at me. "I'm heading back to Karim's. He should know someone willing to drive us into the desert. Locate the others and meet me back there in an hour."

"And the small matter of getting into their building without our brains getting blown out the back of our heads?" Beast asks.

"We'll figure that out along the way," Arden replies.

"Sounds like a *great* plan," Beast retorts, his voice heavy with sarcasm as he throws me a look.

Despite my need to just get to Cyn as soon as fucking possible, I agree with Beast. "Arden, we need to think about this."

"We have eight hours in a car to do exactly that," he replies, before picking up speed and striding ahead of us. In a matter of seconds we lose him within the crowd of people.

"Well that went well," Beast mutters, as Carrick strides past us with a determined look on his face.

"Let me talk to him. I'll see you back at Karim's," he throws over his shoulder, jogging to catch up with Arden.

"Fuck!" I exclaim, dragging a hand over my face.

Beast grasps my arm, forcing me to stop. He jerks his chin towards a restaurant on the other side of the souk that's filled with locals eating delicious smelling food. My stomach rumbles, adding to the grumble of Beast's stomach.

"I don't know about you, but I'm fucking starving. We got time to eat. Let's go."

"No. I want to get moving so we're ready to go as soon as Arden's located a driver," I retort shaking off his arm.

Beast reaches for me again. "Listen, you fucked–," he coughs, grinning. "I meant *talked* some sense into Carrick, the least I can do is look out for you. You look like shit. You need to eat. Gather your strength, mate, because you're going to need it."

I know he's right, my head's fucking splitting from heat,

hunger and dehydration. The last thing anyone needs is for me to get sick. "Fine. I'll make that call to Jakub. The Masks can meet us here. Then we can all head back to Karim's together."

Fifteen minutes later, we're sitting at a round table in a lively restaurant filled with tourists and locals with piles of Morrocan food on dozens of plates spread out in front of us, Jakub sitting opposite me. Konrad and Leon excused themselves five minutes after they arrived to use the toilet and haven't returned yet.

"I sure hope they've only drank bottled water," Beast remarks around a mouthful of lamb and couscous, "Because we do not need to be two men down."

Jakub arches a brow. "We won't be."

Beast laughs at Jakub's confidence. "Okay then, mate. I'll take your word for it. So, what chance do you think we have of not dying in the next twenty-four hours?"

Jakub dabs at the corner of his mouth with a napkin. "Right now. Zero."

Beast groans. "Fuck, I thought you might say that."

"So what's the alternative?" I ask, frustrated. "We know where Cyn is, Karim has supplied us with weapons. Time isn't on our side."

"Why? Did Arden see something?" Jakub asks, shifting forward in his seat, assuming he's had a vision.

"No. I've just got this feeling..." My voice trails off as I take a sip of my chilled beer before resting the cool glass against my cheek. I swear I hear it fucking sizzle.

"Yeah, it's called indigestion," Beast remarks, smirking.

I know he's trying to lighten the mood, but it's not helping.

"I can't seem to shift it," I say, pressing the base of my palm against the centre of my chest trying to soothe the ache there. "Nothing's helping."

"Pretty sure you helped it a little on the plane," Beast jibes, winking at me.

"Relieving our pain together was a temporary fix," I reply with a little more honesty than either of us expect. "It's not the same as having her in our arms."

"You love her," Jakub says, regarding me.

"I wouldn't be here if I didn't," I say, dropping my hand.

"And the others?" he asks. "Do they love her like you do?"

"Without a doubt."

He nods, seemingly satisfied. "We'll get her back."

"I know we will, I just can't see *how* right now. We can't get close without being seen."

"I think I might have a solution," Konrad says as he steps into my peripheral vision.

We all turn to look up at him.

"What the fuck happened to you? Did you take a shit big enough to punch you in the noggin?" Beast says with a laugh. "Where's Leon? Getting rid of the evidence?"

"Funny," he retorts, swiping at the split in his brow. "I think you might want to follow me."

"Ah fuck," Beast exclaims, understanding instantly that shit's about to go down. "I ain't gonna get to come back and eat the rest of this, am I?"

Konrad shakes his head. "The sooner we get out of here the better," he says, unfurling the fingers of his right hand. We all stare at the severed thumb sitting on his palm, tattooed into the flesh is a thumb bone. "Leon and I had just had a chat with a very interesting waiter."

"Is that so? Where's the rest of him?" I ask, chucking him a napkin so he can get rid of the fucking thumb.

Konrad's lip twitches. I'm not sure if it's the start of a smile or a scowl. Either way, I don't much care. "He's stuffed into a dumpster out back. Leon's waiting for us. We need to move. Now," he replies, wrapping the thumb up in the napkin and tucking it into his pocket.

Jakub stands up and grabs his bag from underneath the table. "Let's go then," he says firmly as he slides his chair back under the table.

I drain my beer and get up too. "Lead on." I motion to Konrad before throwing a few notes down on the table for our lunch. It was a good meal, and considering it might be our last I figure it's only right we should pay for it.

It's nearing midnight when the seven of us are seated in a booth in the corner of a traditional shisha cafe in the less touristy part of the city. The air is filled with clouds of smoke, and the chatter of a group of locals congregating at a table on the other side of the cafe. It has dark red brick walls, and small arched windows to maintain a level of privacy not granted by other cafes. Outside the streets are quiet, most of the tourists have headed back to their hotels and only a few locals are still out and about.

"So," I say, to break the oppressive silence between us all. "What time are the buyers expected to arrive?"

Konrad checks his watch. "According to the waiter, shortly."

"So we wait for the buyers who are due to collect diamonds from Soren, jump them and then take their place? Is that how this is going down?" Beast asks, dragging in a deep lungful from the shisha pipe before blowing the scented smoke up into the air.

"That's about the gist of it," Arden replies, his knee bouncing up and down as he casts an assessing look around the space. "Unless you have a better idea?"

Beast shrugs. "I'm easy, man. So long as we don't get arrested by the Gendarmerie."

"Karim is waiting for us out back. Once we find out where the buyers' rendezvous is with the driver, he'll take us there at the designated time so we can pick up their transportation to Soren's stronghold," I explain.

"And can we trust this waiter guy? He could've lied and sent us into a trap. He's working for the Skull Brotherhood after all," Beast remarks.

"*Was* working for the Skull Brotherhood," Leon points out, taking a sip of mint tea as he eyes us all. "He wasn't lying, and he didn't have the opportunity to send us into a trap."

"Leon's right, he got verbal diarrhoea when Leon threatened to chop off his dick," Konrad says with a shrug.

Beast chuckles. "And there's me thinking you were the ones with the shits."

"You really don't give it a rest, do you?" Arden asks, pinching the bridge of his nose.

"Mate, we all need a little comedic relief. Just think of me as your injection of joy and lightheartedness," Beast replies, puffing on the shisha and sending more clouds of blue smoke up into the air before turning to Carrick. "You know, you could learn something about torture from those two. The dick trick gets most men. No one wants to be a eunuch."

Carrick rolls his eyes. "Yeah, great tip."

"What they fail to realise is," Beast continues, without any encouragement, "Is that spilling the beans to save their todger ain't gonna do shit when their throats are cut and they're bleeding out on the floor. Or in this case, in a dumpster."

"Indeed," Leon agrees with a smirk.

"Can you trust Karim? I mean he seems like a sound fella, but you can never be too sure," Beast asks, almost as an afterthought.

"He got us into the country. He's supplied us with weapons. Got rid of the body. We spent the afternoon at his riad without issue. The Skull Brotherhood hasn't jumped us. I think it's safe to say we can trust him," Arden replies.

"Fair enough," Beast retorts, winking as he takes a sip from his cup of mint tea. "Fucking hell, that tastes bloody lovely. I'm normally a Yorkshire tea kind of man, but I could get used to this."

"Okay, so we take the buyer's place," Carrick interrupts, jerking his chin towards the group of men sitting on the far side of the cafe. "What about them?"

"I'm all for a bloodbath," Beast says with a wry grin, "But I'd rather not take out the locals if I can help it. Not their fault they're in the wrong place at the wrong time."

"Leave it with me. I can handle that," Jakub says, getting to his feet and heading over to the manager of the establishment, passing him his rucksack as they talk in low voices. He returns a moment later with a fresh pot of mint tea pouring us all a cup as the manager ushers the men out of the cafe. A minute or so after, the manager leaves with his staff, giving us a brief nod as he exits.

"What did you say exactly?" Carrick asks.

"The truth, that if he wants to live long enough to use the fifty grand stashed in that rucksack I just gave him, then I suggest he clears the building."

"You don't think he's going to contact the Gendarmerie the second he gets the chance?" Beast asks, cocking a brow.

"What and tell them that a group of criminals are waiting to jump another group of criminals in his nice, respectable shisha cafe?" Jakub retorts.

"Point well made," Beast concedes with a smirk.

"He could contact Soren, though," Carrick says.

"He could but he won't."

"How can you be so sure?" Arden asks, drawing his gun from inside his jacket and screwing on a silencer.

Jakub rests his hands on the table, entwining his fingers. "Christy."

"She had a vision?" Beast asks, brows raised.

"Yes," he confirms with a sharp nod of his head, before moving to stand. "I got a call whilst we were questioning the stall holders in the souk. She saw all this play out. How do you think we got the tip-off about the waiter?"

"So we're going to live?" Beast asks, expectantly.

"I believe so," Jakub confirms.

"Don't sound too certain, mate," Beast says with raised brows.

"Christy isn't always able to tell us everything we want to know in case it changes the hands of fate," Jakub explains.

Beast pulls a face. "What's the bloody point then?"

"Just trust me on this, like I trust Christy, okay?" Jakub throws back.

Beast nods his head. "Fine, fuck. What about when we get to Soren's hideaway?"

Jakub shrugs. "That I don't know."

"Bloody perfect," Beast scowls, sliding his hand through his hair. "I guess I'll have to just take this win. I'm all for living in the moment."

Leon slaps Beast on the back, throwing him a look. "Sure you are."

"I'm a dad, things are fucking different now," Beast replies, rolling his shoulders to loosen some of the tension there. "You wait until you have a child then see how shit changes."

"We appreciate you being here," I say, the words rushing out before I have time to think about it.

We all knew going into this that there was a high chance of not walking back out alive. The fact Beast came with us is a blessing in and of itself, despite his constant jokes. He's a good man. Arden was right to squash his and Grim's debt.

"You'd better," he grumbles back. "I don't take on other people's wars lightly."

"I'm beginning to understand that," I reply with a respectful nod.

"Carrick and Konrad should cover the back exit," Arden cuts in, moving to stand. "The rest of you spread out amongst the booths.

"Lucky for us, this place ain't got huge glass windows and the bastards can't see inside easily, because there's no way I'd be stepping into an empty cafe. Talk about fucking alarm bells," Beast remarks.

"You could always pretend to be the waiter," Leon suggests with a perfectly straight face.

"Funny, mate. Funny."

"Positions," Arden instructs, his voice strained as he steps behind the pillar right next to the front entrance, even less entertained by the jokes and banter as Carrick and I.

He's the most vulnerable where he is, and when I look over at him there's a tightness around his mouth and eyes that worries me. I narrow my eyes on him. "What is it?" I ask.

"Nothing that can't wait," he replies, dismissing my concerns as we all take up our positions and wait for the buyers. Once they're dealt with, we can take their place and get Cyn back.

Less than ten minutes later, a group of eight men enter the cafe.

The second the last man enters, Arden has a gun pressed to the back of his head and is kicking the heavy wooden door shut behind him.

"What the fu–?" the man begins, only to be silenced by a bullet ripping through the back of his skull, brain, blood and bone exploding out of the front of his face.

Then all hell breaks loose.

12

C yn

Groaning, I try to blink back the pain throbbing in what feels like every inch of my body as Soren shoves me back into the room I've been sharing with Faith. Bruises bloom across my skin and the right side of my ribcage aches where he punched me so hard I felt bone break.

"Cyn!" Faith cries as I stumble into the room, her wide eyes falling on me as she sits up in bed. "I've been so worried–"

Fear swims in her eyes as she watches me push up from the floor, her gaze lifting from me to Soren.

"I'm okay," I manage to say, before Soren reaches over and

grabs my hair, pulling the strands so hard I feel some of them rip from my scalp.

"You have a day to recover before the fun really starts," Soren sneers, shoving me towards the bed, strands of hair falling from his fingers like confetti.

Faith moves towards me, but I shake my head, warning her with my eyes not to help me. We both know that if Soren thinks her condition has improved to a level he's satisfied with, she'll be back in his private quarters, and this time her baby might not survive his abuse.

"I have matters to deal with in preparation for the celebration, and our visitors, so why not take one of your potions and recuperate," he says with an evil smirk, eying the ingredients and equipment on the trestle table in the corner of the room. "I'm sure there's something you can use to help with the pain, *witch*."

He turns to leave but I push myself upright, ignoring the way my head spins and my vision blurs, and move towards the table. Reaching for the vial of dark brown liquid, I hold it out to him and croak, "For the girl."

My voice is hoarse from my bruised throat and windpipe where he squeezed so hard I honestly thought he'd kill me. Soren drops his gaze from my face to my hand and smirks.

"I don't think so."

I take another step forward, hating what I'm about to say but doing it anyway. "Please."

Snatching the bottle from my hand, he eyes it before twisting his torso and throwing it against the wall opposite. It smashes into tiny pieces, the contents splattering against the wall.

"I said no!" he retorts, rounding on me, his green eyes flaring with hatred and a sick kind of power.

"She will suffer," I grind out, refusing to shed a tear in front of him.

"There's no kindness permitted within these walls," he says, sneering at me before his gaze settles on Faith behind me. "The *only* reason she's alive is because she's carrying my son. I don't give a fuck about the vessel, only what I can get out of it. That applies to every woman here, including you."

I grit my teeth so hard together that I can feel a tooth chip, but I refuse to retaliate with words, knowing that's exactly what he wants. Instead I give him a wall of silence, expressing my disgust and hatred with my eyes.

"That's what I thought," he replies, his hand shooting out as he grips my throat for what seems like the hundredth time today.

When I remain mute, not even gasping for breath, he leans close and presses a hard kiss against my mouth before saying, "I'm going to enjoy fucking you."

Then he releases his hand and shoves me in the chest. I stumble backwards onto the bed, sitting down heavily, and with my fingers curling tightly around the bedsheets, I watch as he strides across the room.

"Cynthia," Faith whispers, but I shake my head and refuse to look at her, keeping my eye on the predator still in the room.

When Soren reaches the door, he throws us both a twisted look, his lips curling up into a cruel smile. "Until tomorrow," he says before hauling open the door and slamming it shut behind him.

The second he's gone, Faith crawls across the bed to me, her arms wrapping around my front as my shoulders collapse inwards and the heavy tears fall. Not one of them is for me, but for the girl whose life will be taken by a deviant man that these bastards are selling her to, and for the woman who'll suffer tomorrow night if the men I love don't hurry up and get to us soon.

"Did he...?" Faith's voice trails off, her unfinished question a heavy weight between us as she waits for me to purge myself of tears.

Eventually I respond.

"No. He beat me. He didn't rape me," I reply hoarsely, picking up the cream I made for Faith and applying it to the bruises that litter my skin. My ribs ache as I move, and I wince, dragging in a sharp breath.

"Thank God," Faith says, reaching around and taking the cream from me, applying some to a fist shaped bruise on my upper thigh. She sighs, whispering softly. "I meant thank god he didn't rape you, not thank god that he beat you."

"I know what you meant, Faith," I reply, laying my hand over hers in reassurance.

"I'm so sorry," she replies softly, tears muffling her words.

"As horrific as my time with him was, I know that if he'd raped me I might not have survived it," I admit, honesty stripping me bare.

"How did you stop him from taking you? Did you refuse to make more diamonds?" she asks.

"No. He's waiting until the celebration tomorrow night," I say numbly, pressing my eyes shut as Faith lifts up my t-shirt and rubs some cream into a particularly painful bruise on my lower back. She's exceedingly gentle, partly due to not wanting to hurt me further, but also partly due to the fact she is still so weak. "He wants to *savour* me. His words, not mine."

"I'm so sorry for what you've had to endure," Faith says, the tremble in her voice matching the tremble in her fingers. Another sob rises up her throat and somehow that's more painful to withstand than any of the bruises Soren inflicted on me these past couple of hours.

Twisting to face her, I take the tub of cream from her hands and place it on the nightstand next to the bed, then curl my fingers around hers. "I'm *not* broken by him," I tell her, steeling my voice as well as my spine. "He hurt me, yes. Did it make me feel powerless when he beat me? Also yes. But I am *not* broken by him. I refuse to be."

She sniffles, swiping at the tears on her cheeks. "You're so strong."

"No. You're the one who's strong. You've survived three years in his company, Faith. Three years," I reply, squeezing her hands. "But I am angry. So fucking angry. That's the only reason I've not withdrawn into myself. The *only* reason. That and knowing my men *will* come for us, and we'll seek retribution together. All of us."

She nods, her eyes meeting mine, the fire and the strength I've seen glimpses of fully blazing to life as she stares at me. "He's going to die, isn't he?"

"Yes. Soren's going to die," I promise her, leaning my forehead against hers. "And believe me when I say it will be excruciatingly painful."

"Thank you," she whispers, her soft breath feathering across my skin.

"For what?"

"For giving me hope."

"I'm not giving you hope. I'm giving you my word," I reply fiercely.

She smiles at me. "*Cras es noster...*"

"What does that mean?" I ask.

"Tomorrow is ours."

A few hours later as Faith and I sip the tea I just prepared, savouring its calming properties that help to soothe our physical and emotional pain, the sun sets beyond the window of our room, its colours bleeding onto the horizon like a bloody wound.

"A bad omen?" Faith ponders, her gaze drifting to mine as she unconsciously rests her hand on her abdomen.

"For the Skull Brotherhood, yes," I reply in agreement.

She nods, lost to her thoughts as she slowly rubs her belly. "What will happen to me when we finally get out of here?"

"What do you want to happen?"

"I don't know. I've been a prisoner for so long..." Her voice trails off as she frowns.

"Do you have any family?"

She shakes her head. "Not any that I want to return to."

"Any friends?"

A soft sigh escapes her lips. "Yes, but I'm not sure they'd be able to deal with my baggage. I wouldn't want to inflict them with my suffering."

"If they're your friends it wouldn't even cross their minds not to take you in," I point out.

"Honestly," she says, giving me a sweet smile, "If I get out of here–"

"When you get out of here," I interrupt.

"*When* I get out of here," she says with a determined smile. "I want a fresh start. I want to become someone new, someone who hasn't lived the past few years of her life as a sex slave, abused and degraded daily. I can't bear to see the pity that I know will be in their eyes, it would kill me."

"I see," I say, frowning.

"I'll figure it out somehow," she says.

"You won't need to figure it out on your own. You'll have me. I know people who'll be able to help you start over."

"Those men who're coming to save you?" she asks, tipping her head to the side, her blonde hair inked in reds and oranges as the last of the sun rays slip past the horizon.

"Yes, the men who're coming to save *us*," I reply, reminding her that I will not leave her or any of the other women behind.

A few minutes of silence pass before Faith rests her empty mug on the nightstand. She pulls up the cover over her thighs as the heat of the day begins to make way for the cool temperature of night, and clears her throat.

"I've been meaning to ask you something, Cyn."

"Sure, go ahead."

"The other day when you asked Soren for the ingredients to help me, you said something that I thought I imagined..."

"What was that?" I ask, knowing full well what she's referring to.

I've been debating whether I should tell her of my plans about poisoning Soren and his men. Part of me thought it would be better if she didn't know, to protect her should it all go wrong, but the other part needs her advice. She knows this place better than anyone.

"You said that not all of the ingredients were for me. What did you mean by that exactly?"

"Hold on a minute," I request, getting up off the bed and stepping into the bathroom.

Crouching down next to the toilet and ignoring the spasm of pain from my ribs, I open up the cistern and fish out the plastic bag containing the small glass bottle filled with poison.

When I reenter the room, Faith watches me curiously as I take the glass bottle out of the bag and hand it to her. She frowns, looking from it then back up to me.

"What's this?"

"That's something I made for the Skull Brotherhood."

"Another drug?" she questions, holding the bottle up to the light and marvelling at the deep brown liquid as it glitters in the fading light.

"No. Poison."

"Poison?!" she hisses, eyes as wide as saucers as she looks up at me.

"That's right."

"What does it do?"

"It mimics dysentery. A few minutes after ingesting it they'll be violently sick, followed shortly after with diarrhoea. It will make them feel like death and hopefully it will weaken them enough so that we can get away."

"Will it kill them?"

"That all depends," I say, chewing on my lip.

"On what?"

"On whether they have the antidote?"

"You have an antidote?" she queries, watching me closely.

"No."

Faith's lips part and a laugh erupts from her mouth like a tinkling bell. It's one of the most beautiful sounds I've heard and I can't help but grin despite my split lip and the dangerous situation we're in.

"If I thought I could hug you without hurting you, I would," she says, smothering the laughter releasing from her lips. Then her smile drops. "Wait, does this mean your men aren't coming for us?"

"Oh, I *know* they are," I say, believing with all my heart that it's true. "But we can't just sit and hope that's going to happen before tomorrow night. I can't let those women die, Faith. We have to act sooner rather than later. If that means incapacitating these men and making a run for it, then that's what we'll do. They must have vehicles to get here, right? We'll use them to get away after we've poisoned the bastards."

"You're right," she agrees.

"But there's an issue with this plan. I have to somehow get it into their food, and there's no way Soren will let me anywhere near their kitchen."

"Does it have to be their food?"

"I can dissolve it in liquid, though food is preferable to disguise the taste. It's bitter."

Faith nods, dropping her gaze back to the glass bottle, her fingers wrapping around it as a slow smile pulls up her lips. "Then I think I can help."

"How?"

"Tomorrow night, during celebration night, Soren will make a toast just before the men are given permission to..." Her eyes meet mine, hardening. I know what she's about to say, she doesn't need to spell it out to me. "They call it the *Drink of Death*."

"Death, how apt?" I laugh. Oh the irony. "What is this drink exactly?"

"I don't know for sure, but I think it's some kind of hallucinogenic alcohol, not dissimilar to absynthe. It strips them of all inhibitions, their humanity."

"Humanity? They're *already* animals."

"What little they may have left, if any," Faith whispers, as her eyes glaze over and I lose her to a memory so painful that she wraps her arms around herself and rocks back and forward as she processes it. Eventually she blinks, her face pale and her eyes brimming with tears.

"The bones in Soren's bedchamber, they're victims of previous celebration nights, aren't they?" I ask softly, knowing it to be true.

"Yes," she nods, meeting my gaze and understanding the silent question I keep inside, unable to voice it. "You want to know why I survived, why my bones aren't displayed in that room too?"

"No, I–" I shake my head feeling so much guilt at the thought, but she's right, I do. It seems unfathomable to me that she's managed to survive this long. I'm glad, of course I am, but how has she managed it?

"The first year, for whatever reason only known to Soren, I wasn't restrained like the other women. He'd already chosen me as his and I guess he just didn't want to share me with his men, so I was locked in my cell until it was over. That didn't stop me from hearing the screams though..." Faith blinks back her tears and drags in a shaky breath. "Every year following that I've been given the *honour*," Faith says with a broken whisper, "Of pouring the *Drink of Death* on celebration night. It became a thing."

"Soren admired you for surviving his abuse?" I ask.

"Maybe, begrudgingly, yes. But more so because he knew how much it hurt me deeply to witness their evil. When I think about it, part of me wonders if he never truly let go in my presence and killed me like he has so many other women because he wanted to see if I would break on the next celebration night. It's become a game to him. Physically he'd broken me over and over, but mentally..."

"You survived," I whisper.

"Somehow."

"Okay," I nod, forcing myself not to tear up at her story, and instead focus on the plan. "I'm going to put the poison in their drink."

"No. *I'll* put it in their drink."

"Faith, no. Absolutely not," I reply, shaking my head. "You're going to stay in here, with the door barricaded. You're not going to be anywhere near the *celebration*."

I spit the last word out, hating the fact Soren's using it to describe a night of violence and abuse against women.

Faith reaches for me. "Listen, I can do this. It's been my job to pour wine for the brotherhood these last few years on celebration night. One more time won't make a difference. Besides, I have to be there, whether I want to be or not."

"You're not strong enough," I say, shaking my head. "No, Faith."

"I'm stronger than I've been in weeks, months even, thanks to you," she replies, taking my hand in hers.

I huff out a breath, my gaze falling to the bruises and sores still littering her body. "It's only been a couple of days," I say.

"I don't mean physically, though I do feel a lot better," she adds quickly. "I mean here, and here."

Lifting her hand she places it over her heart and then against her temple. "I need to be there when it happens. I need to see them suffer. I need to see *him* suffer. Even if that's the last thing I do."

"It's too risky," I counter. "Just tell me how I can get it into their drink."

"It has to be me. It's the only way, Cynthia," she implores, handing me back the vial so that I can hide it back in the cistern until it's ready to use.

Deep down, I know she's right.

13

A^{rden}

Using the buyer's body as a shield, I duck as bullets whizz past my head, some exploding into the brickwork behind me, whilst the majority find their resting place in the man's meaty flesh, slashed open like a pinata exploded into a million pieces. Jakub, Leon, Beast and Lorcan attack quickly and methodically, loading lead into the men with precision. The soft putt-putt of silenced bullets cut through flesh and bone as grunts and sharp cries of pain are instantly muffled with fatal shots. Each man is cut down, until all but one remains standing. Shoving the dead man off of me, I step over his bullet riddled body and pick my way through the carnage.

They didn't stand a chance.

Lifting my gun, I press the butt against the remaining man's head. "Arms up!" I yell.

He raises his arms, blood spilling from a bullet hole that's ripped through his upper arm, leaving a fleshy wound and a nasty hole.

"Who the fuck are you?" he asks.

"Never mind who we are," I reply, as Beast, Lorcan, Jakub and Leon step out of their hiding places and further into the room now that there's no danger of them getting shot. Behind them, Carrick and Konrad re-enter the cafe from the back entrance.

"Karim's man is waiting with the van," Carrick says, his eyes quickly assessing us for injuries. Satisfied that we're all still intact, he focuses back on me.

"And the bodies?" I ask, glancing down at the dead men.

"Clean up crew are all ready to move in, and dispose of the bodies," Carrick replies, cutting a look to the only man left standing. "We need to move, now."

"Then let's go," I agree, grabbing the man's collar so he can't make a run for it, and shoving the gun into the back of his head so he knows that if he makes one false move, he's dead.

"There's something else," Carrick says, looking from me to Lorcan.

"What?" I question, disliking the look in his eyes.

"We've got a visitor. He's in the van with Karim."

"A visitor? What the fuck are you talking about?" Lorcan asks before I'm able to.

Beast slams his palm against the counter and grins. "The fucker made it? I knew he would."

My head snaps around as I glare at Beast. "*Who's* made it?"

"Connall. Figured we could use his help. As soon as we arrived at the port, I told him where we were. Looks like he arrived just in the nick of time."

"Are we talking about *Connall O'Brien*? Cyn's uncle?" I ask, gritting my jaw.

"Yes," Carrick replies with a sharp nod of his head.

"Fuck!" Lorcan exclaims.

Beast frowns. "Look, he ain't informed the rest of the O'Briens about this little hiccup with Cyn, if that's what you're worried about," Beast says. "But whilst I agreed with Christy not to share the fact Cyn's spent the last six months with you, I ain't about to hide the fact his niece is in mortal fucking danger. He'd fucking kill me for keeping that from him."

"You've no idea what you've done!" I exclaim, fuming.

"Done? He's here to help. He's my best mate and I trust him with my life. Not to mention he's one of the good ones," Beast counters, looking at me like I've grown another head.

"I'm not sure Cyn will agree with that statement," I reply tightly. "Fuck!"

"I know Cyn's been estranged from her mother's side of the family and all, but that ain't Con's fault. So what the fuck you on about? "

"Why don't you ask him," I counter, pressing the gun harder into the man's head and striding out of the cafe, ignoring Beast's incredulous questions as the rest of the guys follow me out.

"This has complicated matters," Carrick mutters as he

jumps into the main body of the van alongside Lorcan and The Masks.

"No shit," I reply, cutting a look at Beast who hugs Connall then shoots me a confused look as they slide into the seat upfront beside Karim. "But it's not up to us to tell Beast what Connall did."

"Is there something we need to be aware of?" Jakub asks as I shove the guy into the back of the van. He hits the floor with a thud, and I rest my boot in the small of his back.

"Not something that's any of your business," I say curtly, turning to our prisoner. "Face down on the floor. Arms above your head."

"Very well," Jakub replies, having the good sense not to press the point.

Carrick grabs a couple of cable ties from his rucksack and chucks one to Leon who is sitting opposite us on the bench that runs the length of the van.

"Tie his hands to the bench," he instructs doing the same on his side. Fetching two more cable ties he hands one to Lorcan and chucks the other to Jakub who's sitting nearest to the man's feet. "Now the feet."

Once he's secure, I take a seat between Carrick and Lorcan just as the van picks up speed.

"You'll pay for this," the man snarls, attempting to lift his head to look at me.

"Doubtful," I reply, shoving it back down with the butt of my gun as I lean over him. "I need the location of the rendezvous point."

"Why the fuck should I give it to you?" he snarls. "You're

only going to kill me anyway. I've got fuck all to lose by not telling you."

"Everyone has something to lose," I reply, cocking my head to the side as he looks at me. "Mothers, fathers, sisters, brothers, wives, husbands, children, lovers, a fucking bestfriend..." It's an empty threat. I know it. Lorcan and Carrick know it. We don't hurt the innocent. This fucker, however, doesn't know that.

"You don't know anything about me. This is the first time we've crossed paths and I sure as fuck won't tell you my name. So good luck with that."

"Are you sure about that?" I goad, kneeling beside him as I curl my fingers in his straw-blonde hair and twist his head to face me. "Have you heard of the Deana-dhe?"

The man's face pales, all blood leaching from his skin. He blinks up at me, taking in my appearance, registering my accent. I can literally see his thought processes unfold behind his eyes. First it's disbelief, followed by fear, then finally resignation.

It's times like these that I'm thankful we were savvy enough to allow the beast of our reputation grow into a living night-mare. As I stare into his eyes I wonder which story he's heard about us that forces him to spill the information in one long run-on sentence to save whoever he loves from our wrath.

"You're-to-meet-a-man-called-Remnia-midday-tomorrow-at-a-large-carpet-warehouse-situated-on-the-road-that-leads-out-from-the-old-city-walls-towards-Zegora."

"There are many warehouses dotted along that route, care to be a bit more specific?" Carrick adds, the heel of his boot digging into the man's hand. Despite the sound of bones breaking the man doesn't cry out. He simply grits his teeth and waits until Carrick lifts his boot.

"The warehouse is a large corrugated building, painted a dark blue. You can't miss it," he pants, sweat beading on his brow.

"Excellent," I reply, dropping his head and replacing my hand with the butt of the gun, my finger slowly pulling back on the trigger.

"Wait, there's more," he quickly adds, drawing in a sharp breath.

"Go on," I say, releasing my finger, giving him a few seconds reprieve.

"Soren invited us to collect the diamonds on the night of their yearly celebration."

"Their celebration?" I ask, glancing at Carrick and Lorcan who just shake their heads as baffled by the information as I am. "What is this celebration?"

"It's a tradition of theirs, apparently. There's a feast. Women..." his voice trails off as he twists his head to look at me.

"Women?" I ask, my blood turning cold, my voice icy.

"We were instructed to wear black hooded robes whilst in attendance, as a mark of respect."

"That'll make things a little easier for us," Lorcan remarks, thinking exactly what I'm thinking.

The man nods. "I'm telling you this so there are no surprises and you don't hurt my family... *Please,* don't hurt them."

"You have my word," I reply, then without hesitation, shoot him in the head.

"Lorcan, Carrick... Arden," Connall says, addressing us each in turn as we make ourselves comfortable in the guest apartment of Karim's home, twenty miles outside of the city.

Karim lives a life of luxury inside the walls of a huge twelve bedroomed riad that's circled by fifteen-foot high ochre brick walls and palm trees. It's protected by a small army, so we're relatively safe here for the time being.

"Connall," I reply, taking a seat at the large table situated in the living room, the tension thick between us.

Out of the corner of my eye I can see Beast having a conversation with The Masks who've spent the last hour since we arrived back here talking to Christy via video call. Whatever he says to them has Jakub glancing my way and tipping his chin, before the three of them leave the room and head towards one of the bedrooms situated off the central courtyard.

I'm glad for the headspace. I need a moment to think, to regroup, but as Beast strides over to us, pulls out a seat and jerks his chin at Connall who drops down into the seat next to him, I realise that I'm not going to get it.

"Do you want to tell me what the fuck all this is about?" Beast asks, straight to the point as usual.

Drawing in a stabilising breath I cut a look to Connall. "Like I said back at the shisha cafe, you need to ask him."

"Listen. I don't know what it is you think I've done, but I can assure you whatever it is, I haven't," he says, looking between the three of us, only to be met with stony silence.

"Tough crowd," Beast mutters.

Connall narrows his eyes on us. "Despite my better judgement I came here without telling the rest of the family what was going down. You're friends of the family for fuck's sake, yet you kept my niece imprisoned in your home for the past six months without telling us, and now she's been kidnapped by the motherfucking Skull Brotherhood! You know we've been trying to get Cynthia back for years, and you dare to look at me like *I'm* the one in the fucking wrong?"

His voice rises with anger, and Beast rests his hand on Connnall's arm. "Easy mate. You said that you wouldn't lose your shit."

There's a moment when I debate reaching for my gun and loading a bullet into Connall's skull, but my loyalty and love for Cyn stops me. Connall is her uncle, and given what he's done, only she gets to decide his fate.

"Cyn knows," I say, leaning back in my chair as I study his reaction.

He narrows his eyes at me, but still the penny hasn't dropped. "Knows what? That she can't fucking rely on you three to keep her safe?"

"No. About Aoife," I reply, my voice cool and emotionless.

"Aoife?" Beast pulls a face, looking at Connall whose skin has drained of colour. "Con, what's Arden talking about?"

Connall lets out a heavy sigh, his shoulders collapsing with the weight of the truth. "How?" he whispers.

"How *what*?" Beast asks, his gaze bobbing between the two of us.

"It doesn't matter how we found out. What matters is that

Cyn knows the secret you've been keeping for years," Lorcan says.

"What are they talking about, Con? What does Cyn know?" Beast repeats, more urgently this time.

"That's why you kept her for six months, isn't it? She came to you to find out, and you called in the debt as payment," Connall says, piecing the information together, ignoring Beast's questions.

I nod. "Yes."

"It was an accident," Connall eventually says, pressing his eyes shut, his thumb and forefinger squeezing the bridge of his nose. When he opens his eyes again they're swimming with tears and haunted by memories.

"Accident or not, Cyn needed to know. Now she does," Carrick says evenly.

"Would someone tell me what the fuck you're talking about?!" Beast exclaims, voice rising with frustration. "Mate, what's this all about?"

Connall grasps his hands in front of him on the table, then after a beat begins to tell us his story, one that's been kept secret for years.

"You already know that Aoife was stolen by Niall O'Farrell when I was just a kid. I was ten at the time and I didn't understand why she suddenly left without saying goodbye. She was my big sister and I adored her."

"Yeah, you used to talk about her a lot when we were kids," Beast says, still trying to understand where this is going.

"My family kept the truth from me, that she was stolen," Connall continues. "It wasn't until four years later, the summer

I turned fourteen, I found out what really happened. Tom had made a plan to take her back, and I wanted in," he explains, blowing out a long tremulous breath.

"Ah fuck, man," Beast says, understanding dawning as he stares at his best friend. "That was the time you spent the summer in Ireland, wasn't it. You came back different..."

Connall's teeth scrape against each other as he tries to hold in his emotions, but it can't stop the single tear that trails down his cheek, and drips from his jaw. "Killing your older sister can do that to you," he replies, swiping at his face roughly.

Beast squeezes his shoulder. "Listen, mate–"

Connall shakes him off. "Don't do that. I don't deserve any sympathy. Aoife died because of me. My mistake took her life."

"It was an accident though, right?" Beast says roughly.

"Accident or not, I had no business being there. I'd barely learnt how to handle a gun. I fired a wild shot, aiming for one of Niall's soldiers but it hit my sister. It hit her. Fuck!"

"It's alright, mate," Beast says, trying to console him.

Connall rounds on him, eyes blazing with shame and anger. "It's not alright. I killed my sister. *Me!*" he exclaims, fist clenched as he bashes it against the table. "For years I blotted out the memory, but I can't hide from it anymore. I can't unsee the moment my bullet tore into her and took her life."

"How do you know it was your bullet that killed her? There was a firefight going on. It could've been someone else," Beast says, trying to find a better explanation, trying to comfort his friend.

Connall shakes his head. "It was me. I was aiming for the guard in front of her. He moved just as I fired. I saw her stumble backwards from the impact, and the shock on her face as she looked over at me. In that split second, I knew I had shot my sister, and she knew it was fatal."

"Fuck, man. I'm sorry," Beast says, gripping Connall's arm, squeezing it in sympathy. This time he doesn't shake him off.

"She stumbled into a room just beyond where she was standing, one hand pressed against the bullet wound I'd made, and the other holding onto Cynthia. That was the last time I saw either of them."

Finally, Beast breaks the silence. "What happened after that?" he asks softly, his voice barely audible.

"As the fight continued around me, I went into a state of shock, I suppose. Too fucking scared to fire another bullet, too scared to tell anyone what had happened. We left Ireland empty-handed, our men injured, some dead, my sister gone..."

"Does Tom know?" Beast asks, referring to Connall's older brother, and the leader of the family.

"No one knows," Connall says, lifting his gaze to meet mine. "At least I believed that was true. Until now."

"You didn't tell Tom?" Beast asks.

"I convinced myself that the stray bullet wasn't mine. Call it trauma, call it fear, call it what you want. For a long time I blocked it out. I let Tom and the family believe what they wanted. I didn't tell them. I didn't tell *anyone*..." Connall's voice trails off as he looks at me. "So I ask you again, how did you know?"

"Does it matter?" I ask. "Cyn knows the truth, and it's up to her what she does with that."

"Fuck," Beast says, his voice soft as he regards his best friend. "How are you gonna deal with this?"

"The only way I can," Connall replies, heavily and resigned. "*Whatever* punishment Cynthia deems appropriate, I'll take it."

"Connall," Beast warns, shaking his head. "It was an accident. You were a child."

"It doesn't matter."

"It matters, mate," Beast argues, but as he doesn't get the response from Connall that he needs, turns to me and says, "Arden, you can't hold him to this."

"You're right, I can't. But Cyn, *she* can," I reply, before rising to my feet and gesturing for Lorcan and Carrick to follow. "Get some rest. Tomorrow we take down the Skull Brotherhood."

With that said, we head to our room in silence. A few hours later, as Carrick and Lorcan sleep restlessly beside me, there's a gentle knock on the door. I ease off the bed and pull the door open only to find my arch nemesis standing before me.

"What do you want?" I grind out, stepping out of the bedroom and pulling the door closed behind me.

"Not me, *Christy*," Jakub says, handing me his phone.

I frown, lifting it to my ear. "What is it?" I ask, cutting to the chase.

"There's something you need to know," she says, and even though Christy's thousands of miles away, I get that same strange tug in my chest, the one I always get right before a future yet to unfold is revealed.

14

C^{yn}

"Cynthia. Wake up."

My eyes snap open as Faith's sweet voice is drowned out by the sound of a bell ringing. The incessant ding-dong is like a hammer to my skull. Rubbing at my face, I hiss at the sudden, sharp stab in my ribs, as I twist around to face her.

"What's going on? What's that noise?" I ask, blinking away the grogginess and doing my best to ignore the aches and pains all over my body. Fuck, I hurt. I hurt so bad that my vision darkens at the edges and I have to suck in several deep breaths to keep myself from fainting.

"It's almost time," she replies softly, the tremor in her voice unmistakable.

"Time? For what?" I ask, pushing upright with a grimace as Faith looks down at me. She's standing beside the bed dressed in a blood red robe that covers her entire body, the hem brushing across the stone floor at her feet. "What are you wearing?"

"Robes for the celebration. It's time, Cynthia," she repeats, her voice soft, filled with trepidation.

The last dregs of a restless sleep float away and reality hits me like a punch to the gut, winding me. "But the celebration evening isn't until tomorrow," I say, looking out of the window onto a dark and starry night, blinking back the grogginess and needling pain over every inch of my skin.

"It *is* tomorrow evening. You've slept almost twenty-four hours," Faith tells me.

"What?!"

She gives me a sympathetic smile, her pretty eyes filled with concern. "It's the trauma you've been through, the stress. I've not long since woken up myself."

"I'm sorry," I murmur.

"There's no need to apologise. You needed to rest, to gather your strength. Just like I needed to gather mine."

"But I was supposed to be looking after you!" I exclaim, anxiety crawling up my spine at the thought of what could've happened whilst I was out cold. It doesn't bear thinking about.

"You don't owe me anything. You've done more than enough."

"If anything goes wrong, you blame me for all of it, okay?" I urge her, forcing strength into my voice despite feeling far from strong.

She shakes her head. "No. I won't let you do that. If it goes wrong then we stand together. We fight until we can't anymore."

"You won't be fighting anyone. You have a life inside of you, Faith. That is what you protect. If it comes to it and you can get away, you run. Don't look back. Get out of here. Do not try and help me or the others," I say, taking her hands and squeezing tightly. "Promise me, Faith."

"This is going to work," she replies instead. "Right?"

I don't answer. I can't.

"Right?!" she insists.

"Right!" I nod, willing myself to believe it.

I would be a liar if I said I wasn't scared. The truth is I'm terrified. Not because I fear for my own life, but because I fear this plan won't work. Even if Soren and the Skull Brotherhood ingest the drink without noticing we've poisoned it, they could still kill any one of us before the effects truly take hold. These women could die anyway and all of this would be for nothing. Faith rests her hand on my arm, her thumb circling over the patch of skin not discoloured by bruises.

"Perhaps I should've woken you up sooner, given you more time to get ready mentally for what's to come, but you looked so peaceful, and I just wanted to give you that before..."

Her voice trails off as tears clog her throat, and I shake my head, reaching for her. Pushing away my own anxiety and doubts, I force myself to believe that we will succeed. That the effects of the poison will give us all a fighting chance.

"We'll get through this," I say firmly.

She nods. "I trust you, Cynthia."

Giving her one last squeeze, I slowly unravel myself from her arms and reach for the heavy robe spread out across the end of the bed. It takes immense concentration to pull it over my body and not pass out from the pain. The fabric is coarse and thick, but it will conceal the vial of medicine without issue.

"When did these arrive?" I ask, adjusting the robe to sit more comfortably on my shoulders. It has long, wide, bell-like sleeves that hang over my hands, and the arm holes are big enough for me to tuck my arms inside the robe if I wanted to.

"I'm not sure. When I woke up they were lying at the foot of the bed."

A chill passes over my skin at the thought of one of Soren's men stepping into this room whilst we were asleep and vulnerable, but I refuse to allow my thoughts to wander to such a dark place and focus on our plan instead. "Do you have the poison?"

She nods, lifting up the hem of the robe and showing me how she's strapped the vial around her waist with a length of material ripped from my skirt that I'd left to dry in the bathroom the other day. Thank God they didn't search the cistern whilst we were sleeping.

"They won't search you?" I ask.

She shakes her head. "It's unlikely. Soren is too arrogant to believe we'd try to take him out."

"But not improbable?"

"Let's not worry about that, okay?" she whispers, taking my hand in hers.

"But–," I begin, just as the door to our room slams open and

Half-skull walks in, his gaze scanning over Faith before finally settling on me.

"I see you're ready," he says in a low voice as he sneers at us both.

His lascivious gaze makes my stomach churn, but I clench my teeth together and straighten my spine, forcing myself to stand tall and not cower before him.

"We're ready," Faith says, her voice soft as she reaches for my hand and squeezes it gently.

"Then follow me," he replies, turning towards the door and leading us out of the bedroom and along a maze of corridors until we eventually reach the entrance of a large assembly hall.

The space is dimly lit with gas lamps dotted around the edges of the room, bringing life to the shadows that spread out like an evil stain across the stone floor. The air is thick and heavy with tension, but Faith's grip on my hand is strong, and I find comfort in her presence. That comfort is short-lived as my eyes adjust to the light and I take in the five large circular tables, ten chairs surrounding each.

"Oh God, no," I whisper, a sudden wave of dizziness hitting me as my stomach rolls with nausea.

On each table, naked, with their arms and legs spread wide, are the women Soren made me examine two days ago. Some tremble with fear, sobbing quietly, whilst others are deathly quiet, as though they've already checked out, their conscious minds retreating to the depths to protect themselves from what's to come.

"Stay strong, Cynthia," Faith whispers as I look across at her.

Tears tremble on her lashes but she brushes them away, forcing her gaze ahead. I take her lead, and blow out a long breath, allowing my gaze to take in the rest of the details of the hall, if only to distract myself from the true horror about to unfold.

Running along both sides of the room are long tables filled with plates of steaming food, platters of cold meats, and bowls of cooked vegetables and stewed fruit. There's even a hog roast turning on a spit over an open fire, its skin sizzling, fat dripping from the carcass. Warmth spreads out from the flames but my stomach churns uneasily as my gaze is drawn to the top of the assembly hall.

Sitting upon a throne made of human bones, wearing nothing but his tattooed skin, is Soren. He's flanked by two rows of hooded figures which make up the Skull Brotherhood. Vomit rises up my throat, and I press my hand against my mouth, choking back the acrid taste.

"Cynthia?" Faith whispers.

"I'm okay," I mutter, feeling far from it.

Half-skull looks over his shoulder at us. "Shut the fuck up," he snarls. "You speak when given permission to speak, and not before."

I meet his gaze, glaring at him, a sudden, overwhelming anger overriding any dizziness I feel.

"You really are begging for it, aren't you?" he asks, lip curling up into a cruel smile as he steps towards me.

"Bring them in!" Soren booms, his voice laced with anger and impatience.

Half-skull reluctantly drags his attention away from me and motions for us to step further inside.

"Sir," Half-skull replies, circling behind us, his large hands shoving us both in the back, aggravating bruises already inflicted by Soren's fists.

We stumble past the naked women strapped to the tables, their whimpers a desperate plea for someone, anyone to save them. I want to tell them it's going to be okay, but right now all I can do is focus on placing one foot in front of the other.

As we pass by the tables piled high with food, I notice another five women standing in the shadows just behind them, their bodies covered in a patchwork of scars and bruises, naked except for thick iron chains strapped around their ankles. They must be the other women who've been kept in the bowels of this building, the ones whose screams and cries of distress were carried through the thick brick walls to my cell.

"On your knees before your master," Half-skull orders, forcing us both to kneel before Soren the second we reach him. My teeth clack from the vibration of my knees hitting the hard stone, but the pain shooting up my spine barely registers as Half-skull grips my hair and forces me to look upon the monster responsible for so much abuse and cruelty.

"You've been brought here to serve me," Soren declares, his voice booming so that it echoes off the walls and high ceiling. "Tonight the *witch* is mine to fuck. She's off-limits to anyone else in this room."

I swallow hard, refusing to cower from his glare, boldly meeting his gaze whilst cursing his existence with every last cell in my body. I'd sooner die then let him fuck me.

Shifting his focus to Faith, his lips curl up in a grimace as he grabs her face and digs his fingers into her cheeks. "My bitch will serve us the *Drink of Death* as she has done each year previously. She too is off-limits. No one touches her. Understood?"

"Yes, Sir!" the men reply in unison.

"However, the women at your tables are my gift to you all. Sit, eat and drink. Once your bellies are full, and your cocks are hard, then we'll feast on the flesh."

Soren waves his hand in the air, and his men file past, filling up each seat surrounding the five tables. Now it's just me and Faith left kneeling before him.

"Rise," he commands, gesturing to Faith. "Do your duty, *bitch.*"

Out of the corner of my eye, I watch Faith slowly rise to her feet, her expression blank, her green eyes dull, and without emotion. I daren't watch her as she heads towards the table of pitchers for fear of giving away our plan. Instead, I stare at the ground beneath Soren's feet and wait. Behind me I hear the sounds of food being served and men talking and eating, raucous laughter fills the air pitted with the muffled sounds of the women sobbing. I feel their fear and humiliation as though it's my own.

"Look at me," Soren orders, his fingers pinching my chin as he forces my head up.

My gaze meets the darkness of his. His usually green eyes are swallowed up by the blackness of his pupils. My throat tightens. I recognise that look. He's under the influence of diamonds.

"I want you to observe what happens when those bitches

are given your drug, and my men consume the Drink of Death," he says, an evil smile stretching the skull that's tattooed onto his face.

I shake my head, my last act of defiance. "No."

"TURN AROUND AND SIT AT MY FEET, WITCH!" he roars, spittle flying from my mouth as he throws a punch that smashes against my eye and cheek and sends me crashing to the floor.

My head rings, my brain sloshes around inside my skull from the impact. I blink back the pain, retching. When he stands and kicks me in the side right where he already bruised my ribs, my stomach empties, nothing more than bile splattering across the stone floor.

"Next time I won't be so lenient," Soren says, grasping my hair and forcefully turning me around to face the scene unfolding.

Black spots dance in my vision as I try to remain conscious, but everywhere hurts. Every muscle aches, I can barely drag in a breath without feeling like I've been stabbed. But I do as he demands, my heart thudding painfully against my chest, fear and dread clawing at my insides as I watch the men devour their food brought to them by the naked women in chains. They stop eating to grasp at the women tied to each of their tables, bruising their skin, violating them with their fingers, shoving the drug I was brought here to make, into their mouths.

More bile burns the back of my throat as guilt lacerates my skin.

Something I made to bring me and the Deana-dhe together

is being used to tear these women apart. It hurts knowing that I'm responsible.

One woman cries out, her sobs cracking my heart in two. She's quietened by a punch to her cheek, snapping her head to the side as she's knocked out from the blow. It takes every last bit of restraint not to get up and rush to her aid. I can't act, no matter how much I want to.

"Bring me my drink!" Soren orders as Faith enters my field of vision, carrying a large wooden pitcher.

She has to hold it with both hands, the weight clearly too heavy for her weakened state. Trembling from the exertion, Faith pours the liquid into the goblet Soren holds up, spilling some over the lip as she does so.

A droplet hits my arm, and with it the familiar scent of the flowering herb, lobelia, wafts under my nose. My heart rate spikes. She did it. Faith has poisoned their drink. Now we have to hope Soren doesn't notice the slight, but distinctive smell.

"Now serve the brotherhood," Soren commands, resting the goblet on the arm of his throne without taking a sip.

My heart thunders in my chest as Faith moves between each table, pouring each of the men a glass until eventually they've all been served. Returning the pitcher to the table she got it from, Faith takes up her position at Soren's feet, keeping her gaze downcast and her demeanour subdued.

Out of the corner of my eye, I see Half-skull striding towards Soren, his cold, hard gaze resting on his leader. "Sir, your visitors have arrived," he utters.

"Excellent," Soren responds, his voice dripping with antici-pation. My body tenses as his fingers weave through my hair, sending a chill up my spine. It's an intimate touch, gentle almost, and that makes it far more disturbing than any violence he's previously inflicted on me. "Now the fun really begins."

Fun? What does he mean by that? What if they're here to partake in this celebration night too? My blood runs cold at the thought, panic running rampant. There's no more poison left...

"Should I bring them in?" Half-skull's voice slices through the air, disrupting my thoughts.

"Yes, they can observe the festivities before we give them what they came for," Soren's replies, his voice morphing into a vicious snarl as his fingers dig painfully into my scalp.

My stomach drops as I struggle to contain my reaction. I bite on the inside of my cheek so hard that I can feel the bitter taste of blood in my mouth, every nerve in my body now buzzing with dread. Fear takes hold of me, like a vice, and it's all I can do not to let it crush me.

"Very well," Half-skull replies, twisting on his feet and striding from the hall, returning a couple of minutes later with a group of men. There are eight in total and all of them are dressed head to foot in the same black robes, the hoods pulled up over their heads, hiding their faces from view.

Curling his fingers into my hair, Soren stands, yanking me to my feet with him. I let out an involuntary yelp of pain, but I don't try to fight him off, not when he's holding his goblet of drink aloft. I can't risk him spilling it.

"Brotherhood, before you take a sip from your glasses, I want to welcome our guests who are here tonight to collect their order of diamonds, made by *my* very own *witch*," Soren announces, dropping the strands of my hair, and hauling me to his side. Leaning over he presses his nose into my hair, a deep rumble rising up his chest as he says, "I'm going to enjoy fucking you in front of your men until you pass out from the pain."

My men?

I audibly gasp. My gaze darting back to the line of hooded visitors.

"No!" I whimper, hope draining from my body as I realise the imminent danger they're in.

"And when you wake up I'm going to make you wear their blood and internal organs as a reminder of what I've taken from you. No one fucks with the Skull Brotherhood and lives. No one."

"Run!"

But my warning comes out as a strangled cry as Soren barks out a laugh, places his hand around my throat and squeezes the warning from my lips.

Holding me captive, he raises his goblet with the other hand and says, "To our guests."

"To our guests," the members of the Skull Brotherhood repeat with a malicious roar, before they all take a sip.

I can only hope the effects of the poison take hold sooner rather than later.

For all of our sakes.

15

Carrick

Rage narrows my vision into a sharp point as Soren yanks Cyn to her feet by her hair.

MOTHERFUCKER! I scream internally, my whole body vibrating with the need to kill the cunt and have Cyn safe in my arms.

"Brotherhood, before you take a sip from your glasses, I want to welcome our guests who are here tonight to collect their order of diamonds, made by *my* very own witch," Soren exclaims, sending a pulse of searing hot hatred shooting up my spine as he hauls Cyn roughly into his side.

How dare he abuse her!

How dare he fucking claim her as his!

It makes me want to throw up. It makes me want to rip at my own face in anguish because I recognise the veiled admiration that he wished he didn't feel for her. I recognise the darkness thrumming in his blood for a woman he wants but doesn't wish to understand.

I recognise it, because once upon a time, I'd sneered at her in the same way.

I was afraid of her too.

The only difference is deep down I'd also loved her.

I'd fucking loved her.

I *still* love her. So fucking much.

That fucking monster, Soren, he doesn't love. He doesn't feel. He abuses. He takes. He owns. He ruins and destroys.

Cyn might be a witch–and I mean that as a compliment for all the fucking amazing ways she can heal, cure and repair what's broken–but she's not his.

She's *ours*.

Our beautiful, kind, courageous, talented witch.

Our Cyn.

Our soulmate.

Ours god-fucking-damnit.

Fury boils my blood to dangerous levels as my fingers curl into fists, and my body vibrates with the need to kill.

I'll take great pleasure chopping off Soren's fingers for daring to touch her. I will enjoy removing his tongue for daring to speak her name. I will savour the moment when I gouge out his eyes for looking at her the way he is now. I will cackle in fucking glee as I slice off his erection and shove it in his empty eye socket for being turned on by her fear. And I will relish every fucking moment as I carve out his motherfucking heart and crush it in my hand for taking the woman I love from us.

He will suffer.

I will make him suffer.

Soren drops his head, pressing his nose into Cyn's hair. He's whispering something to her, something that makes her gasp.

It's so quiet, the sound.

Barely audible.

But she may as well have screamed, because I hear the terror in her voice.

And the look she gives me. Fuck, it tears me in two.

I see the abject fear she holds, it's etched into her features like a stone carving that no amount of polishing will ever remove. He's marked her permanently, and I can't fucking bare it.

I can't fucking stand here a second longer.

My body moves of its own accord and I know I'm blowing our cover, but I can't... I *can't* watch this. I need to act. I need to act now.

"To our guests!" Soren booms, pulling me up sharp.

"To our guests!" the brotherhood responds.

Then like a well-oiled machine, the Skull Brotherhood all take a drink from their glasses before pulling their guns and aiming them at our heads.

"Ah, fuck!" Beast groans next to me. "Looks like the game's up."

A deep growl rumbles up my chest as I push back my hood and take a step forward.

"LET HER GO!" I roar.

Soren's grip tightens around Cyn's throat as he says, "You think I don't have my own spies in the city? You came here on a fool's errand. You lose. I win. She's mine."

"She will never be yours!" Arden shouts from somewhere to my left. "Let her go and we'll make your death quick."

A dark, monstrous laugh breaks free from Soren's fleshless lips. "If it hasn't escaped your notice, there are almost fifty of us, and only eight of you. We're armed. You're not."

"Let her go and we'll make your death quick," Arden repeats, eerily calm.

Releasing Cyn's throat, Soren shoves her forward. She stumbles, gasping for air, tears tumbling down her cheeks. The other woman, also wearing a red robe, rushes towards Cyn but Soren grabs her arm and forcefully throws her backwards, she lands awkwardly against his throne, a cry ripping out of her throat as Soren grasps Cyn's hair and yanks her back up against his chest. She reaches up to scratch at his face but he grasps her fingers, breaking them.

"MOTHERFUCKER!" I roar, earning a gun to my temple by the big bastard who escorted us into the hall just a few minutes ago.

"Just give me a fucking reason," the Skull says, digging the metal into my skin.

"Carrick, no!" Cyn cries, shaking her head fiercely, clutching her broken fingers against her chest.

"Easy now, mate. Our moment will come," Beast says under his breath.

If I wasn't so fucking incensed, I'd laugh at his confidence.

They could shoot us all dead right now. He knows it as well as me.

"Please don't," Cyn whimpers, as she implores us not to act.

Soren meets my gaze as he pulls on Cyn's hair, licking her cheek. "You should listen to the witch," he says with a smirk.

"Carrick, please. Just *wait*," she chokes out, her voice hoarse, a mixture of fear and anger blazing in her eyes. "Just wait," she repeats with a croak.

It makes no sense given the dire fucking situation we're in.

We need to act. Now.

I look over at Arden, who glances at me. He shakes his head, flicking his gaze back to Cyn, trying to make me understand something. But I'm too fucking angry to try and figure it out.

He's hurting her! He's fucking hurting her.

I can't fucking hold it inside. I tip my head back and roar.

Releasing my rage.

I let it pour from me in a torrent of anger and promises of death to every fucking man in this room. I don't give a fuck that my reaction earns sniggers from the cunt pressing his gun against my head because he'll die, like all the fucking rest.

Chest heaving, I glare at Soren, waiting for the moment when I can kill him.

Because it's coming.

"This is what's going to happen," Soren says, his eyes narrowed as he looks between us. "Before you all die, I'm going to fuck your pretty little witch whilst you watch me ruin her. Then my men are going to string you up and gut you, and I'm going to dress your whore in your entrails."

Most of the Skull Brotherhood laugh, their breath coming

out in huffs of air, but a few of them wince, their smiles twisted with sudden pain. One man at the back of the room covers his mouth with his hand, gagging. Two men next to him suddenly bend over, clutching at their stomachs as a strange coppery smell fills the air.

As if on cue, one by one Soren's men turn puce, colour draining from their skin as guns clatter to the ground and they bend at the waist, a bright neon yellow gore spraying from their mouths and splattering across the floor.

"What the fuck?!" Soren exclaims, eyes widening. He looks from his men then to Cyn with murder in his eyes. "You fucking bitch!"

In that moment, Soren comes to the same conclusion as I do, but rather than feel fury like him, I feel pride.

My clever, clever little witch.

She's given us an opening. One we all take.

Dropping low, I elbow the big bastard next to me in the stomach, then twist my body in front of him and throat punch him as hard as I fucking can. It has the desired effect and as he gasps for breath, I relieve him of his gun, loading a bullet into his face, parting his skull like a machete through a watermelon.

One man down.

Around me chaos erupts, but I don't have time to check on the rest of the guys as I pull the dead man's body over mine, take aim and fire at the other Skulls nearest to me. I watch as they fall, one by one. The violent spray of blood mixing with the acrid smell of puke as their bodies crumple to the ground.

Six bullets. Six men, dead.

I pull the trigger once more, but the barrel is empty.

"Fuck!" I swear, shoving the dead man off me, then crawl like a fucking soldier on a battlefield until I'm beside the nearest table.

Behind me, Beast is in a brutal fist fight with a huge fucking man who's as wide as he is, and just as tall. Both of them are roaring in rage as they grapple with each other. The man takes a punch to his gut, triggering a violent spray of puke that Beast just barely dodges but uses to his advantage as he severs the man's spinal cord with a serrated knife. A little way over, Connall is picking off more Skulls, aiming at their heads and loading bullets into their bodies.

To my left, Lorcan and Arden are back to back as they move through the men, using each other as protection, working in tandem to cut them down. One of the skulls launches at Arden, managing to slice a blade across his bicep, blood spurts from the cut and for the briefest of moments terror grips my throat. But Arden doesn't even register the pain as he shoots his attacker dead. To my right The Masks are battling another group of Skulls, a controlled kind of fury emanating off of each of them.

Shots ring out.

Men roar in anger, in pain.

Violence permeates the air, thick and bloody, mixing with the putrid smell of vomit.

Women scream.

Chairs are upended.

Silverware, plates and cutlery crash to the floor, all adding to the cacophony of sound.

Fists break bones. Knives slice skin. Bullets rip through flesh and muscle.

The Skulls literally shit their pants.

It's fucking carnage.

But none of that matters other than getting to Cyn. She feels like a million miles away as she grapples with Soren, who for whatever reason hasn't succumbed to her poison yet.

One quick look over the table I'm crouched behind, and past the woman staring blindly up at the ceiling, her throat slit open by one of the Skulls just seconds ago, my gaze hones in on Cyn.

Soren has both hands wrapped around her throat, squeezing the life from her. Her face reddens from lack of oxygen, but still she fights, clawing at his wrists with broken fingers whilst the other women Soren threw to the ground a few minutes ago tries in vain to pull him off of her.

He's killing her.

He's killing the woman I love.

A mist descends.

It's not red, but black.

I will rip that cunt to shreds with my hands and teeth.

I'm beyond rage, beyond fury. I'm past the point of no return.

I am fury incarnate. I am the embodiment of revenge. I am death.

My heart thump-thumps in my chest as a buzzing sound fills my ears like a swarm of bees.

Grabbing a steak knife from the table, I make a run for it, only to be grabbed by one of the Skulls from behind. He catches me off guard and manages to get me to the floor, kicking me in the stomach. I barely have time to react when a shot rings out and the Skull goes down, half his face blown off. Flesh, blood and bone splatters across my body, but I don't fucking care about that.

"Cunt!" I roar, jumping up and looking around me wildly.

Across the hall I spot Jakub, his gun pointing in my direction.

"Go, I'll cover you!" Jakub shouts as he shoots at another Skull stumbling towards me, puke drooling from his mouth.

I fucking run.

Barrelling through Soren's men, I slash as many as I can with the steak knife, dodging others as Jakub fires shot after shot. Some hitting home, some narrowly missing me. The danger barely registers. I don't give a fuck about anything other than reaching Cyn.

I'm only metres away when Soren throws off the woman on his back, landing a backward kick to her stomach. She crashes back to the floor, a scream parting her lips as she curls into a ball on her side, but I don't have time to help her, not when Soren's hands tighten further around Cyn's throat. I hear her desperate gasps for breath, her skin flushing a darker red, her eyes bloodshot from the pressure. I see the fear and horror in her eyes as death approaches.

Soren's so fucking busy trying to strangle the woman I love, he doesn't know I'm coming.

He has no fucking idea.

Until I'm upon him.

With a fierce, primal roar of rage, I stab the bastard in the side, plunging the blade deep, feeling it pierce flesh, muscle and organs. I don't stop there, I thrust the knife into him again and again and *a-fuckin-gain*, until his grip loosens and he drops to his knees clutching at his ruined stomach as blood gushes from his belly, the blade in my hand slick with the stuff.

I drop the knife, knowing he'll be dead in minutes, and reach for Cyn, pulling her away from him. She gasps for air, her knees buckling as she crumples.

"Cyn!" I cry, catching her in my arms, holding her close as she chokes and coughs, tears sliding down her cheeks. "We're here, we're here. You're safe now."

I hear myself saying the words having no idea if that's true, trusting that my brothers, that The Masks, and Beast and Connall are dealing with the rest of this fucking cult. Hoping and fucking praying they're okay too.

"Carrrrr," she croaks out, lifting her trembling hand, sliding her broken fingers into my hair.

"I've got you. I've got you," I whisper, my thumb gentling over the deep purple bruise on her cheek. Our eyes meet, my vision blurring with tears, and I know that I will spend the rest of my life doing everything in my power to heal her wounds. To give her a place of safety and love.

Cyn's lips move, but the sound that releases from her lips is cracked and brittle. It doesn't matter though, I understand what she's trying to say.

You came.

"Always. No matter what. We'll always find you."

The words barely leave my mouth before a loud, heart-wrenching scream pierces through the air. I look up to see the other woman who tried to help Cyn staggering to her feet, her robe pulled up over her waist, revealing a river of blood streaming down her bare legs and pooling on the floor beneath her.

"Noooooooo!" she screams, clutching her stomach, her face twisted in torment as she collapses to her knees. "My baby's gone. She's gone. She's gone. She's gone."

Cyn thrashes wildly in my arms, desperate to break free and reach the woman. Even in her frail state her instincts are to help, but even I realise that there is too much blood and no way to stop it. Regardless, I carry Cyn to her, knowing that she doesn't have the strength to move on her own. I don't know who this woman is, but given the grief spilling from Cyn's lashes, I know she's important to her.

A fractured sob escapes Cyn's lips as I drop to my knees and she reaches out to take the woman's hand, desperately trying to form words, but they come out broken, shattered.

"Don't cry for me," the woman murmurs, a deathly hue shadowing her features.

But Cyn does cry.

She sobs and sobs and sobs, doubled over, wracked with pain.

In my arms she breaks.

I feel her heart splintering, and there's nothing I can do about it.

I can't stop the blood from pouring from this woman anymore than I can stop the river of grief spilling from Cyn's eyes.

"Hold on. We'll get you help," I say, knowing it's a lie,

knowing that there's too much blood and we have no means to help her. She's fading fast. Colour leeches from her skin. Her lips are tinged blue, her eyes glazing over.

Cyn pushes off me and presses her broken fingers against the woman's stomach, her voice scratching, hoarse, as she tries to form words.

"Pl-eeaass-eee," she sobs.

"It's too late," the woman says, her lips wobbling as Cyn clutches the material of her robe and cups the woman between the legs if that alone will stop the bleeding.

"N-O!" Cyn cries, shaking, trembling, as she crawls up the woman's body, reaching her face, smearing blood across the woman's pale cheeks.

"Cyn–" My voice cracks as I reach for her.

But she shakes me off, glaring at me with angry, grief-riddled eyes.

"I w-want you to l-live," the woman whispers, her shaking hands reaching up to cup Cyn's face.

Cyn shakes her head vehemently, her tears dropping and mingling with those of the woman.

Death isn't far away. I recognise the grip it has on this woman, the cool dark fingers drawing colour from her skin and light from her eyes.

She's almost gone.

Bowing over her body, Cyn cups the woman's face, begging her to live with her kisses and her tears, her sobs and wretched cries of agony.

Loss and grief pours from the woman I love and it tears a hole right in my chest. Tears stream down my face as I cry for them both. I cry for the trauma they've so obviously shared and bonded over, for the friendship that has so cruelly been taken from them, for the loss of an innocent life that never got to live, and the chance for a woman who's obviously been through hell, to heal.

In my peripheral vision I see Arden and Lorcan approach, the sickening scent of blood thick in the air, eyes wide with horror as they watch the scene unfold. Our ragged breathing is another chorus of suffering as we all bear witness to the devastation unfolding before us. Beast and Connall join us, their ragged, blood-soaked bodies testament to the violence they've endured. And then, The Masks step forward, our sworn enemies for so many years, standing side-by-side with my brothers, and my friends. Their silent support and sympathy is worth so much more than a past filled with vengeance and hate. Together we watch life fade away, an unspoken bond forming between us.

"*Live* for me and my baby..."

And with those parting words, her hands fall from Cyn's face like lead weights, eyes staring, chest still, a pool of blood forming around them both.

Cyn screams.

She screams and screams and screams, the sound coming from a voice broken by trauma and a heart annihilated by loss. I feel her pain cut through me like a white-hot poker, my heart breaking alongside hers. The pain is relentless even after Cyn faints in my arms, consumed by an unbearable, shattering grief.

16

C^{yn}

P^{ain.}
So much pain.

My body aches.

Every breath is a sharp stab to my side.

My throat burns, my ribs throb.

I can't swallow without wishing I could pass out.

I can't breathe without longing for oblivion.

My fingers brush against soft material, and I reach for it, trying to hold on, but it's agony.

This hurts too much.

Everything hurts too much.

I try to open my eyes but I don't even have the strength to do that.

Am I dead?

Is this what death feels like?

No, this is worse than death. So much worse.

This is Hell.

A vicious memory slams into my mind in full technicolor. A man... No, a *skeleton* has me in its grasp. Its bony fingers tighten around my throat in a vice, its strange green eyes ablaze with fury and wrath. Panic rushes through my body and I convulse at the memory. My subconscious mind cowering from the trauma.

No. No. No. No.

My lips part.

A tiny whimper escapes.

"Cyn?"

A voice. A male voice. Lyrical, warm.

I recognise it, but I can't place it.

Why can't I place it?

Why can't I open my eyes?

I'm seized by panic as oxygen is sucked from my lungs. I feel like I'm drowning, sound and vision distorted as I gasp for breath.

"It's okay. You're safe now. You're safe," he reassures me.

Gentle lips press against my temple.

Soft. Loving. Welcome.

"We've got you. You're safe."

I fade away, drawn back into the arms of oblivion.

Time passes. Minutes. Hours.

I'm carried, passed from one set of strong arms to another until someone lays me down on a bed, a warm breeze passing over my skin.

Even that hurts.

"Karim's doctor is going to examine you now," that same voice from earlier says as fingers gently press against my bruised skin.

It hurts.

"She must be in incredible pain," a foreign voice says. "Her injuries are fresher than some of the other women I just examined. These have been inflicted in the last day or so."

"Has she been...?" Another familiar voice asks, voice cracking.

Gentle hands press against my upper thighs, but don't reach between my legs. "As far as I can tell, no," the doctor says. "But I won't do a full examination, not whilst she's unable to give her consent. That alone could do more harm than good given what she's been through."

I black out, coming too when my eyelids are gently pried open and a bright light passes across my vision.

"Pupils are reacting as expected. It's a good response. I will need to reset and splint her fingers though."

Pain. Sharp.

"She's fit to travel after she's had some fluids and more analgesia. But she will require a lot of rest and recuperation. This won't be easy..." His voice trails off, and the air stills as though holding a trembling breath.

What won't be easy?

My internal question dissolves as I feel a sharp scratch to

my inner elbow, followed by cool liquid flooding my veins. My body welcomes the darkness again.

Some time later, I rouse as murmured conversations brush against my ears like velvet, the occasional hushed whisper floating over my skin. Around me sounds and smells trickle into my subconsciousness as a warm breeze drifts over me, carrying with it the earthy scent of spices, mingled with the light aroma of flowers coming from the distant sound of a busy city.

Pain lances my chest as I hear the sound of women crying, only ebbing away when reassurances come from voices I recognise but for some reason can't place right now.

Images appear in my mind. Memories of naked women, afraid, tied to tables. My heart races, my pulse becomes erratic until darkness returns, sucking me beneath its blissful surface once more.

Sometime later, my subconscious mind is drawn to the surface as the repetitive sound of a train passes over metal tracks. More voices. More murmured talk. Plans are being made. Lives rearranged. A promise of safety given.

Next there's a gentle rocking, accompanied by the swishing sound of waves. I sleep, dragged back beneath exhaustion and trauma.

The roar of a plane's jet engines jerks me awake. Wherever I am it's dark, warm, safe. I have no concept of time, no real understanding of what's happening around me, just that I'm no longer gasping for breath, no longer fighting to live.

I'm kept safe. Held in warm arms.

Never alone.

I hear murmured words. Feel gentle hands and soft kisses peppering my temple. It's as though whoever's holding me needs to check I'm actually real and not a mirage.

"We're nearly home. Hold on, Cyn," he says as I fall back into oblivion.

More time passes.

Then I'm lifted into a spacious car with heated leather seats, and cuddled against another strong, warm chest as muscular arms wrap around me. This man smells of freshly laundered cotton and strangely, suntan cream. He talks to me, words of comfort washing over me in a gentle caress, soothing me back to sleep. I curl into his body, finding solace in his arms. My body responds to him, my heart recognising him, but my mind isn't ready to acknowledge him just yet.

Later, I stare up at a different man with a shock of dark brown hair and obsidian eyes. Despite seeing him through only one eye because the other is swollen shut, I don't really feel in control of my body or my actions. There's a physical disconnect that I don't understand. I can see, hear, touch, taste, and yet it's as though those senses belong to someone else.

"We're back in London, Cyn," he says softly, tucking me into a warm bed. "Grim is letting us stay overnight at her place until we can get you back home."

Home? Do I even have a home?

Concern etches a deep line between his brows. Dark shadows reflect the exhaustion in his eyes. He stares at me, waiting for some kind of response. I don't answer. I can't.

"Cyn, it's me, Carrick," he whispers, laying down beside me.

I face him. Seeing, but not responding.

Deep down inside, I know who he is. I recognise him. Yet, I can't seem to bring myself to acknowledge that fact. I'm both within my body, but separate from it. Feeling and unfeeling. Aware and unaware. Both me and not me. I can't think too deeply or remember too much.

There's something agonising, something that will break me, just out of reach. I don't want to remember. It's easier to just close my eyes. So that's what I do. The last thing I hear before sleep drags me under is the sound of an angel singing.

As time moves on voices come and go.

Male. female. Some are familiar. Others are not.

But all are concerned.

"Like the doctor in Marrakech told you," an unfamiliar, older male voice says somewhere nearby, "Cynthia has bruised ribs, and four broken fingers on her right hand. She's covered in bruises from head-to-toe where that bastard beat her. Her left eye is swollen shut, and she's lost some hair on her head."

"Fucking bastard!" A female voice says. She too is angry, concerned, and I recognise her voice but can't place it. "I hope you left his body to the vultures to pick at."

"I promise you, we made sure they were nice and barbequed for the wildlife," a gruff voice responds.

"Good," the woman replies. "Come on, Beast, we've got families to locate and women to get home. Leon and Konrad have already made a start."

"What about her unresponsiveness?" the voice I know to be Carrick's asks as I hear footsteps leave the room.

"I thought perhaps it could be a delayed concussion, but I

suspect this is more than likely something else far more concerning..." the old man's voice trails off.

"More likely what?" another voice asks, a deeper timber.

My heart thunders in recognition. That voice belongs to one of the men who took it in turns to carry me to this bed from the other side of the world. I'm beginning to remember now, passages of time like polaroid snapshots developing in my mind.

"Trauma, Arden."

Yes, that's it, Arden with the amber eyes.

Arden Dálaigh.

"Is that why she's not really with us even when she's awake?" another female asks, her voice gentler than the other. Sweet. Kind.

I know that voice... Don't I?

"Yes. Right now her mind is trying to protect her. It's not uncommon after a traumatic event such as this."

"And what about...?" Carrick asks. He can't finish his question, his voice thick with concern.

"The bruising around her throat will eventually fade, but until she comes around fully I can't tell you what the long term effects on her voice will be."

"Fuck!" he exclaims, the crack in his voice opening up the chasm in my heart.

"She *will* heal. She will come back to you. Cyn is strong," another male voice says, foreign, sharp almost, but I don't fear it. It reminds me of my childhood.

Is that Jakub?

"But it will take time," the older voice intercedes. "In the meantime, she'll need some help. I've prescribed some drugs to help her to rest, to manage her emotions until she's strong enough to deal with what's happened. She needs sleep. She needs fresh air. She needs time and space to grieve. She needs love and care. That most of all."

"And she'll get that from us. I swear to you," Arden replies with conviction. "We're taking her home. We'll heal her, the three of us."

"What about Connall and the O'Briens? What about her father?" that same foreign voice asks.

"I don't care about them. I only care about Cyn. You heard what Joey said, she needs to heal, she can't do that with the O'Briens and the O'Farrells still at each other's throats," Arden continues, his voice determined, certain.

No more words are said, but the air is swollen with unspoken thoughts as I blink open the eye that isn't swollen shut. My vision is blurred as several figures move around me. I groan.

"She's coming to," the woman with the gentle voice and fiery red hair says as she reaches for my good hand, gently squeezing it. "Cynthia?"

Christy?

I open my mouth to speak. I know her. She's my friend.

My friend.

Wait!

Then like a freight train being derailed, disturbing memories barrel towards me, smacking me right in the centre of my chest as my breath is snatched from my lungs.

I remember a smelly, cold cell.

I remember making diamonds and being watched by men with skulls tattooed onto their faces.

I remember women screaming late at night, begging to be left alone.

I remember a skeleton brought to life.

I remember a woman bruised and battered, in a state far worse than me.

I tried to heal her. I promised to keep her safe.

She's *pregnant.*

Faith!

Where is she? Where's Faith?

"Ffff!" I try to call her name, but my voice won't sound, the pain in my throat is too much.

It hurts.

It hurts so much.

Tears well in my eyes, tipping over my lashes.

There's something else, something painful just at the edges of my consciousness. I struggle against the memory.

Then it hits me.

Blood.

So much blood.

"Don't cry for me. I want you to live... Just live for me and my baby..."

She's dead.

My friend's dead.

I promised she'd be okay. I promised I would save her.

But I couldn't.

I didn't.

Pain unlike anything I've known rushes over me and I'm

sucked into a whirlpool of grief, sinking beneath the waves, drowning from the agony.

"Cynthia, it's okay. It's okay," Christy says, panic littering her voice as she strokes my arm, but I don't feel her touch. I'm numb. "Arden. Get over here."

"Cyn, I'm so sorry," he says, the amber eyes of Arden–a man my heart knows but my mind refuses to fully remember–flicking with concern as he snakes a hand through his coal black hair. "We couldn't save her."

We couldn't save her.

Faith.

Behind him another man stares at me. He has white-blonde hair and silver-blue eyes.

I know him too, of course I do. It's *Lorcan*. Next to him is the man who said he was taking me home. *Carrick.*

They're the three men who captured me to pay a debt, then wanted to set me free. Who hated me as a child but rescued me from the Skull Brotherhood and held me in their arms across land, sea and air.

They're the Deana-dhe.

And like a key turning in a stiff, rusty lock, more memories come flooding back.

All of them. Not just the recent ones.

My whole life is playing like a movie in my mind. I'm flooded with the good and the bad, the disturbing and the uplifting.

Rushing in like a tidal wave.

Drowning.

Gasping.

Panic rushes through my veins as terror grips my throat and squeezes, my thoughts circling back to that woman who tried to pull Soren off of me.

She's dead!

The sound of her scream rips through my memory, yanking me from oblivion and forcing me back in my body. Panic and overwhelming grief has me pushing Christy away from me as I try to climb out of bed, her name nothing more than a strangled sound on my lips. "Ffff!"

Christy moves away, concern etching her features as Arden takes her place on the mattress.

"Hey, Cyn. It's me. It's Arden," he says, reaching for me, cupping my face in his hands.

I push angrily against his chest, my broken fingers shaking as I press against him forcefully. I register the pain, but I don't *feel* it. His unmoving strength makes me cry out in frustration and desperation. It's such a broken, pitiful sound.

"Look at me, Cyn," he says, his voice full of authority now. It snaps my attention back to him and away from the memories of Soren and his cruelty, of Faith and all that blood. "Breathe."

I blink through my tears, dragging in a wavering breath. It hurts to expand my chest but I keep going as he breathes with me. Dark thoughts grip at my mind, trying to trap me with memories I don't want to remember

She's dead.

"I'm sorry about your friend," he whispers, his gaze burning into mine.

I draw in a shaky breath, shuddering, shaking, pain ripping through my chest.

"Just keep breathing, in and out, in and out. Listen to my voice. I'm here. I'm here."

He tries to soothe me, and I try my hardest to focus on just his voice, just him.

"Good girl. Just keep breathing, okay? Just keep breathing."

Tears stream down my cheeks. Pain lacerates my chest. I'm raw, bleeding out grief.

"Live for me and my baby," her voice in my head urges me.

Faith.

I mouth her name, a painful sob breaking free from my throat.

"I'm so so sorry," Arden repeats, as he gently strokes his thumbs across my skin. "For everything."

For everything?

"We'll leave you for a moment. Come on, let's give them some space," Christy says, slipping away in my peripheral vision, the other men walking out behind her.

"Cyn," Carrick whispers, a mixture of emotions stuttering across his face as he sits on the bed to my left. His shoulders slump as he reaches for me. "We've been so fucking worried about you."

It was him. It was Carrick who killed Soren. Who fought his way through the Skulls to get to me. Who carried me to her broken and bloody body so I could hold her hand whilst she died. He looks as haggard as I feel, his coal-black eyes pitted with sorrow. My chest heaves, another broken sob parting my lips as more tears cascade down my cheeks.

"I'm sorry we couldn't save her too," he says, reaching for

me, his thumbs pressing against my pulse, measuring my heart rate.

Doesn't he understand? It doesn't matter if my heart is still beating, it's already shattered. My head drops, my hair falling over my face as I cry silently.

I couldn't save her.

"It's not your fault. None of this is your fault," Arden says, trying in vain to comfort me.

I see him look over to Lorcan, a silent conversation occurring between them as a heavy weight hangs in the air. It's oppressive, suffocating. It isn't just me who feels it. It's them too. I blink up at them trying to convey with my eyes what I need to know, mouthing the words when they don't answer right away.

Tell me they're all dead.

"They're all dead," Carrick replies, meeting my gaze unflinchingly. "We killed every last one of them."

But instead of giving me some form of comfort I just feel overwhelmingly sad and my body starts to tremble, my teeth clacking with the force of it.

"Here, take this. It will help you sleep," Arden says, holding up a pill to my lips.

I open my mouth automatically, the bitter taste of man-made drugs sits heavy on my tongue, but my need to sink into oblivion is too strong to spit it out. When Arden places a bottle of water against my lips, I swallow.

"Rest, Cyn. We'll be here when you wake up," Arden says, his voice thick with emotion as he sits down in the seat beside my bed.

I settle under the covers as a sudden overwhelming exhaustion washes over me.

"You're never leaving our side again," Carrick reassures me, his brown hair falling over his forehead, his dark eyes filled with concern as he lays down on the bed next to me.

"Sleep now," Lorcan says, his weight compressing the mattress behind me. "When you wake up, we'll be home."

Home, I mouth before exhaustion drags me under.

17

A rden

"Right now, I don't give a fuck about the O'Briens," I say, my voice rising with every word, furious that it's even a suggestion that Connall takes Cyn back to his family home to recuperate.

Fuck that. "Cyn will not be a pawn between two warring families!"

"She's *my* niece. She's *my* blood, Arden. She doesn't belong to you!" Connall retorts angrily.

"Listen, lads, no need to start a war in my fucking living room," Beast says, a warning in his voice as he grips Connall's shoulder, preventing him from taking a step towards me.

Behind me Lorcan and Carrick get to their feet, ready to fight. The O'Briens might be old family friends, but when it comes to Cyn we're not fucking budging.

"She's ours. We fought our way to get her back from those cunts. She's coming home with us," Carrick grinds out, brooking no arguments.

"I think you'll find that Cyn very much belongs to herself," Grim says, folding her arms across her chest and narrowing her eyes at us as she watches this all play out. Next to her Christy and The Masks sit quietly, taking it all in.

"You heard what Joey said, she needs rest, recuperation, love and care," I continue. "She doesn't need to be a victim of another fucking war. You've done enough damage as it is."

Connall snorts. "Love and care? By all accounts you've made her life hell in the past. What makes you think you're capable of looking after her any better now? Why would she even want you to, after how you've treated her?"

I throw Beast an angry look and he holds his hands up. "Mate, you were cunts to her as kids. I'm not about to keep that from Connall. He needed the complete picture, so I gave it to him."

Drawing in a ragged breath, my arm fucking hurting like a bitch from the eight inch slice to it that's been patched up by Joey, I try my best to calm the fuck down. "Look, I know what we did in the past when we were kids was out of order," I admit, some of the anger deflating a little at the truth. "But we made peace with that. Cyn forgave us. We were just starting to build our relationship before they took her from us."

"She forgave you to give *them* time," Connall cuts in, pointing at Christy and The Masks.

"Are you saying to me that what we have is a fucking lie?" I ask, his comment angering me as much as it does because I've asked myself that question over and over again these past few weeks. We'd told Cyn the truth that night when she finally revealed her voice to us, but had she done the same in return? My heart, my fucking soul, tells me she was being truthful, but my head isn't so sure.

"If the shoe fits," Connall throws back.

"You know shit about how we feel for each other," I argue, my blood boiling with frustration, with guilt, with anger. All I want is Cyn home with us, so we have the opportunity to make this right.

Lorcan steps forward, gripping my shoulder. "Easy, brother," he says, stepping around me and placing himself between us. He's as riled up as I am, yet he's able to hide it a lot better than me.

"When we say that Cyn is ours it's because she always was. You of all people know how that feels," he says looking between Grim and Beast.

"He's got a point," Beast adds with a shrug, winking at Grim. "You *are* mine."

Grim cuts him a look that would shrivel the balls of even the hardest of men. "And you're lucky I love you enough to let that caveman statement go. I'm only yours because I want to be."

Beast smirks. "Exactly my point, babe."

"From the very first moment we met Cyn, she belonged to

us," Lorcan continues, ignoring their flirty-banter. "Back when we were kids we didn't fully understand that what we felt for her was love. It was twisted up into something ugly because of our history with the Brovs, with the O'Farrell's. We fucked up. We want to make it right. That was beginning to happen before the Skulls took her. We need the opportunity to fix things, but we're not asking for permission. This will happen regardless."

Connall scowls. "How can I trust that you won't fuck this up again?"

"Have we not proven that we love Cyn?" Carrick asks, locking eyes with Connall. "Have we not shown you that we will move heaven and earth to protect her? You know us. You know the Deana-dhe, and you know that we don't care for many people, but we care for her. We *will* love her."

Connall shakes his head, swiping a hand over his face. "I'm not sure your definition of love is the same as mine."

"You're right, it's deeper. It's *more*," I add fiercely, feeling that love for Cyn inside of me like a living, breathing entity. It's the truest thing I've felt in a very, very long time.

The atmosphere is heavy with unease, neither side willing to back down. I don't want to hurt Connall, or Beast if he chooses to take his side, but I will if I have to.

"Maybe you can't trust them, but perhaps you can trust me?" Christy says, the soothing calm of her voice a balm that seems to dissolve the tension enough for us not to start a fucking fight to the death. She looks between us knowingly, and something lifts off my shoulders when she gives me a soft smile.

"Oh damn. If Christy knows shit, then you'd better listen," Beast remarks, slapping Connall on the back like this isn't the most tense fucking situation since stepping into the Skull Brotherhood's lair.

"I don't believe in any of that shit," Connall says, causing Leon and Konrad to scowl at him and Jakub to pin him with a dark stare.

"You'd be wise not to insult the woman we love, Connall O'Brien," Jakub warns. "But we'll allow that one slip-up out of respect for Grim and Beast, given you're their friend."

Beast looks wide-eyed between the two, but there's a hint of a smile playing around his lips that tells us he's less bothered by the threat, and more entertained.

"Seeing as you motherfuckers aren't going to get in the ring anytime soon now that you're besties," Beast says looking between us and The Masks, "A three on one fight could be quite entertaining. What do you reckon, Connall?"

"Fuck off, Beast," he replies.

"Seriously though, that'd bring in the punters. Don't you think, love?" Beast says, turning his attention to Grim now.

She rolls her eyes. "What I think is that you should stop talking and start listening... *Christy*," Grim urges.

"Whether you believe me or not, is irrelevant," Christy begins in that quietly-calm, yet assertive way of hers. "Cyn and the Deana-dhe are meant to be together. It really is as simple as that."

"So I'm supposed to just trust your word?" Connall asks.

"You don't have to do anything. I'm simply stating a fact. She is theirs, as much as they are hers. Nothing can change that. Not you. Not your brother or the rest of your family. Not Niall. Not any of us."

"And what about Cynthia? Doesn't she have a say in this, doesn't she get to choose?"

Christy meets Connall's gaze with a steady one of her own. "She already made her choice. She did that the night of the Brònach Masquerade Ball."

"Wait, what?" I ask, as we all turn to look at her. "Is this about the letter your mother wrote to her? You've seen something? When?"

Christy nods. "Last night after I left Cyn, I had a vision. It was of the past this time. Whatever my mother wrote in that letter, it made her choose you three that night. She did it to save your lives."

"Our *lives*?" My skin prickles with goosebumps as though someone has just walked over my grave.

"Yes. Her choice to leave with you that night saved your lives, and now your choice to let her go with them," Christy says, looking pointedly at Connall, "Will save hers."

PART II

CURES

"Nothing can cure the soul but the senses, just as nothing can cure the senses but the soul."
The Picture of Dorian Gray, Oscar Wilde.

18

C^{yn}

The salty, seaweed scent of the ocean trickles through the tiny cracks around the window frame as cool air feathers over my skin, drawing me awake with its tentative touch.

I blink at the bright light that pours through a gap in the curtains as tiny motes of dust lift up in the air, sensing other people in the room about the same time as I do. My gaze is drawn to Arden, Lorcan and Carrick who are sitting around the open fire on the other side of the room, its flames crackling in the hearth.

"According to Beast the O'Briens are getting restless," Arden says, a dangerous edge to his voice. "They want to see Cyn."

"It's only been a week. She's slept most of that time. Been barely lucid the rest of it," Carrick replies, swiping a hand through his sleep-tousled hair. "She's not ready."

A week? I have no recollection of any of that time passing. None.

But I do remember why I'm here and a sudden, overwhelming sadness pulls at my senses, threatening to drag me back under a deep sea of oblivion.

Faith is dead.

Her baby is gone.

And I'm crushed by the pain of it.

A huge part of me wants to fall back into the arms of darkness. It's safer there. Quiet. There's no pain, no memories, just a vast expanse devoid of colour. It's peaceful too, like a gently lapping ocean under a midnight sky.

Yet their voices keep me in the present.

Anchoring me for the time being.

And for the first time in a long while, I don't allow the ever present tide of my grief to draw me back into the ocean's embrace. I tread water just enough to keep listening.

"She just needs time," Lorcan says. "*We* need time."

"And what about Niall?" Carrick bites out.

My father... If I could laugh bitterly, I would. We haven't talked in almost two years. Not since I went to live with The Masks. He doesn't care about me. He never did.

"So far nothing," Arden says. "I'm not sure if it's because he never really gave a shit about Cyn, or if it's because he's waiting for the right time to act."

"How can he not love her?" Lorcan asks angrily. "Why can't that fucking arsehole see how incredible she is? I don't get it."

"I've no idea, but the O'Briens are different. They'll come for he eventually," Arden replies, swiping a hand through his hair. "Beast won't be able to hold them off forever."

"And we'll be ready when they do." Carrick stands, pushing back his chair roughly. "They can't fucking have her."

He moves to leave, but Lorcan grasps his wrist. "Brother, they won't take her if she doesn't want to leave. We just need to get her better and give her enough of a reason to stay."

Carrick nods tightly, flicking his gaze over in my direction, I keep my gaze fixed on him as he cocks his head and frowns.

"Cyn?" he asks, pulling out of Lorcan's hold and striding towards me. I can feel the tension in his body even from the otherside of the room, the barely restrained hope. "Cyn, can you hear me?" He drops to his knees beside the bed, his rough fingertips feathering over my cheek as he dips his head closer.

I blink up at him, feeling his touch, yet I don't acknowledge him. I don't know why. I just keep staring, waiting for my body to react, for my lips to part on a whisper. For something to happen.

"Cyn, please come back to us. We need you," he says, softer now, pleading with me as Lorcan and Arden step up behind him.

I don't look up at them either. I just keep my gaze fixed on Carrick, and the water swimming in his dark eyes.

"Why won't you come back to us?" he whispers, his fingers pushing into my hair as his thumb rubs against my cheek.

I don't have an answer for him because I don't know myself. There's such a big part of me that is still so numb, unable to react to his question, his touch, his intensity. But there's another part, this tiny small spark that keeps me in the present, listening, watching, *feeling*.

His touch anchors me, the warmth of his breath keeps me held captive. I hang onto that feeling with feeble fingers, wishing I had the strength to pull myself up and into his arms, to whisper his name like he's whispering mine.

"Cyn, Cyn, Cyn," he murmurs, his thumb making circles across my skin, sparking something to life within me.

"Carrick, come on, let her rest," Arden says from behind him.

"Give me a minute, goddamn it," Carrick retorts, flashing a look over his shoulder before refocusing on me. "You can hear me, I know you can, Cyn. Don't let the darkness take you. Remember what Faith said. *Live.*"

And I do remember. I remember it all, and it's too much. It's too painful. I'm not strong enough to live with the memories of what happened to her. It was so brutal, so callous. *She* deserved to live. Her baby deserved to live.

"Please, Cyn," Carrick begs, peppering my face with kisses that I can't respond to, but need to feel.

Keep kissing me. Touching me. Don't stop.

"She just needs time," Arden adds, but there's a frailty to his words; they're without any strength as though he doesn't believe them himself. I'm not sure any of them do. I'm not sure I do.

Carrick shakes his head, pressing his warm lips against my cool cheek as they slide up to my ear. "Come back to us, Cyn. Just come back to us."

His voice cracks, and a single tear seeps from between my lashes and slides down my nose.

I want to. I do.

But I'm not strong enough to hold on.

Not without something to keep me here.

Carrick removes his touch. His warm lips leaving my skin, his hands pulling back as he stands, and the absence of his touch has me freefalling back into oblivion.

I wish he knew. I wish they knew that I need their touch to keep me with them.

But it's too late.

The dark void calls out to me like a siren's song, an irresistible pull drawing me closer and closer until my skin is slick with inky blackness. I feel the velvet embrace of the darkness as it swallows me up, muffling the voices of reality until they are silenced, fading away to a distant island where seaweed clings to the shore and salty tears mingle with the ocean.

19

L^{orcan}

Rain beats against the windowpane like a thousand tiny hammers, echoing Cyn's sadness as she lay on her bed, staring off into the distance. Thunder rumbles above a stormy sea, a shard of lightning illuminating a grey, cloud-filled sky. Despite the fire roaring in the hearth, there's a coldness that lingers in the room, in all of us, creeping into the gaps split open by Cyn's grief.

"How's she fairing today?" Arden asks me as he stands in the doorway of Cyn's bedroom.

I place the tube of arnica cream back on the bedside table, lowering her pyjama top.

"She's no better than yesterday, or the day before that," I reply sullenly.

The truth is she's getting worse.

For the last two weeks, Arden, Carrick and I have been taking turns watching over her, but instead of improving, she seems to have withdrawn into herself further with every passing day.

We've kept her alive by spoon feeding her soup and soft foods throughout the day. She chews and swallows, following our instructions to eat, but she's never really there. Never present.

She hasn't made a sound as I've guided her to the bathroom so she can use the toilet. Not a murmur when I soothed her bruises with cream, helped her to bathe, washing her with a gentle touch and soft words of encouragement.

There are no words. Not even the attempt at any.

If speaking was the only thing she wasn't able or willing to do, I could live with that. But seeing her like this. So fucking numb. Completely and utterly checked out. That kills me.

She's a ghost, a fucking wraith, a shadow.

And I'm at a loss of what to do. We all are.

Arden nods tightly, a muscle flicking in his jaw as he steps into the room. I watch him as he flicks through Cyn's recipe book, showing me a double page spread. Her intricate drawings and neat script makes my heart pang.

"I'm going to make this," he says, finger hovering over the page.

"*A tonic to ease a broken heart,*" I read. "Do you think it will work?"

"This is Cyn we're talking about, of course it'll work," Arden replies, an edge of desperation in his voice as his gaze drifts from me to Cyn.

"And you think you can pull it off?"

"I've spent the last two weeks since we got back studying this book and Cyn's recipes. I can do this."

"But you're not Cyn. It could go wrong."

"What choice do we have? Cyn is slipping away from us and I refuse to just sit by and watch."

"None of us are equipped to deal with this, Arden. Cyn was the one who was capable of healing others, not us. Who the fuck do we think we are?" I reply with frustration.

Arden's expression darkens, his fingers tightening around her recipe book. "We're the men who love her and we're *going* to be the men who'll heal her, understand?"

I take a deep breath and try to steady myself. I want to believe him, I really do, but it's so damn hard. Cyn is the healer, the one who understands the human body, mind and soul. Without her guidance we're floundering in an abyss of help-lessness.

"Do you truly believe that we're capable?" I ask quietly.

Arden pauses for a moment before answering. "I take it you don't?" he counters. "I thought we were on the same page."

We were, and yet I look at Cyn, at the blankness of her stare and the paleness of her skin, and want to fucking rage at the world. We might've rescued her from Soren, but now that she's here in our care, nothing has been able to bring her back from this darkness that has settled over her like a shroud.

"Fuck," I exclaim, scraping a hand through my hair as I get up and walk to the window, needing a moment.

Arden follows me, resting his hand on my shoulder. "Lorcan, don't fucking lose it now. I need you to keep it together."

"Lets just say that by some fucking miracle she does come back to us," I say, turning back to face him, and lowering my voice. "What do we tell her about the woman who died? We met her that night when we delivered the diamonds, Arden, and we didn't help her."

His face pales, regret burning in his eyes. "The only thing we can do. We tell her the truth."

"We could lose her," I counter.

"We could." He grits his teeth, casting his gaze to Cyn before turning back to me. "But I promised Cyn that there would be no more secrets between us, and I intend on keeping that promise."

"Okay," I agree, my stomach churning at the dire situation we're in. I don't want to lie to Cyn either, but this truth? This one is going to hurt. Her and us.

Arden grips me on the back of the head and pulls me into a hug, his lips brushing against my neck in warm affection as I wrap my arms around his back. We remain like that for long moments before he eventually pulls away.

"Would you mind sitting with Cyn a bit longer? I want to get started on this right away."

"Of course. Where's Carrick? I haven't seen him all day."

Arden rubs the back of his neck, more worry piling on top of the growing mountain of it. I know how he feels.

"Arden?"

"He's in the chapel."

"The chapel? We locked the doors to that part of the monastery years ago."

"Well, he's unlocked them," Arden murmurs.

"Fuck," I mutter.

"Yeah," Arden agrees.

An hour later Arden still hasn't returned with the tonic. The fire in the hearth has died down to a dull ember, and the rain has settled into a light patter as the clouds part above a gently lapping sea, revealing a star splattered sky.

At some point during my conversation with Arden, Cyn had drifted off to sleep. I look at her now, her expression troubled. She looks so small and helpless lying there, her skin pale and wan against the sheets, and my heart wrenches inside my chest as I slowly trace circles against the back of her hand with my thumb, needing to touch her.

"Come back to us, Cyn," I say, repeating what we've all said to her over and over again these past couple of weeks.

A small moan parts her lips, and I lift my head up. "Cyn?"

Her lashes flutter against her cheeks, the long, dark fronds soft against her skin, but she doesn't open her eyes. Another moan releases, louder this time. I reach for her hand drawing it to my lips, kissing her knuckles. Pressing all the love I feel for her through my lips and into her skin, begging her silently to come back to us. She moans again, and the pain I hear in it has my heart racing.

"Cyn, I'm here. It's Lorcan," I say, reaching up to cup her face.

She frowns, her mouth parting as a sob is wrenched from her chest, and tears seep out from between her lashes.

"Cyn, it's just a dream. I'm here. I'm here."

But it isn't just a dream. It's a nightmare that she's lived over and over again these past couple of weeks. Even in sleep she can't get any respite. I watch helplessly as she thrashes around, my hand knocked away as she fights an invisible force.

"Cyn!"

Panic litters my voice as a hoarse scream rips from her chest and she jerks awake, her eyes opening, blinking rapidly as more tears pour down her cheeks. She could form an ocean with all the tears she's cried.

"Hey, hey, you're okay. I'm here," I say, knowing it's fruitless, knowing that when she finally calms she'll retreat back into herself once more just like she's done every occasion before now.

I ease her back onto the bed, brushing her hair back off her face, my thumbs gently swiping away at the tears as she blinks up at me.

"It's okay," I soothe, needing to touch her as my fingertips glide over her skin, cupping her shoulders, my thumbs gently rubbing circles across her collarbone.

Instinct takes over, something within me telling me to keep touching her when before I'd been too afraid to. So I keep stroking her skin, cupping her arms, sliding my fingers up and down their length urging her to *feel*, trying to imbue all the care and love I feel for her into my touch.

Slowly her breathing settles, the trembling subsides and the tears stop falling. She blinks up at me, but this time she doesn't retreat into herself completely, there's a glimmer of life in her eyes that just wasn't there before.

"Cyn?" I question gently, daring not to hope.

A sob escapes her throat, and then she reaches for me, her arms spreading wide, wrapping around me as she pushes upwards and climbs into my lap.

"Cyn! Oh, fuck, Cyn!"

I don't hesitate, I haul her against my chest, my damn heart near beating out of my ribcage as she curls her body against mine and I wrap my arms around her. There's strength in her grasp that surprises me, life in her limbs as she shifts closer. Her breath rushes over the bare skin of my neck, and I hear her croak as she tries to use her voice.

"I've got you. Shh, I've got you," I whisper against her hair, feeling the wetness of her tears seeping through my top. "It's okay. You're okay."

She shakes her head and clings to me even tighter, her fingers curling into my shirt, fisting the fabric as if she's never going to let go.

Gently I run my fingers through her hair, soothing her with a gentle touch until eventually she begins to relax in my arms, her breathing evening out.

"That's it, I've got you."

When she's calm, I gently cup her chin, hoping and praying that when I look into her eyes that the Cyn I know and love is staring back at me and not a ghost.

This time it's her.

"Cyn," I lament, my voice thick with emotion.

Her grey eyes swell with tears like storm clouds before rainfall, but she blinks them away and beneath the glistening sadness I see something I haven't seen since before the Skull

Brotherhood stole her from us. A spark, a memory of who she was before that day. If I can remind her of who she was then, maybe I can bring her back to the surface for good this time.

I feel my throat close up with emotion as I take in her appearance, the bruises on her body a testament to the horrors she has endured. Whilst they've faded from a deep purple to a greenish-yellow, healing with every passing day, it still kills me to look at her mottled skin, knowing what she's been through at the hands of that evil cunt.

"Cyn," I choke out. "I thought I'd lost you."

She reaches up, cupping my face with her broken fingers, her thumb running across my bottom lip as she looks at me, really looks, instead of staring right through me.

"I'm h-here," she manages to get out, her voice nothing more than broken shards of glass in a smoky room. "I'm s-sorry."

"Don't apologise to me," I murmur, my mouth pressing against her forehead, my shoulders sagging as the tension seeps out of me.

I wrap my arms around her tightly, burying my face into her hair. She stays there for a few moments before gently pushing against my chest until I look at her again. Her grey eyes meet mine and then she speaks, each word is an effort that seems to cost more energy than she has within her exhausted body.

"Where am I?"

"Home, Cyn. You're home."

She frowns, her fingers dropping from my face and feathering against the bruise that rings her throat. She begins to tremble, the lingering pain from her still healing fingers triggering the memory of what happened to her.

"We've been back on our island for two weeks now," I say quickly, trying to distract her, to keep her focused on the here and now.

"The Masks, Christy? I remember hearing her voice..." she frowns.

"They've gone home to Ardelby Castle. Christy said we needed our space. They send their love. They'll come visit whenever you're ready," I add.

"And Connall?"

"We told him he could speak to you when you were ready, and not before."

"I see..." she coughs, her eyes watering from the pain.

"Would you like some painkillers?" I ask, shifting her on my lap so that I can grab the glass of water from the side table, passing it to her.

"No," she replies, taking a sip, wincing as she swallows. "I'd like a bath."

"A bath?"

"P-please..." She pauses, her eyes wavering with uncertainty. "If you'd help me."

"Anything you need. I'm here," I reply, my arm wrapping around her back as I take most of her weight. Her breathing is shallow and her body is tense from stiffness and pain, but she manages to move forward with my help. At least this time she's conscious of what she's doing, instead of robotic. "Easy now. Just lean into me. I've got you."

A tremulous breath parts her lips and she clings to me as we make our way into the en-suite bathroom. "I feel lightheaded."

"Sit here for a moment," I say, closing the lid to the toilet and easing her down on it so that I can fill up the bath. "Take deep breaths. Your body's not used to being up and about. The only time you've gotten out of bed was to use the toilet and bathe. You had my help each time."

Her cheeks heat and I immediately regret my words. "Hey, don't be embarrassed. You needed me, so I helped you."

She nods, watching me as I roll up my sleeves and turn on the taps, checking the water every so often as it fills to make sure it's not too hot. Once it reaches a level I'm happy with, I pour in some bath salts, swirling the water until puffy white clouds appear on the surface and the scent of orange blossom and sandalwood fills the air.

"It's ready," I say, the heat from the steamy water enveloping us as I help Cyn up, and ease her onto the ledge of the bath.

She reaches for the hem of her t-shirt, then winces at the pain from her bruised ribs, and just for the briefest of moments I see her slip away from me, the pain triggering more memories.

"Look at me, Cyn," I say, unable to hide the desperation in my voice.

I can't let her leave, not yet, *not ever*. Her mouth parts and her eyes refocus at the sound of my voice and she looks at me with trembling lips as I crouch down in front of her, resting my hands on either side of her hips.

"I'm going to remove your clothes, if you're okay with that?"

She nods, blinking at me. "Okay," she rasps.

Reaching for her feet, I remove the thick woollen socks Carrick dressed her in this morning to keep her warm. Her toes curl and flex at my touch, but she doesn't flinch away from me as I place them back on the floor and gently rub my palms over the top of her feet, needing contact.

"Can you lift your hips for me a little so I can remove your pyjama bottoms?" I ask.

She tries but her arms tremble like a newborn foul.

"That's okay. It'll take time to build your strength. Here, let me."

Getting to my feet, I slide one arm around her back and lift her enough so that I grab the hem of her waistband and gently tug both her pyjama bottoms and her knickers down, my fingertips burning as though a live wire connects us. She lets out a plaintiff cry, the movement most likely aggravating her injuries, extinguishing my desire as quickly as it appeared.

"Let me settle you back down," I say, leaving the material around her thighs whilst I lower her back onto the edge of the bath. She lets out a long, shaky breath, watching me as I drop back onto my knees before her. "Okay?"

"Yes," she whispers.

"Good girl," I murmur, forcing myself not to look at the apex of her thighs and the soft thatch of curly hair covering her pussy.

Gently, I pull off her pyjama bottoms and knickers the rest of the way, my knuckles grazing over her bare thighs and calves, my touch sending a rash of goosebumps across her skin. Easing her feet out of the material, I discard her clothes and find myself staring at the fading bruises scattered across her thighs. Swallowing the burning anger rising up my throat, it takes me a full minute before I'm calm enough to touch her again.

"Your shirt next, okay?" I say, my chest hitting her knees as my fingertips hover over the top button. "Okay?" I repeat, needing to make sure I have her consent, knowing that it's important for her recovery after Soren stole her choices from her so brutally. She nods, biting on her bottom lip as I reach up and undo each button slowly, one by one. The material parts, revealing the curve of her breasts. I swallow hard, jerking my eyes up to meet hers, ignoring how aroused I am. How fucking wrong it is to want her so badly when she's so vulnerable like this.

"Will you look at me?" she croaks, tears pooling in her eyes.

"I am," I reply, pinning her gaze with mine.

"No. I mean, my body."

"Cyn, I–"

"Am I that revolting to you?" she asks, a tremor in her smoky voice that burns me with its heat.

"No. God, no!" I say, shaking my head. "That's not how I feel when I look at you."

"Then how do you feel?"

I swallow hard, my gaze dropping to her body as I slide my fingers under her shirt, easing the material off her shoulders, the yellowish-green splotches still marking her beautiful skin. A sudden rush of anger and guilt tightens my chest as I discard the shirt at her feet.

"Lorcan?" she insists, clearing her throat. "How do you feel when you look at me?"

"Angry," I bite out. "What happened to you makes me so fucking angry, Cyn."

Even after the bruises disappear I know that the memory of her injuries will remain a constant reminder that we almost lost her, that we we're too fucking arrogant when it came to her safety. We assumed that because we're the infamous Deanadhe no one in their right mind would try to steal her from us. We were wrong, and we all paid for our arrogance. Cyn most of all.

"What else?"

"Guilt." My shoulders sag with the weight of it. "Fuck, we thought we were so damn untouchable. We truly believed that no one would try and take you from us. We were wrong."

"You always did think you were above everyone else," she says, a hint of a smile in her voice that almost has me smothering her in a hug through sheer relief.

Lifting my gaze back up to meet hers, I say fiercely, "No one will ever hurt you again. *Never.*"

She nods. "I believe you."

Then, when I don't fill the silence, when I keep my gaze fixed on her body, she brushes her shaking fingers gently against my arm.

"Is there anything else you feel when you look at me?" she asks softly.

I resist the urge to palm her breasts, to soothe her, to replace the hurt with something else. I wish I could remove every last memory of that bastard's hands on her. Truth be known, it's taking everything in me not to carry her back into the bedroom and fuck her pain away.

"Lorcan?" The vulnerability in her eyes cuts me up, and I force myself to swallow back the lump in my throat as I cup her cheek in my palm.

"I see a strong woman. I see someone who's lived through

trauma and survived. I see grace, beauty, power. I see intelligence and kindness. I see a woman I want to fuck," I admit.

"You do?"

"You think I don't? Fuck, Cyn, I want you more than I've ever wanted anything in my life."

"Good," she whispers and the smile she gives me makes my cock jerk in my pants and my heart swell with love.

"Let me help you into the bath," I say, reaching for her hand because, despite what I've just said, there's no way I'm going to fuck Cyn until she's ready, both physically, mentally and emotionally. And by fuck I mean make love.

She nods, sliding her hand into mine so that I can keep her steady as she steps into the bath. I don't let go until she's fully submerged, a strange sound parting her lips, somewhere between a hiss and a groan as the water gently sloshes around her.

"Is it too hot?"

"It's fine," she replies, her voice no more than a wisp of smoke.

"Then I'll wait outside, let you enjoy your bath in peace," I say, but she reaches for me, her fingers grazing my forearm.

"Don't go. *Stay.*"

"Cyn–"

"Please, Lorcan," she whispers.

How can I deny her? She could ask anything of me and I'd give it to her.

"Faith told me that she used to dream about laying in a warm bath. Such a simple need, and he took that from her too," Cyn says softly, her eyes glazing over a little as she goes to some faraway place. I see her shutting down right before my eyes and I can't let her go.

Kneeling beside the tub, I take her hand in mine, drawing circles on her palm with my thumb, trying to keep her in the present with soft touches.

"She was so brave," Cyn adds, her voice filled with sorrow.

Right now I don't know how to respond without admitting that Arden and I didn't try to help her friend when we had the opportunity to do so. I don't want to hurt Cyn anymore than she already is, and selfishly I don't want her to hate me.

I will tell her, just not yet.

"Do you want me to wash your hair?" I ask, forcing the self-loathing deep inside.

She nods, grasping onto the side of the tub and lowering her upper body beneath the water, I reach over and cup the back of her head, helping her to wet her hair. Water droplets slide over her skin as she sits back up and I grab the shampoo, squeezing some into my hand, the scent of peaches filling the air.

"Is this okay?" I ask, gently massaging the shampoo into her scalp in a slow circular motion.

"Yes," she whispers, closing her eyes, her face relaxing into an expression of serenity as the foamy white bubbles cling to her strands.

Christ, she's so fucking beautiful.

I want to kiss her, this sudden overwhelming urge begging me to press my lips against her bare skin. But I restrain myself, determined to show her that I'm not ruled by my lust, that I can be her place of safety for as long as she needs it. So I turn on the shower attachment and rinse her hair free of suds instead. When I'm done, I grab the body wash resting on the ledge next to the bath.

"Here," I say, nudging her arm gently.

Peeling her eyes open she looks from the bottle of body wash back up to me in silent invitation.

"Do you want me to wash you?"

In answer she takes the bottle from me, flips the cap and pours some of the liquid into my open palm. "I need you to wash away every memory of his touch," she says.

Fuck, she's killing me.

My cock twitches, my balls a heavy weight at the base of my dick as I begin to massage her shoulders, gently kneading her muscles, mindful not to press too hard as I work my fingers down her back before working my way back up again.

She lets out a gentle sigh so I grab more of the bath wash, lather up the liquid and gently work my fingers along her collarbone and the expanse of skin above her breasts. Her moans of pleasure intensify as I stroke down her arms, massaging her hands and fingers.

Next, I reach under the water and grasp her ankle, gently resting her foot on the lip of the bath so I can massage her legs too. Her gaze softens, her eyes heavy-lidded as she watches me.

"Is this okay?" I ask once again, making sure I'm interpreting her reactions correctly.

She nods, and when my fingers brush the inside of her thigh her eyes flare with something that surprises me.

Need.

Reaching for my hand beneath the water, she locks eyes with me and slowly sides my hand upwards.

"Cyn, I'm not sure..."

But my voice trails off as she guides my fingers to the soft folds of her pussy.

Fuck.

I can't think straight.

My heart is racing, my dick rock hard as she rocks against my hand.

"Cyn. It's too soon," I whisper hoarsely, pulling my hand away, fighting the need to sink my fingers inside of her.

"He didn't..." she begins.

"I know." I reply, thanking whatever greater power there might be that he didn't rape her. "But you've been through so much, Cyn. He hurt you in other ways. I don't want you to regret anything. I'm trying to protect you."

"Please, I need to *feel* something," she begs.

"Let's talk this out instead."

"You don't understand. I need your touch most of all," she explains, the scratchy sound of her voice hoarse as she continues. "I don't want to feel numb anymore. This is what I want, Lorcan."

"There are things I need to tell you, Cyn—"

"I don't want to know. Not right now," she rasps. "Please, just do this for me."

My resolve crumbles at her words. I can't deny her this.

"At any point if this is too much, or you change your mind, tell me and I'll stop, okay? I'll stop."

She nods, then grabs my hand once more and guides it

between her legs. Her lips part as I gently rub the pad of my thumb against her clit, circling her delicate flesh, watching her face for signs of distress.

But when she moans in pleasure, not pain, I continue, encouraged by the way her body rocks against my hand. Slowly I explore her, gently inserting a finger inside of her when she spreads her legs a little wider. She whimpers, her nipples puckering as she arches her back.

For long minutes, I gently touch her, my own body trembling with need as I watch her mouth part on a moan and her head tip back as she arches her spine.

"Lorcan," she utters, voice coated in pleasure, steeped in emotion.

My hand stills as I look up at her, a single tear slides down her cheek.

"Cyn, I'm sorry. I shouldn't have--"

"No," she replies, reaching for my wrist, holding me against her, looking at me like I'm her fucking savour. "Please, don't stop. Kiss me."

With a thundering heart, I lean over the bath and press my mouth against hers, continuing to stroke her. She whispers my name in pleasured exhales as I begin to gently glide my finger in and out of her folds, intensifying the sensations coursing through her body. She chases the pleasure, rocking against my hand, sliding her tongue deeper into my mouth whilst I continue to draw out an orgasm from deep within her body.

Replacing pain with pleasure, sadness with lust, depression with joy.

"I've got you, my love," I whisper, drawing back, needing to watch her come undone.

Two pink spots of colour highlight her cheeks, as her internal walls tighten and her chest heaves with the oncoming orgasm.

"Come for me," I demand, pressing against her clit until she cries out in rapture; an expression of both surrender and bliss on her face.

It takes my breath away to see it—to witness such absolute beauty and abandon after suffering so much pain, sadness and loss. As our eyes lock, a million emotions pass between us: understanding, empathy and something much deeper than physical pleasure.

Love.

A few minutes later, I wrap a soft towel around Cyn's body and carry her back to bed, holding her against my chest until she's fast asleep. Eventually, I drift off myself, feeling at peace for the first time in weeks, having hope that one day soon we'll get our girl back fully–whole, healed and free from the sorrow that holds her hostage still.

20

C^{yn}

Stirring, my eyes flutter open as wakefulness draws me to the surface of my consciousness and a stream of pink sunlight cuts across my chest and face. Beyond the window, dawn rises, bathing the sky with pinks, oranges and golds.

It reminds me of another, more blood-red sky in a country far away from here, and my heart pangs at the memory of Faith doused in the dying embers of the sun.

"*A bad omen?*" she had asked.

For her it had been, despite my promise that it wouldn't be.

I'd believed with everything I had that she would survive,

that her baby would be born into the arms of a mother stronger than any woman I've ever met.

But she didn't. Soren had taken from her one last time and I can't... I don't know *how* to live with the unfairness of that, the brutality. I'm the one who's supposed to help people, take care of them, and when she'd needed me the most, I couldn't help her.

My throat tightens with tears, and I feel the stitches in my broken heart that Lorcan had sewn with his care and attention yesterday begin to pull apart at the memory.

If I had the power to turn back time I would've found a way to stop her from attending that awful night. If I hadn't been so badly beaten by Soren, I would have had the energy to make her a sleep tonic instead of passing out myself. There are a million things I could've done to save her. But I hadn't, and I'll have to live with that somehow.

Tears form in my eyes, and I can feel myself retreating back into that same dark headspace I've been in when the sound of someone singing pulls me up sharp.

Haunting.

Beautiful.

Familiar.

It's the voice of an angel. It's *Carrick*.

The sound is so raw, so pain-filled that it forces something within me to awaken, the part of me I've felt slip away since I'd witnessed Faith's death: my intense need to heal what's broken.

Next to me Lorcan stirs, and I watch him for a moment, allowing Carrick's voice to wash over me as I study Lorcan's sleeping form. His silver-blonde hair is a mess of strands across his face, and his lips are parted as he softly snores in a deep sleep. My heart squeezes at the sight of him and I reach out, gently resting my fingers against his cheek knowing he put his life at risk to save me. That he must be so emotionally exhausted given insomnia hasn't kept him awake this time.

"Thank you," I whisper, and I don't just mean for coming to rescue me, but for last night, and all the hours before when he looked after me as I drowned beneath sorrow and grief.

I'm aware that they've all spent time with me, taking it in turns to keep me company whilst I tried and failed to come back to them, so devastated by memories that even now haunt me, will continue to haunt me. There are pockets of time that I don't consciously remember these past couple of weeks since we returned to the island, but my body, my heart, my soul, they haven't forgotten what my mind has blanked out.

Concern, care, affection, worry, desperation, love.

I've felt that from them all, despite feeling numb myself. It's for that reason I slip out of bed on unsteady legs, pull on a dressing gown hanging on the back of my bedroom door, and go in search of Carrick. My legs are still weak from lack of use and my head dizzy from not eating enough these past few days, but I push on, determined.

Passing by Arden's bedroom, I see the steady rise and fall of his chest as he sleeps, still fully clothed on his bed. Clutched in his hand is my recipe book. He hangs on to it like a lifeline, and something about that makes the pain in my chest ease a little.

As I continue onwards, my bare feet pressing against the

cool wooden floorboards, Carrick's voice carries through the house like an ethereal lullaby, somehow both calming and soothing to my soul. Words that are not sung but intoned with sadness, with heartbreak and passion, love and hope, and despite the heaviness of my limbs and the lingering pain in my body, I press onwards.

My feet carry me downstairs, past the kitchen and dining room, past the office and the door leading down into the basement, towards a part of the old monastery that I've never ventured in before. Carrick's voice grows louder as I near, and at the end of a long, dimly lit corridor is a door that has always been locked, now standing ajar.

I *was afraid of dying, afraid of falling,*
    Afraid of loving, silently grieving
But you came along, healing.
Stealing my heart...

H is words wash over me and I stumble a little, so profoundly affected by his voice. Steadying myself, I place my hand on the thick wood and push the door open to find myself standing on the threshold of a tiny chapel.

In front of me, Carrick's tall frame is silhouetted against the large window opposite, rays of warm light streaming around him as the sun continues to rise.

His head is thrown back and his eyes are closed as his voice lifts up into the arched ceiling, scattering goosebumps across my skin and taking me back to that time when we were kids.

Back then I'd been affected in much the same way by his voice, drawn to him by its purity and the secrets he kept hidden inside of him. That hasn't changed. In fact, when I look at him now, I sense something he's tried to hide, rising to the surface with every note that releases from his lips.

It isn't just the melody of the song and the words he's singing that touches something deep within me, it's the pain buried beneath it, the trauma. And just like when we were kids I approach him, my silent footsteps gliding across the stone floor.

Carrick finishes with a long trembling note that scatters the dust motes around him and shakes his body to the core.

"Carrick?" I whisper, reaching for him, my hand squeezing his shoulder gently.

"Go away," he cries, knees buckling as he falls to the ground. "You're not real."

My heart tightens painfully, and I remove my hand as his head bows, uncertain what to do next.

"Now I'm imagining your voice, your touch," he mumbles, a broken laugh escaping his lips.

"Carrick, you're not imagining things," I whisper, my voice hoarse as I step around his body and kneel before him.

Slowly he looks up, his eyes wide with shock and disbelief. I gasp at the scar that carves across his face, something I remember seeing at some point over the last few weeks, but not really comprehending. When they took me, he fought so hard, and they hurt him.

"Carrick..."

"Cyn?"

The second he realises that I'm real and not a figment of his imagination, he lunges for me, hauling me into his arms, holding me close. It's not tender, this hug, it's a clawing kind of hope, desperate.

"Fuck, I was going insane waiting for you, Cyn," he mutters into my neck, his lips sliding across my skin as he talks. "I thought you'd never come back to us, so I came here to sing in this place I hate, hoping that whatever mighty power exists would somehow hear my prayers this time.

"And I dreamt of an angel singing. I guess that was you," I reply, his fingers curling into the material of my dressing gown and clutching me closer.

"I'm no angel," he answers at the exact same moment his fingers hit the tender spot on my ribcage and I hiss with pain. He jerks back, letting me go as though scolded. "Fuck. I'm sorry. I'm sorry!"

I raise my hand, tears smarting my eyes as he falls onto his arse and scoots away from me, regret, fear, and pain twisting up his features.

"Don't do that," I say.

"I hurt you," he counters, scraping a hand through his hair, tugging on the strands.

"You didn't mean to."

"Just like he hurt you," he continues, fisting his hair, pulling.

"No. Not like that," I reply, reaching for him.

I hold my hand out, a peace offering. "Take my hand, Carrick."

He shakes his head. "I can't do that. I want you too much... Fuck!" he exclaims, slapping his hand against the cold stone. "Ever since you've been back, I've had this urge to–"

"To what, Carrick?" I croak, my voice a pile of rocks and boulders in my throat.

"To bury myself inside of you. To connect not just my body, but my soul with yours. I've never needed anything more in my life. It's wrong to want that after what he did to you, after what I failed to do."

"Failed to do?" I ask, shocked at how his truth affects me.

I'm not scared by it, or his honesty. This isn't a brutal man who wants to rape and abuse me like Soren, this is a man so in need of human contact and connection, love and affection, that he's literally beating himself up for wanting it.

"I didn't protect you from them. I should've fought harder."

"Don't blame yourself."

"He beat you, Cyn!" he argues. "I don't even know if he raped you, and I'm here wanting to fuck you. What kind of person does that make me?"

"He didn't rape me," I confess, lips wobbling.

"He hurt you so badly. You had to watch your friend die in the worst possible way. That's on me!"

"No!" I shake my head furiously. "You saved me."

"Did I though?" he asks quietly, looking at me, really looking. His penetrating gaze bores holes into my face as he studies me. "Are you really here? Or will you fall back into that place where we can't reach you."

"I'm here now," I reply, holding my hands out once more. "I

can't promise you tomorrow or the day after that, but I'm here now."

"Then we'll just have to make sure that we give you a reason to stay," he replies, crawling back to me and taking my hands. His thick fingers sliding across my palms, cupping my wrists as though he needs to feel the steady beat of my pulse to be certain I really am here with him.

"I'm so fucked-up over this," he admits.

"Me too," I reply.

"How do we fix it?" he asks.

"I'm not sure," I reply honestly. "I need time."

He nods. "I can give you that. I *will* give you that..."

"Thank you."

"When I said I wanted to fuck you," he swallows hard, his Adam's apple bobbing up and down as guilt stutters across his face. "It came out wrong. I don't want you to be scared of me."

"I'm not," I say. "How can I be afraid of a man who tore through a herd of monsters with no concern for his own safety just to save me?"

"Don't make me out to be a hero, I'm not one, Cyn."

I ignore him, continuing. "How can I be afraid of a man who sings like you do, who makes me feel like I've been torn apart and put back together again in one song? You truly are gifted, Carrick."

He shakes his head. "It's just a voice."

"You and I both know that isn't true," I croak, my own voice cracking under the strain. I swallow hard, wincing, my throat is so sore.

"It hurts?" he asks, reaching up to press his fingers gently against the skin on my neck.

"A little," I lie. It hurts a lot.

"Then rest your voice, we can communicate the way we used to if you want?"

"I'll rest later. There is one question I want to ask you, if that's okay?"

"Sure," he replies, cupping my neck gently, his thumb rubbing over my pulse as it flutters wildly beneath my skin from his touch.

"What secret are you hiding? Why does it hurt you so much to sing?"

"That's two questions," he replies, dropping his gaze so he doesn't have to meet my eyes.

I wait, sliding my legs out from beneath me to get more comfortable. We're both steeped in the sunlight that warms the small patch of stone we're sitting on. Carrick's dark brown hair is highlighted with streaks of mahogany, his eyes lit with shards of sunlight as he replies.

"I've never told anyone this," he admits.

"Not even Arden or Lorcan?" I whisper, forcing the words out even when they hurt me to speak.

"Not even them... Though I suspect they know and have respected my choice not to talk about it."

He drops his gaze to our joined hands, his thumbs rubbing across the back of my knuckles. I wait, giving him time to summon the courage to tell me what haunts him so badly.

"I was sent to Silver Oaks Institute because I almost killed a man when I was fourteen," he whispers, pausing for a moment, as though waiting for me to get up and run at his confession.

I don't.

I keep still, quiet.

"Arden and Lorcan know about that, just like the whole village where we grew up did, but no one knows the real reason why I almost beat my singing teacher to death. Arden's family suspected, and that's why I was sent to Silver Oaks for rehabilitation and not jail. They pulled some strings. My singing teacher was threatened. No one spoke of it again."

Carrick absentmindedly reaches for the spot on his collarbone where I bit him all those years ago, as though the reminder of the pain soothes him. Given what I already know about Carrick and his needs, it probably does.

"I loved singing in the choir at church. I loved it so fucking much," he continues, stroking my knuckles once more. "It was like I was a different person when I sang. I could hold the attention of the whole congregation every time I opened my mouth. They were enraptured, and it made me feel so good about myself. But it wasn't just that, I felt at peace when I sang. I knew I was special... The problem was so did he."

For a long minute silence spreads out between us as a deep sense of foreboding settles in my stomach. I already know where this is heading, my body sensing the impending horror as nausea churns in my stomach. I so badly want to soothe away his trauma, but I know if I move a muscle or say a word he might not continue. So I keep silent and wait.

"The first time my singing teacher touched my dick, I was so shocked that all I could do was let him. They say in times of great stress and trauma you either fight or you run. I did neither. I clammed up. I became a statue as he fisted my cock and made me hard."

Carrick's fingers squeeze my wrists tightly as he blows out a deep exhale. He's trembling now, and it takes a great deal of effort not to climb into his lap and hold him, soothe him.

"I couldn't understand how my body could betray me so much. I didn't run. I didn't make a sound, but I came all over his hand nevertheless. He abused me for another three weeks, always fisting my dick, always making me come, until one day I didn't let him. That day I beat him so badly he was left unconscious with a fractured skull, shattered jaw and cheekbone, and several broken ribs. I didn't sing again willingly until that night in the chapel at Silver Oaks. You found me at my most vulnerable and I hated you for seeing what no one else had," he admits, lifting his gaze to meet mine.

The pain and regret I see in his eyes has me cupping his face gently as I try to imbue him with care and affection, understanding and forgiveness. "It's okay," I whisper.

"You tried to run, and I wanted to hurt you for witnessing what you did," he continues. "Then you bit me, and it was like all the memories and the trauma just disappeared, replaced instead with pain. I remember thinking afterwards how cruel it was that you, the person I hated, were the only one who'd given me respite. Not the therapist at the school, not my best friends, but you. I thought you'd put a spell on me, and in a way I guess you had."

"I'm sorry for what you've been through," I say, forcing his chin up to look at me.

"You saved me that day, Cyn. You provided me with a way to cope with the trauma, and I repaid you in the worst possible way. Will you ever forgive me?"

"I forgave you a long time ago, Carrick," I croak.

"How will I ever repay you?" he asks, drawing me into his arms.

I climb into his lap willingly, curling my body against his, burying my nose in the warmth of his neck, breathing him in. "You saved my life," I whisper in response. "We're even."

"Then how can I help you to heal? Lorcan has always been the best at knowing what you need. He's kinder than I am, far more patient. He has a soft touch, has looked after your body these past couple of weeks whilst your heart and mind had time to heal. Arden has taught himself herbology so that he can make your recipes. He's spent every spare moment when he's not been watching over you, practising. He's determined. What can I offer? I'm not like them."

"Your voice," I reply without hesitation.

"My voice?"

I nod. "If you're willing to share it?"

For a long time Carrick just sits quietly, his strong arms wrapped around me as he mulls over my request. I get the sense that he's going to deny me, and I understand why that might be, given that his love for singing is tangled with trauma. So I offer him a trade.

"If you sing for me, I will give you what you need," I reply, brushing my lips across his throat, tentatively running my teeth over his collarbone before releasing a long, trembling breath. He remains quiet, waiting, sensing I have more to say. "You weren't the only one who felt different after that night in the chapel. Biting you, feeling you surrender beneath me like that, it made me feel like I had control for once in my life, it made me feel powerful. Since what's happened, I've felt powerless, Carrick," I admit. "Maybe together we can rewrite the narrative. You can sing without associating it with your trauma, and I can give you the pain that you so desperately need without associating it with mine."

"You'd do that?" he asks, rubbing his cheek against mine. I can feel his heart hammering beneath his ribcage as I shift a little in his lap and reach up for his collar, pulling it to one side.

"Sing for me," I whisper, and when the first note releases from his lips, lifting the hairs on the back of my neck and soothing my soul, I sink my teeth into his skin, soothing his.

Warm blood trickles into my mouth as Carrick's voice lifts up into the air around us. He doesn't miss a note as I suck on his skin, my lips and tongue capturing the blood that trickles from him like beaded jewels. He simply holds me closer as I shift in his lap, my hands pressed against his chest as he breathes in and out, a musical organ brought to life with sound.

Tasting him like this as he sings, his chest vibrating, is beyond sexual, it's spiritual. I feel the notes caressing me, soothing my pain and slowly binding the tears in my heart as a part of him becomes a part of me. I feel power in his submission, honoured that he trusts me enough to try this when I know how hard it must be.

Between us I can feel the hard length of his erection, but it doesn't distract him from the singing. If anything, his physical reaction tells me that my instincts were right, that he needs the pain to help him find pleasure in singing again. That his trauma shouldn't stop him from doing what he loves, and that mine shouldn't be allowed to have power over me either. So I bite him as he sings and when the last note falls from his lips and I gently lick over the tiny wounds my teeth have made, peace settles between us.

For long minutes we sit wrapped up in each other's arms, sunlight through the window warming our skin until, eventually, he pulls back a little.

"Thank you," he murmurs, stroking my hair and pressing featherlight kisses across my brow.

"Thank you," I whisper back, tipping my head back as I look up at him, and he down at me.

"I really want to kiss you," he says, his dark brown hair falling into his eyes, a little of the tension in them gone now. "Can I?"

I nod, reaching up and cupping his cheek, my fingers gently tracing over his scar, forever reminding me that this man fought so hard to protect me, and later killed a monster to save me.

He slowly lowers his mouth, brushing his lips tentatively against mine. It's the lightest of touches, searching almost. When he draws back a little, our breaths mingle as he stares deeply into my eyes, a well of emotion in his.

"I'm afraid if I really kiss you, I'm not sure I'll have the strength to stop there," he admits.

"I trust you," I reply, telling him in so many words that I want his kiss, but I'm not ready for more. Not yet.

He frowns, wanting to kiss me but not wanting to break my trust in him. Eventually he makes a decision and presses his lips against mine, groaning when I open my mouth and welcome his tongue.

And so we kiss.

We kiss with mutual trust, with passion, with the soft swell of our hearts beating in unison.

We kiss and kiss and kiss.

And between those kisses he mutters words of affection and love, he talks about a future filled with warmth and laughter, hope and joy, and in return I place my trust in the man who hurt me as a child but promises to love me as an adult.

21

Arden

Bleary-eyed and needing a cup of coffee to wake me the hell up, I walk into the kitchen a few hours after I left it, pulling up sharp when I see Cyn standing at the kitchen island, stirring the pot of ingredients I'd left overnight to steep.

"Cyn!" I say, rubbing my eyes just to make sure that I'm not seeing things.

I blink back my exhaustion, expecting her to disappear, but my fucking heart near beats out of my chest at the vision I see before me.

"Cyn," I repeat, sounding like a fucking moron. I'm so

shocked I can't seem to do anything more than repeat her name.

She gives me a soft, tentative smile, and despite the dark circles that ring her eyes, there's a softness around her features that just wasn't there the last time I saw her. I rock on my feet, wanting to take her in my arms and pull her close, but not really knowing if that's what she needs.

"I heard Carrick singing…" she replies, her voice rough as it scratches out her words.

"He's been singing more since we got back," I reply, internally cringing at my awkwardness.

Get a fucking grip, Arden.

"I'm hoping that he'll keep doing so. It's soothing."

"So that's what finally woke you?" I ask, swallowing down this surprising surge of jealousy at the thought. I didn't realise how badly I wanted to be the one to bring her back until now. It makes me feel like a dick for even feeling this way.

"No, it kept me here in the present. It was Lorcan who drew me out of the darkness," she says softly.

I nod my head, unable to form any words because of this toxic feeling growing inside of me. It's petty, this jealousy, I should be grateful to my brothers. I *am* grateful, but I can't deny that it hurts that I wasn't the one to bring her back around.

"You've been busy," she says, dropping her gaze back to the large pot before her.

"I was making you a tonic, but I can see you don't need it now," I reply, the words coming out more harshly than I'd intended.

"You don't seem too happy about it," she says roughly, her

face betraying the fact I've hurt her with my careless comment, her voice hoarse and cracked.

"Cyn–"

"I understand."

"No. You don't," I retort, my heart pounding like a drum as I take a few quick steps towards her, desperate to make amends but not knowing how to fully express the guilt and shame I feel. Not just over this jealous remark, but for everything.

My arrogance got her beaten and almost raped and killed. My selfishness meant her friend died brutally when perhaps Lorcan and I could've done something to prevent that. My need to bring her home and keep her cloistered has most likely stirred up the war between the O'Briens and the O'Farrells. Not to mention all the mistakes I made as a kid. The fact of the matter is, I've fucked up over and over again when it's come to Cyn, and I just wanted to do right by her one fucking time. I wanted to heal her after causing her so much pain.

Me.

I owed her that much at least.

"That came out wrong. It's *really* good to see you up and about," I say earnestly, meaning every word of it, wanting to pull her into my arms and kiss her until she forgives me, but not wanting to overstep. "How do you feel?"

With her eyes trained on me, her expression is one of guardedness, and it only serves to amplify my regret for making such a thoughtless remark. I hate that I put that look on her face.

"I feel... Better isn't exactly the right word. I guess, not as lost?"

She chews on her lip as her gaze drops back to the table and all the ingredients scattered across the surface.

"Not being lost is a good thing," I point out.

"It's better than feeling numb."

"Cyn, I–"

"What were you making?" she asks, cutting me off as she picks up a sprig of Motherwort, a herb with tiny lilac flowers and slim green leaves that look like the pointy end of a letter opener. She already knows the answer–of course she does, it's her recipe after all–but I tell her anyway.

"This," I say, opening up the pages of her recipe book and showing her.

"Ah, *a tonic to heal a broken heart*," she reads, a sad laugh releasing from her lips.

"Doesn't it work?" I ask, tucking my shaking hands into my jean pockets. I don't know what I expected to happen when she woke up, but this awkward kind of tension wasn't it.

"It depends on how you look at it," she replies. "This tonic helps with insomnia which some people get when they're grieving a loss, or trying to heal from a break up. It can calm a racing heart caused by anxiety, and settle an overworked mind, but actually healing a broken heart? I'm not so sure there are any medicines, natural or otherwise, that can do that."

"If anyone can do it, you can," I counter. "You're incredible."

"So incredible that the Skull Brotherhood fed women diamonds so they could heighten their emotions, their *fear*, when they raped them?" she shakes her head, tears clogging her throat.

"Fuck, I'm sorry," I reply, more guilt piling on top of the guilt already weighing me down.

"Diamonds were never meant to be used like that, Arden. They were supposed to bring people together in a good way, not be one of the ingredients in a nightmare."

"Don't you dare blame yourself. This is my fault. What happened to you, what happened to your friend, to the women Soren held captive, all of it. It's my fault. I took advantage of you, Cyn, and even after I realised how much I wanted you, *needed* you," I correct myself, "I still didn't do right by you. I delivered the diamonds right into his hands. I didn't protect you. I didn't protect your friend–"

"Stop!" she says, holding her hand up. "I knew what I was doing coming here. I knew what it meant. I was dishonest."

"You came here to give The Masks and Christy time. You did that out of *love*," I counter. "You're not in the wrong here."

"Aren't I?" she mutters, taking her recipe book from me and flicking through the pages. "I didn't tell you everything."

"Are you talking about the letter from my aunt?" I ask.

"You know about that?" she asks me, clearing her throat.

I see how she winces. I hear how rough the sound of her voice is, as though she has swallowed shards of glass that cut up her voice box every time she speaks. Grabbing a glass, I fill it with water from the tap, passing it to her.

"Drink," I urge her.

Our fingers brush against one another as she takes the glass from me, and I feel that brief touch all the way done to the marrow of my bones. I want to hold her so badly. So fucking badly. Yet I hold back. She swallows a mouthful, her throat bobbing under the fading bruise ringing her neck, which only serves to remind me how close we were to losing her.

"How did you know?" she asks me, placing the glass of water onto the kitchen table.

"Christy. She told us that her mother wrote you a letter too. We understand now that you didn't just leave with us that night of the masquerade ball because you wanted to give Christy and The Masks time to heal, you also left because you chose a path which saved our lives," I explain, reaching for her, my fingers pressing against her arm as she looks up at me. "Is that right?"

"Yes. Two paths. Two choices. Two lives. Nessa said that one choice led to a life of happiness, where I would heal many people but you, Lorcan and Carrick would die," she explains, her grey eyes billowing with secrets and swirling emotions.

"And the other path," I whisper, stepping closer, my palm running up her arm as she turns to face me fully. I lock eyes with her and I swear I can see right into her soul. There's no guard up, there are no walls, nothing to hide behind, just complete honesty.

"Would lead to here, with you all alive."

Her eyes well with tears as I pull her into my arms, holding her against my chest in a fierce hug.

I don't deserve her. I don't deserve her bravery, her selflessness or her kindness.

"You chose the path to protect us knowing that you'd have to sacrifice yourself in the process, didn't you?" I ask on an unsteady breath, feeling so much fucking gratitude, feeling utterly unworthy. "You lost too much, and I'm afraid that we won't be enough."

Her tears seep through my shirt, her sobs tear at my heart as her body shakes with grief. I wish I could erase what happened, but I can't. All I can do is live in her grief alongside her, show her how much I love her, and prove to her that our future together was worth the sacrifice.

But first, I owe her the truth.

"Cyn, there's something I need to tell you, something important that might change how you feel about us," I say, gently easing her out of my arms, and pulling out a seat at the table so that she can sit down.

"What?" she asks, as I take a seat next to her and angle my body towards her.

"I made a promise to myself to always be truthful, even if it's hard."

She blinks up at me with uncertainty, afraid of what I'm about to say. "This is going to hurt, isn't it?"

"Yes," I admit, taking her hands in mine. "But I wouldn't be doing right by you if I didn't tell you this one last truth. I hope you'll forgive us."

Cyn swallows, then nods. *Go on*, she silently urges me with her eyes, because like me she's suddenly lost the ability to speak.

Swallowing back the brittleness in my throat, I force the words out of my mouth. "On the night Lorcan and I delivered the diamonds to Soren, the same night his men came here and stole you from Carrick, we met your friend, Faith."

Cyn gasps, her eyes widening as her face drains of colour.

"She was in the room with Soren, naked except for a chain wrapped around her waist linking her to him. We knew she couldn't have been there of her own accord, but instead of trying to do something to help, we delivered the diamonds, and we left. On the way out, I began to have a vision. Lorcan got me to the car just in time. I passed out. When I woke up we were on the boat back to the island."

Cyn's bottom lip begins to tremble, and her eyes mist with tears that I wish I didn't cause.

"I'm sorry. I'm sorry we didn't try to help her. I'm sorry we were too selfish to think about anything else apart from getting back to you. I'm sorry we put you in a position of danger. I'm sorry for your loss. I'm so fucking sorry for it all, Cyn."

She stares at me for a long time, and with every second that passes it's like she's removing layer upon layer of skin and muscle until I'm just a heart beating wildly, waiting for her to crush it.

She has the power to do that. She always did.

But instead of doing that, she takes my hands in hers and says, "I left my journal for you to find not just because I wanted you to find a way to co-exist with The Masks, but because I knew the only chance you had of saving me was with their help. Knowing that, how could you have done anything differently that night. You couldn't have."

"Maybe you're right, but the honest to God truth is, we could've tried. We didn't because all we wanted was to get back to you. It was a selfish act."

Cyn sighs heavily, and I feel the weight of her grief as if it's my own.

"I could lie and tell you that hearing you say that doesn't hurt, because it does. It hurts deeply, not because I feel betrayed by your decision but because Faith was a good woman, strong, brave. She *deserved* to live. It hurts so much to know she suffered for so long and never got the chance to be a mum, that she lost her life and that of her unborn child so brutally. I'm not sure I'll ever get over her loss."

"We should've tried."

"You could've died and then what would've happened?"

"We should've tried," I insist.

"Can I ask you something?" she asks softly.

"Anything."

"If you'd known what Faith would mean to me before you walked into that room, what would you have done?"

"We would've fought to save her. No question."

"But if you had, they would've killed you, and then who would have come to save me, the other women?" she asks, her voice imploring me to understand. "Do you see what I'm trying to say?"

"I'm not sure that makes me feel any better, that our selfishness saved us. You're different, Cyn. Your instinct is to help, to heal. You chose a path you knew was going to be painful, to save us."

"Because I knew what the outcome would be. Nessa told me. You didn't know Faith before that moment. You didn't know how much she'd mean to me or what would happen to her. All you knew was that Soren and his men were dangerous. That there were just two of you and many of them. In that moment you had to live. You had to live so that later you could save me, and those other women you set free."

"I appreciate what you're trying to do, but I don't deserve your excuses."

"It isn't an excuse. It's the horrible, unfair, brutal truth. Sometimes terrible things happen to good people. Do I wish with all my heart it wasn't true? Of course I do," Cyn says, her voice cracking as tears stream down her face.

She drops her head, her shoulders shaking and I reach for her, thumbing away her tears as I draw her onto my lap. She comes willingly, settling against me as I hold her, fucking breathing in her scent. To hold her in my arms like this, it's a wish come true. I never, ever want to let her go.

"She was a good woman, Arden. So brave. So strong. I think you would've liked her."

"Tell me about her."

"One day, but not yet," she croaks back, her tear-clogged voice brittle.

"So what do we do now?" I ask, respecting her request for more time so that she can grieve and heal.

She pulls back slightly, sliding her hands up and over my chest, then cupping my cheeks as she brushes her lips softly over mine, and says, "*We live.*"

Then she kisses me, and that jealousy I felt earlier disappears, hope taking its place as our tongues dance, our lips meld, and our breaths mingle.

"That smells... interesting," Lorcan says as he steps into the kitchen a little while later. His gaze flicks to Cyn who's eating a bowl of tomato soup whilst I stir a pot of bubbling herbs on the stove under her watchful gaze. "I woke up and you were gone," he adds, not angry, just relieved that she's here, safe.

"That was my fault," Carrick says, stepping into the kitchen behind him. He's bare-chested, his hair wet from a shower as he squeezes Lorcan on the shoulder and sits down beside Cyn. "I was singing. Cyn found me in the chapel."

"You didn't hear him?" I ask Lorcan.

He shakes his head. "I was sleeping."

"You slept?" Carrick's look of shock is almost comical.

Lorcan grins. "A solid six hours straight."

Carrick returns his smile, before brushing a soft kiss against Cyn's temple. "How are you feeling?"

She nods. "Okay. You?" her gaze flicks to his collarbone and the new teeth marks indenting his skin.

Lorcan's heated gaze flicks between them both and I can tell he has questions, but for the moment he refrains from asking them as he presses a kiss on top of Cyn's head then pulls out a seat at the table and sits down too.

She smiles at him and it damn near floors me that she's back here with us and capable of interacting like this. Just a few hours ago, Cyn was pretty much catatonic. Now she's alert, present and eating, thanks to Lorcan and Carrick, both of whom somehow pulled her out of the darkness and kept her here. I suspect there's more to what happened between them, but I'm not going to pry. We all love the same girl, and there was never any question that we're willing to share, that doesn't mean we have to share every interaction we have with her individually.

"Arden is helping me make a syrup to ease the pain in my throat," Cyn explains, placing her spoon on the table next to her empty bowl. "This is the first step of the process. I would do it myself but..." She lifts up her hand, showing us her broken fingers. "I need a little help."

Lorcan nods, unable to completely hide the flare of anger that he feels every time he sees her injuries. I know how he feels. Carrick too, given the look on his face.

"Are you sure you trust him?" Carrick asks, trying to lighten the mood, but his joke quickly falls flat when Cyn shifts uncomfortably in her seat. He winces. "Too soon?"

Lorcan flashes me a look and I blow out a breath as Cyn looks between us. She takes a sip of water, then clears her throat.

"I wanted to thank you all," she begins. "For rescuing me. For not killing The Masks in the process. For looking after me these past couple of weeks. It means more than you know..." Her voice trails off and the room falls deathly silent as she blinks back the emotion in her eyes before continuing. "I don't blame you for Faith's death," she says softly, looking up at Lorcan as the colour drains from his face.

"Cyn, I'm sorry," he says, grasping her hand and kissing her knuckles. "I should've told you the minute you woke up."

"Maybe not the minute I woke up," she whispers, giving him a soft smile as she blinks back the tears brought forward by the mention of Faith's name.

"You're not leaving us then?" he asks.

"Not unless you want me to," she replies, chewing on her lip, unsure of our answer in that moment.

"Never. We're never letting you go," Carrick says fiercely,

reaching over and hauling Cyn into his lap.

She lets out a soft gasp, and for a moment I think she's going to stiffen at his touch, disappear into herself. Instead, she lets out a shuddering sigh and melts into his body, her fingers feathering over the bite on his collarbone.

"I know you won't hurt me."

Carrick brushes his lips over her hair, locking eyes with me as he does so. There's so much fucking love in his gaze that it chokes me up. We love few people, but when we do it's fierce and real and everlasting.

"You can feel safe with us," Lorcan says, twisting his body and resting his hand on Cyn's knee. "Whatever you need, we'll provide it."

"I want you to know that I want what you want," Cyn continues. "I want to forget the mistakes of our pasts and move onwards from this point. I want to build a relationship with you all. Individually. Together. I don't know exactly what will happen from this moment on. Nessa never went into detail, but I'm hopeful."

She laughs softly then looks at me, and I know she remembers the drawing I did way back when we were kids. The one she stole that night I saved her from falling from the roof of Silver Oaks institute, and kept all this time folded up in her recipe book.

"I know what's going to happen," I say, reaching for the picture, pulling it from the book. Unfolding it, I lay it flat out on the table. "You do too, Cyn."

Carrick whistles low, and Cyn's cheeks pink up as we all stare at my drawing. In the centre stands Cyn, completely naked surrounded by the three of us. I'm standing behind her, my lips pressed to her shoulder, my arm around her waist. Kneeling at her feet is Lorcan, his head buried between her spread legs, one of his hands grabbing her breast whilst the other grips her hip, and Carrick stands to my right, his cock fisted in his hands whilst he kisses Cyn fiercely.

"*This* is our future, tomorrow and the next day, and the day after. This is where we get to love you every day for the rest of our lives."

She nods her head, her eyes meeting mine, a sad, almost wistful look in them, before she draws in a shuddering breath and says, "*Cras es noster*... Tomorrow is ours."

"Tomorrow is ours," I repeat.

22

C^{yn}

My hands are covered in dirt as I part the soil and drop a bulb into the hole I've made before piling the earth back over it and patting it down, careful not to aggravate my broken fingers too much. They're still strapped up, but I'm pretty sure in another week or so I'll have full use of them again.

A little way along, Arden has the sleeves of his denim shirt rolled up and is planting a rose bush that was delivered this morning alongside enough tinned food, fresh fruit and vegetables, and staples to keep us going until next winter. Donovan, the captain of the fishing boat that sails between the island and the mainland, won't be back again until the beginning of summer, but even he was surprised by the volume of food and other supplies.

"Know something I don't?" he'd asked cheerily.

Arden had just grinned and tapped his nose.

That was a few hours ago, and Lorcan and Carrick are currently in the kitchen sorting through the delivery, restocking the pantry with herbs, spices and other ingredients needed to replenish what Arden and I've used over the past week working together making tinctures and tonics, lotions and salves. It's been a distraction that I've desperately needed and has brought us even closer together. It hasn't been easy, but I've slowly learnt to be present in the world once more. There have been times where I've slipped into moments of absence when a memory hits me full force, but the difference is, I don't stay there, and I owe that to the Deana-dhe.

During the day Arden has kept my mind busy helping me practise my herbology, he's a quick study and has an instinctual understanding that is hard to find.

At night, Carrick has soothed my soul with his beautiful voice so that I can drift into a peaceful sleep.

And all the hours in between Lorcan has taken care of my body with his gentle hands, kind words and endless patience.

Each of them gives me what I need, all of them loving me in their own way. In return I've fully accepted my place here, and whilst we've shared kisses and affection it hasn't gone any further than that. Lorcan might have fully awoken my body with an orgasm, but he's not attempted to touch me that way since. Neither have Carrick or Arden. They've all respected my need to take it slow, to seal our bond as friends before we become lovers.

Sitting back on my haunches, I swipe my hands over my skirt as I stop and admire Arden. He has his sleeves pulled up to his elbows, the muscles of his strong forearms tensing under his skin as he wrangles the rose bush into the ground. My heart does a funny little flip as he manages to get it straight and starts piling dirt over the roots, compacting it around the base, just like I taught him. We chose this particular rose bush because it's called *Faith*, and it will be surrounded by flowers and herbs that will be used in my remedies to heal ailments in honour of my friend's life.

A beautiful idea that Arden had suggested.

Chewing on my lip, I continue to study him enjoying the feeling of safety, friendship, and love blooming inside my chest.

He must sense me watching him, because he sits back on his haunches and smiles over at me, the cool sea breeze rushing over the bluff, bringing with it the scent of the ocean and ruffling his already wind-tousled hair. This time attraction stirs within me as I stare at the strip of dirt across his forehead and the broad smile across his face. He looks young, carefree, happy, and a warmth blooms out from my stomach, matching the spread of heat that rises up my chest and neck.

"What?" he asks me, a smile curving up his plump lips, the scruff of his week-old beard only adding to his attractiveness. "Have I got something on my face?"

"Just a little dirt," I reply, pointing to my own forehead to indicate where the smudge of dirt is.

"Here?" he asks, reaching up and swiping the back of his hand against his forehead, making it worse.

"Yeah, right there," I reply, laughter bubbling out of my mouth as he looks at me with such joy that I'm momentarily lost for words.

"That sound, Cyn," he says, his amber eyes lit with happiness. "It's so good to hear it."

"It feels good to laugh," I admit, enjoying how the warmth has evolved into a simmering heat, burning brighter with every moment that passes.

"I'm not sure I've ever made you smile like that before," he says, cocking his head to the side as

something shifts in the air between us.

"I like smiling like this, *feeling* like this," I reply, the electric current of attraction that's been building slowly over the past week we've worked alongside each other, sparking to life. "I like it, a lot."

"Me too."

Our eyes lock and I feel that flame within me burn even brighter. My gaze drops from his eyes to his lips, to the butterfly tattoo on his neck, the wings fluttering as he swallows. The top two buttons of his shirt are undone and I can see a smattering of dark chest hair where the dip of his throat meets the top of his chest. I can't help but remember how it felt to touch him there all those weeks ago when I stripped naked in the den and the three of them made me come.

"Cyn..." he begins, but a sudden gust of wind snatches the words from his lips as the distant sound of thunder rumbles out to sea.

"A storm's brewing," I say, brushing my hands together and knocking off the loose dirt gathered on my fingers, a nervous energy coursing through me suddenly.

"It is," he replies, his heated gaze directed at me, and I get the distinct impression that he isn't talking about the one brewing in the sky above us. "I feel it too."

A sudden shyness creeps up my spine at the intense way he looks at me, and I chew on my lip, dropping my gaze. By the time I look back up, Arden is staring at the horizon.

"It'll be a few minutes before the storm reaches us. We've got time to plant the last handful of bulbs before we need to get back inside," he says, before picking up a fork and turning over some more soil.

The way he shoves it angrily into the dirt has my heart rate spiking for another reason and I grow restless as he works, side-eying him as I plant the rest of my bulbs with shaking hands and this irrational feeling that I've done something wrong.

Another rumble of thunder sounds as a flash of lightning carves through the sky, sending a rash of goosebumps over my skin. The hairs on my arms stand on end from the strange energy building in the air, invisible yet so potent I can almost touch it.

Not able to stand it any longer, I climb to my feet and walk towards Arden, feeling jittery, nervous. When I reach him, I gently press my fingers against the broad slope of his shoulder as more thunder sounds, getting louder, closer. The wind picks up the strands of my hair and they turn into little whips around my face as I look down at Arden.

"Just a few more minutes and I'll be done," he barks out,

dropping the fork and making a hole with his hands before dropping a bulb into the newly dug earth, covering it over.

"Arden," I whisper, dropping to my knees beside him, my ankle length skirt billowing out around my legs as I reach for his arm, pressing my dirt-flecked fingers against his skin, forcing him to stop. A muscle in his jaw flexes as he grits his teeth and drops his head, fingers buried in the dirt as he lets out this strange wounded sound.

"What did I do wrong?" I say. "One minute we were both smiling, the next you look like you want to murder somebody. Are you mad at me?"

He shakes his head. "I'm not mad at you. Never you."

"Then what is it?" I ask, my fingers gliding over his skin, tracing the thick veins on his forearms, sighing at the touch. He visibly trembles, and I move to pull away but he reaches up, gripping my hand and pressing it back against him, dirt smudging our skin.

"I'm mad at myself."

"Why?"

"Because one smile from you and I'm as hard as stone, Cyn," he says looking up at me, his black hair drifting into his eyes, that show his struggle; pained, yet heated with lust.

"And that makes you mad at yourself?"

"I should be able to control myself around you, but fuck Cyn, when you smile like that, laugh like that, I just want to take you in my arms. I want to lose myself in you. I just want to fucking love you, Cyn."

His fingers curl into the soil, and the thumping beat of my

heart is engulfed in a surge of passion, billowing inside of me like an out of control fire.

"Then love me," I whisper. "I'm ready."

He stiffens beneath my touch, another bolt of lightning flashing across the ever darkening sky. Thunder as loud as an earthquake rumbles across the ocean, the scent of salt and seaweed, soil and rain, lifting into the air between us.

My skin prickles as Arden slowly turns his body towards me, his dirt-stained hands reaching for my face, grasping my cheeks, smearing soil across my skin as he meets my gaze.

"Are you certain?"

"Never more certain of anything in my life," I whisper.

Arden's gaze flashes with hunger before he slams his mouth against mine in a kiss as powerful as the crack of thunder overhead that brings a curtain of rain, drenching us both in seconds. His fingers tangle in my wet hair, his hot mouth sliding over mine, detonating the attraction between us in a passionate, toe-curling kiss.

Teeth clash, lips bruise, tongues slip and slide.

We grasp at each other, his chest pressed against my chest, my arms wrapped tightly around him as we claw at each other desperately, the sky above erupting in a brilliant, fiery display of lightning and thunder. We kiss, and kiss and kiss, the air shaking with the intensity of our embrace, melding together in a passionate display of lust and love. My fingers curl into Arden's shirt as I press my body against his, electricity sparking between us, around us, above us.

The wind blows harder, whipping my hair and skirt about my body until I feel almost airborne, rain needling our skin and heightening our senses. But neither of us move to escape the deluge, content to let the storm rage on as we ravage each other's mouths. My heart pounds in my chest as his tongue twines with mine.

"Cyn, fuck, Cyn," he gasps, his breath hot, his dick heavy between us as he reaches up for the collar of my shirt pulling the material apart. Buttons fly off in all directions, lost beneath the dirt that's quickly becoming mud.

"Arden, I don't have many clothes," I laugh, joy bubbling up my chest as I push back his hair, rivulets of water running down his face, staining his light denim shirt a dark blue.

"Do that again," he demands, cupping my breasts through my drenched bra, his thumbs rubbing over my nipples, dirt and rain running over my skin.

Instead of laughing, I tip my head back and moan. A growl rips up Arden's throat as he leans forward and pulls down the cup of my bra, taking me in his mouth. I clutch at his head, pulling him closer as his free hand slides down my chest and towards my thighs, gripping the material of my skirt. It's stuck under my knees, so I grab at it, shuffling to pull it out from under me.

Arden laughs roughly and I let out a giggle that has him groaning against my chest, warm huffs of air floating over my skin like little plumes of sunshine.

"We're so wet," I mutter between gasps and moans, as Arden pushes up my sodden skirt over my hips and sucks my nipple back into his mouth.

"Not wet enough," he mumbles against my skin, urging me backwards onto the grass.

Another laugh bursts free, as mud sticks to our clothes, our skin, in our hair, but none of that matters as he slides his hand up my thigh and reaches between my legs, stroking me over the drenched material of my knickers.

"I'm going to make you come so hard, our plants will grow with your pleasure running through their stems. They'll be so fucking beautiful, Cyn. They'll be a reminder of how we made love in the dirt with a storm raging around us. They'll be a reminder of how we chose to *live*," he says against my mouth, then lowers his head between my legs, shoves the material of my knickers to one side and parts my folds with his tongue.

"Arden!" I gasp, my eyes rolling back in ecstasy.

His fingers find my hips as he grabs me there, a rumble of pleasure rising up his throat as he licks and sucks, circling my clit with the tip of his tongue, lapping at my wet centre before sliding two fingers inside of me. I buck up against his face, barely feeling the pulse of pain from my fingers as I grip his head with both hands. Broken fingers or not, I'm not letting him go. I won't.

Water beats down on my bare skin, exposed to the elements, but I don't feel the cold, I only feel this surge of heat building within me, gaining intensity with every stroke of his tongue and every slide of his fingers.

I gasp and moan, unable to control the noises I make or the rhythm of my body as I move against his face. At one point I fear I'm suffocating him, so I push up onto my elbows to find him staring at me, a feral look in his eyes as he eats me out. I watch him, my clit pulsating with an oncoming orgasm as he grinds his dick into the sodden ground beneath him, needing relief himself.

Above us, lightning flashes just as he crooks his fingers inside of me and sucks my beaded clit into his mouth. I come. I come so hard I have no strength to hold myself upright, so I fall back onto the wet earth convulsing with pleasure.

My fingers fall to the earth as my chest heaves, rain falling in sheets as I blink up at the sky, the clouds as tumultuous as the emotions billowing inside of me now.

This is what it means to live.

This intensity. This letting go of pain. This connection.

This.

Arden climbs up my body, his powerful arms locking tight as he straddles me.

"If we don't go inside right now, I'm going to fuck you here in the dirt," he says, pushing upwards as he stares down at me, his chest heaving, kiss-bruised lips parting on a heaving breath.

"Do it," I demand as lightning flashes in the sky above him, lighting him in a brilliant white halo. "Fuck me here in the dirt. Do it."

Arden eyes alight with lust as he tips his head back and roars, ripping at his muddy shirt, more buttons flying off into the air as he bares his chest. Panting, he looks down at me with a fierce kind of love in his eyes as he reaches for his zipper. The material is so wet, it's clinging to his skin, and I watch with amusement painted on my face as he tries to wrangle the wet clothing past his hips, loving how a man so cool and controlled, is so uncontrolled in the moment.

"Can I help you?" I ask, a laugh caught in my throat.

"I've got it," he replies, brows pressed together in concentration, hands ripping at his trousers and boxers in his haste to free himself until I'm faced with his beautiful dick. It stands proud, its bulbous head an angry red as he grips it at the base. My clit flutters at the precum beading on the tip, a rush of heat flooding my sex at the virility I see before me. God, he's big.

"See what you do to me?" he asks, his voice low, strained. "No one has ever turned me on as much as you. Look at you."

"I'm covered in mud," I say, biting my lip.

"You'll be covered in more than mud soon when I come all over your pretty tits," he replies with a smirk as he lowers himself over me, somehow kicking off his shoes and pushing his trousers and boxers past his knees, getting rid of them too.

"Arden Dálaigh, you have a dirty mind," I mutter, biting my lip, a smile playing around my mouth as his dick presses against my opening.

"Do that again. *Smile*," he commands, the rumble in his voice a tender beat in my love-swollen heart.

I can't contain it. Happiness pours out of me, lighting me up from the inside out as I smile.

"Damn," he mutters, pressing his lips to mine in a brutal kiss as his fingers cup my head.

Beneath him, I widen my legs, giving him room to settle between them. I don't feel the cold, all I feel is fire running in my veins.

All I feel is *alive*.

"Look at you," Arden grinds out against my mouth, water cascading from above, running over his skin, dripping onto mine, raindrops melding, hearts pounding in unison. "So fucking beautiful."

"Please, Arden," I beg, needing him inside of me.

"Please what?" he jokes.

A growl rips from my throat this time as I reach between us and grasp his dick, angling him towards my body. It's warm and heavy in my palm, throbbing and pulsing as I stroke him up and down, up and down.

"Don't, I'll come too soon," he mutters against my lips, licking inside my mouth as he adjusts himself above me.

"Then come inside of me instead," I say, our eyes clashing as the words spill from my lips. I know what that could mean, and I know that I don't care. There's a question in his eyes, so I grab his arse.

"Fuck the happiness into me, Arden. Make love to me."

He doesn't hesitate.

With one brutal, earth-shattering thrust he's buried to the hilt inside of me. My back arches, I cry out, digging my fingers into his arse, spreading my legs as he kisses me deeply.

"I will love you like this over and over and over again," he promises, pulling out to the tip and then ramming back into me until we're both gasping and groaning, holding on to each other for dear life. He slams into me so hard, so deep, that I can feel the tip of his dick hitting my cervix.

There are no words as he stares down at me, fucking me with almost wild abandon, our bodies melding to each other as we make love. This might be raw, powerful, filled with lust, but there's no mistaking the feeling inside my chest or the look in his eyes.

We're making love.

My body welcomes him. I'm open, willing, wet and slippery as his velvety cock glides inside of me, the ridges and curves hitting all the right spots along my delicate flesh. With every stroke, he grows, his cock expanding with blood as he fills me up so deliciously.

"Arden!" I scream, wild, frantic now, as we lose all conscious thought and our bodies take over.

I needed to feel this...

This *alive*.

Arden thrusts faster and harder, pushing us both towards the edge as we climb higher and higher towards the pinnacle, towards the magical, wild, earth-shattering moment when our bodies fuse together as one.

"Cyn!" he roars, his head tipped back, the veins in his neck protruding as a bright white light forms behind my closed eyelids and my internal muscles spasm with my own orgasm.

I scream his name again, my nails digging into his back as he thrusts into me, his dick jerking, his come filling me up, and for one blinding moment time stills.

It pauses on a breath as we both hold ours.

And in that moment I allow myself to really, *truly* live.

I open my heart completely. I fall irrevocably, unconditionally in love.

"Cyn. My love, my love," Arden whispers, his chest heaving against mine as we collapse into the dirt, exhausted and utterly spent.

"I love you," I whisper, my lips pressing against his ear.

Arden lifts up onto his elbows, searching my face. "And I've *always* loved you," he replies.

We remain there for what feels like an eternity, our breath intermingling as we become one in the mud and rain, with each other. Eventually, Arden peppers gentle kisses over my face and slowly pulls out of me.

"You're my forever, Cyn," he says, hauling me upright with him.

He presses his lips against my soaked hair before picking me up bridal style and striding towards the house, naked but for his sodden denim shirt that sticks to his skin. Once inside my teeth begin to chatter as my body finally registers the cold.

"You need a warm shower," he says, striding with me in his arms along the hallway leaving mud and rainwater in our wake.

Out of the kitchen step Carrick and Lorcan, their eyes widening as they take in our appearance. Arden grips me closer to him. I can feel his still erect cock bobbing against my arse with every step he takes. But there's no embarrassment or shame as he meets their shocked gaze with a fiery one of his own.

"You're needed," he says.

"What the fuck–"

Carrick's mouth drops open in shock, his eyes flaring with lust.

Behind him Lorcan grins. "Nothing like a thunderstorm to get the blood pumping," he says.

"Bedroom, now!" Arden commands, striding past them both.

There's no hesitation, they follow.

23

L orcan

Carrick flashes me a heated look, his eyes blazing as we follow Arden into his bedroom, feeling the same lust coursing through my veins, seeing the same hunger reflected back at me.

My skin buzzes with desire, my cock twitches with excitement, my pulse races with need, and my heart pounds with love.

I'm turned on, impossibly so.

My dick hardens as my gaze roves over Cyn, taking in her kiss-bruised lips and the stubble rash across her skin from where Arden's kissed the sin back into her body. Her nipples are pebbled from a mixture of cold and desire, as water runs in rivulets down their bodies, and her hair, skin and clothes are covered in splotches of mud.

"Can you add some logs to the fire?" Arden requests, meeting my gaze as he gently lowers Cyn to her feet. She tucks a strand of matted hair behind her ear, smiling, her eyes bright. They're both filthy, in the best possible way. There's something so incredibly raw about the fact they fucked in the garden whilst a thunderstorm raged overhead. I've got to hand it to Arden, he certainly knows how to give a memorable fuck.

"Of course," I nod, reaching for a few logs from the basket beside the hearth and chucking them on the dying embers, adding a couple of firelighters so they catch alight, instantly throwing off an intense warmth as the flames grow higher and higher.

"Carrick, turn on the shower," Arden bosses, removing his shirt, standing naked before us. His cock is still hard, the tip leaking jewels of precum, the base surrounded by a thatch of dark hair that matches the smattering of hair on his chest. They may have fucked, but I know Arden, he's not done yet.

"On it," Carrick replies, striding across the room, the sound of water hitting glass half a minute later. When he reenters the room his shirt is off and the top button of his jeans is undone. He leans against the frame watching Arden as he cups Cyn's face, kissing her deeply.

"Take Cyn's clothes off," Carrick orders, taking charge as they break apart. "I need to see her, every last inch."

Arden flashes him a grin, then reaches for Cyn's shirt, slowly peeling it off her skin. The muscles in his back flexing as he moves. His naked body is familiar to me, the tattoo on his back a reminder of our childhood and the many summers we spent running wild through fields filled with wildflowers back home.

"Like this?" Arden teases, as his hands smooth over her shoulders, running down her bare arms. She shivers as he steps behind her and drags the wet material from her hands, discarding it on the floor, kissing every inch of her bare skin as we both watch.

Cyn flicks her gaze to Carrick, cheeks burning with splotches of pink as the temperature in the room rises along with our desire. With his lips pressed against Cyn's shoulder, Arden meets Carrick's gaze, heat burning in his eyes as his hands disappear behind Cyn's back and he unhooks her bra, sliding the straps down her arms. It falls to the floor in a wet slap as Arden gently cups her breasts, tweaking her nipples between his thumbs and fingers.

"Like what you see, brother?" Arden rasps, pulling on her nipples, drawing them into hard points. Cyn gasps, her spine arching, pressing her breasts into his hands as she turns her head to the side.

"Kiss me," she demands.

Their mouths clash seconds later in a wet, tongue-lapping, dirty-as-fuck kiss. I have to squeeze my dick to stop myself from coming, I'm that wound up. I'm fucking desperate to make love to Cyn the way I've been dreaming of for weeks now, years even.

"Damn," Carrick mutters, biting on his knuckles, his

stomach muscles tensing as he watches them tongue-fuck each other.

"Now her skirt," I demand, drawing Arden's attention back to me as their lips part and his heated gaze meets mine. "Show us our girl."

I've seen her body a lot over the past few weeks. I've soothed cream into her skin, easing the pain with a gentle touch. I've watched the bruises fade. I've watched the brutal marks made by a man who hated her, who hated women, slowly heal. Now I want to see her, *Cyn*, our beautiful woman who's been hiding away inside of herself. Meeting my gaze, seeing the fire, the desire, the hope, the *life* inside of them, I know that she's ready to break free from the pain and the trauma like a butterfly emerging from its chrysalis.

She's ready to live. Fully, completely, wholly.

Arden unzips her skirt, peeling the sopping material down her legs, taking her knickers with it. She steps out of the material, leaving her naked apart from her ankle boots, knee high socks, and mud-splattered skin.

"Allow me, Cinderella," Carrick jokes, stepping towards them both, dropping to his knees as he unties one boot and then the other, discarding them both before peeling off her socks.

Her chest rises and falls as she looks down at my best friend with a whole dose of love in her eyes. There's no mistaking it. It's as clear as the sky after a summer storm.

"You're everything," Carrick says as he presses a kiss against her mound and slowly rises upwards, dragging his mouth over her belly, across her breasts, and up her neck until he curls his fingers into her hair and kisses her deeply, only stopping when Arden twines his fingers in their hair, angling their heads together as he leans in, pressing his mouth against theirs in a three-way kiss.

If I wasn't brutally hard before, I sure as fuck am now.

When they finally pull apart, Cyn's cheeks are suffused with colour, bright spots of pink sitting high up on the apple of her cheeks.

"You're mine," Arden breathes, swiping his lips across Cyn's shoulder before nipping Carrick's neck, and grinning widely. "You too."

"And you're filthy," she replies with a grin.

"Oh you have no idea," Carrick interjects, drawing laughter from all our lips.

Shifting her gaze from Arden and Carrick, back to me, her smile grows and my heart jolts inside my chest. I'm so fucking gone for this woman, but still I wait, needing her to say the words, wanting to hear them, needing her to want me too.

Next to her, Arden palms his dick. "What's up, brother, need me to tell you that you're mine as well?"

"We're each other's, always were, always will be," I retort, wetting my lips.

He arches a brow. "But you're not joining in?"

"That depends on Cyn," I reply, swiping a hand through my hair. "Do you want me too?"

She gives me this look that shreds my heart, then fixes it back together again. "I *want* all of you. I *love* all of you," she says without hesitation, her arms widening. "Come to me, Lorcan."

Her words pull me into motion as I stride across the room

and lift Cyn at the waist, she wraps her legs around me as I kiss her and fucking kiss her, our tongues lapping and licking in a deeply passionate kiss.

"Enough, get in the shower," Arden commands.

"Is he always this bossy?" Cyn asks with a giggle, her lips sweeping over mine briefly.

"Arden likes to take command in the bedroom," Carrick explains as I carry Cyn into the bathroom. "He likes to think he has *all* the big dick energy. But they both know I've got the biggest dick."

Cyn snorts, her giggles turning into full blown laughter. "I think I like it," she says.

"I think you'll like my big dick more," Carrick replies, earning him a light smack to the back of the head from Arden.

"We'll let Cyn be the judge of that," Arden counters with a smirk.

"Get in the shower," I urge, lowering Cyn to the floor as steam billows in the air, the huge shower cubicle roomy enough for all of us. With a central rain showerhead, and two more jet sprays with adjustable settings on opposite walls, it's the Mercedes Benz of showers.

Cyn twists in my arms, lifting her big grey eyes up to mine before pressing a firm kiss against my lips. I grin down at her, my voice rough as I say, "Get clean for us, so Carrick and I can make you filthy with our come."

She gasps, her cheeks heating as she twists on her feet and steps into the shower, her peachy arse begging to be bit.

"You too, swamp man," I joke, pointing at Arden as Carrick

and I undress, stripping off our clothes and discarding them on the bathroom floor, eager to join them.

Arden is soaping up Cyn's hair with coconut-scented shampoo as Carrick and I step into the cubicle. She groans as his fingers massage her scalp, her back pressed against his front as he rocks his dick between her arse cheeks. She watches us enter with smoky grey eyes, sparks of fire brimming within them.

"Wash her, brother," Arden urges.

He doesn't have to tell me twice.

Lathering up some body wash from the bottle on the sunken ledge behind me, I massage it all over Cyn's body, taking care to pay special attention to each erogenous zone. My hands cup her breasts, tweaking her nipples and making her gasp, as Arden tips her head to the side and nibbles her neck, drawing moans from deep within her chest.

Sliding my hand over the silky smooth skin of her stomach, I reach between her legs, cupping her there. She gasps, then rocks against my hand.

"Look at me, Cyn," I demand. "Look at me when I fuck your pretty pussy with my fingers."

Arden chuckles, his eyes flicking from mine to Carrick who has stepped up close behind me. I can feel his warm breath on my neck as he presses his chest against my back, the tip of his hard shaft grazing my lower spine before he presses it fully between us.

"I'm so fucking turned on," Carrick mutters, his mouth brushing over my shoulder as I stroke my thumb over Cyn's inner thigh, parting her pussy lips with my thumb, before circling her clit.

"Oh!" Cyn exclaims, her pupils dilating as I dip a finger inside her wet heat.

"That's it, brother, fuck that tight pussy..." Carrick breathes, reaching between us and fisting my dick, his cock rubbing against my lower back. "I'm going to get you ready so that when Cyn comes, you can slide inside her and she can fist your cock as tightly as I am now."

Cyn gasps at Carrick's dirty talk, biting down on her lip as they lock eyes.

"When we fuck, we fuck with pleasure in mind," Carrick says, fisting my dick, his own cock sliding up and down my arse crack. "We'll fuck each other, we'll fuck you, but every single time you'll be our focus, the one woman who owns us. Pleasure is meant to be shared, and we'll share you and each other every day for the rest of our lives if you'll let us."

"Every day?" Cyn gasps on a breath, her pussy walls tightening around my fingers as I stir up an orgasm.

"Twice a day, *more*," Arden promises, grinning against her skin as he teases her earlobe with his teeth.

"That sounds... Ohhh!" she cries, her words cut off by the pleasure I'm stoking between her legs.

"What, Cyn?" I ask, almost choking out the words too as Carrick runs his thumb across the slit of my dick, then corkscrews his fist down my shaft.

"*Exhausting*," she breathes, her hips rocking against my hand as our breaths mingle on a laugh.

"Don't worry," Arden whispers against her neck whilst he

plays with her tits, "We'll make sure you'll get plenty of rest in between."

Cyn smiles, but that smile is soon replaced by another groan as her internal muscles tighten around me and her legs begin to shake from the impending orgasm.

"Fuck her now," Carrick demands, releasing my throbbing dick as Arden crouches slightly and lifts Cyn up at the same time I grab her arse and Carrick holds her behind the back of her knees.

Between us we hold her weight as I look down, sliding my cock along her glistening slit, my body trembling with need.

"What are you waiting for?" Carrick asks. "Fuck our girl!"

And with his command, I line my dick up against the entrance of her pussy and slide into her in one hard thrust. She cries out and her core tightens its grip around my dick, almost making me come there and then.

"Fuck, Cyn. Fuck!" I cry, adjusting my position, pumping into her.

"Take her," Arden demands, supporting the top half of her body, her upper back leaning against his chest as her hands wrap around the back of his neck, and I pound into her.

"That's it, brother," Carrick says, slapping my arse with his hand, before moving around to the side as he fists his dick and watches as I drive my cock inside of Cyn. "Fuck our girl. Let me see your massive cock send her over the edge."

She gasps and moans, her mouth dropping open as I fuck her.

"That's it, love. Take him deep," Arden says, looking up at

me as I grip her hips tighter and fuck her with every last breath in my chest.

Cyn's eyes roll, her chest heaving as my heart races. I can feel her internal muscles fisting my dick as my pulse thump, thump, thumps to the rhythm of our love.

"Please," she begs, her nipples sharp points as Carrick leans over and captures her lips with his, kissing her with a sensual swipe of his tongue, his hand fisting his dick.

I slow my speed matching the rhythm of their kiss, loving how my best friend gently pulls her lip between his teeth, nibbling, smiling, tongue-fucking her.

Warm water rains down over us all as Arden cups Cyn's breast in his hand, squeezing her tit, twisting her nipple as he casts his gaze to the detachable shower head. I know what he's thinking before he's even voiced it. My balls fucking tighten, my dick swelling with the thought.

"Grab the shower head, Carrick," Arden bosses.

Carrick draws back, a grin spreading across his face. "Hell, yes," he says, grabbing it and switching it on. Warm water rushes out in pulsing spray and he aims it at Cyn's nipple, the needling water hitting her. She gasps, her core tightens like a fist around my dick, and the massive ball of sensation in my lower spine builds.

"Fuck!" I growl as Carrick grins, then lowers the powerful spray to our joined bodies.

Cyn bucks up against me, a cry ripping from her lips as the needling spray hits her swollen clit this time. My knees almost buckle from the way her insides ripple with pleasure.

"Do it. Make her come," Carrick demands, removing the

spray and lowering it to his balls whilst he pumps his dick. "Fuck," he grunts.

I look up at Arden through heavy-lidded eyes, trying to keep myself together long enough to steal every single star from the night sky and put them in her eyes. He nods, his tongue licking sensually against the skin of her shoulder, her neck, her ear.

"I've got her," he says shifting backwards, bracing himself against the wall of the shower, taking us with him.

"Look at me, Cyn," I demand, drawing a deep breath through my flared nostrils, still slowly pumping inside of her.

She rolls her head across Arden's shoulder, lifting her eyes to meet mine. They swarm with emotion, billow with lust, her storm-grey eyes stuttering with pleasure.

"Lorcan," she whispers as her body trembles, sliding her fingers up my arms.

"Do not take your eyes of mine, understand? I want you to see what you do to me, and I want to see you come undone."

She nods and my fingers tighten on her hips, then locking eyes with hers I ram my cock deep inside of her. A rough laugh rips out of Arden's throat as I fuck Cyn against Arden's chest.

"That's it, come inside our girl," he says, and Cyn gasps, her eyes blazing.

Pumping, rutting, fucking her, I bury myself inside of Cyn as deeply as I can all the while keeping my gaze fixed on hers. Beside us Carrick gasps and moans, pleasuring himself at the sight.

"Ride her sweet pussy," Arden growls.

"You're mine. You're ours. You're forever," I grind out until a galaxy of sensation builds up in the base of my spine with every thrust, every moan, every gasp, every flicker of life in Cyn's eyes. Her core tightens in an eye-rolling, toe-curling grip. Her breath becomes harsh, fast, desperate, as she grips the back of my head, pulling my forehead against hers.

"I'm yours forever," she replies and just like that, a star explodes behind my eyes, that same imploding star appearing in Cyn's gaze seconds later as she comes screaming my name.

Heavy breaths mingle, fingers stroke and slide, lips slip and suck as I slowly pull out of Cyn and Arden lowers her to the floor on shaky legs. She bites on her lip, pressing her hand against my chest, right over my heart, as she pushes me back against the opposite side of the shower.

Then reaching up onto her tiptoes, she kisses me, the curve of her stomach brushing over my sensitive cock.

"I love you," she whispers.

"Fuck, I love you too," I reply, feeling that love tightening the connection between us. Knowing that I will never love another human being more than I love her, love us.

Behind her, Carrick's eyes blaze with need, with love too. I've seen that look before. He's not going to hold back. He's going to fuck her now.

"Arden," I warn, glancing at my brother who cocks a brow.

"Cyn can take it," he says, knowingly.

"Take what?" Cyn says, her breath snatched from her chest as Carrick swoops her up into his arms and strides from the shower cubicle out of the bathroom and into Arden's bedroom.

Arden laughs, the love in his eyes so fucking powerful that I drag him into my arms and kiss him hard on the mouth before striding after the pair.

"What was that for?" Arden asks me as I swipe a bath towel from the rail and wrap it around my waist.

"Because I love you. I love *us*," I reply, pulling up sharp as I watch Carrick lay Cyn down on Arden's bed, lower his mouth to her glistening pussy and eat her out like a starving man.

"She's going to sleep for a week after this," Arden jokes, naked, dripping water as he grips his dick next to me.

"We're all going to sleep for a week after this," I reply, licking my lips as I watch Carrick drag Cyn's hips to the corner of the bed and lift her legs over his shoulder. No doubt tasting me as much as her on his tongue.

"Hmm," he rumbles out, and I know that I'm right. "My beautiful witch. You taste like home."

We watch with heaving chests and rock hard dicks as he eats her out with the kind of lustful aggression that has her body shaking, and her coming explosively seconds later. But he doesn't give her a minute to come down from the mind-altering high, he simply grabs her legs, flips her over onto her stomach, drags her to the edge of the bed so that her toes hit the floor and fucks her from behind.

There's no hesitation. No holding back.

Carrick drives into her, their bodies slapping together in a beautiful symphony. Cyn's cries are guttural now, from some ancient place deep within. Animalistic, feral.

It's a fucking beautiful sound.

She cries out, her fingers gripping the duvet, her chest pressed against the mattress as he fucks her, his arse muscles flexing, his thighs and calves strong.

"Fuck me," Arden exclaims, his fist tightening around his dick as he wanks off to the display of pure, unbridled need.

My own cock twitches and lengthens, ready to go again. "Fuck indeed," I reply, reaching over and grasping Arden's dick. He looks up at me, a smile on his face and love in his eyes.

I love him. He loves me. We love Carrick and Cyn.

This is how we love. There are no boundaries between us, no rules. Just feeling, emotion, need.

He groans as I fist him. I moan as he takes my dick in his hand and rubs me with expert hands.

We get each other off as Carrick fucks the woman we love. We become unbearably hard as Carrick grabs her hair in his fists, slides his arm around her stomach and pulls her up against his chest, holding her close as he fucks her standing upright. I let out a deep groan, and Carrick, sensing what we're doing behind them, twists on his feet, taking Cyn with him.

"Look at them," he says, cupping her jaw in his hands, still fucking her from behind. "Look at how they fist each other, Cyn, all the while thinking of you, of fucking you, of *loving you*."

Cyn sobs, her cry of pleasure breaking free from her lips as she watches us watching her.

We're hard for her. Hard for our Cyn, our sin, our soulmate.

"All these years before you, when we've fucked other women, fucked each other, we thought of you. We could never admit it to ourselves, to each other, but you were *always* there, tucked deep inside our hearts. Ours souls bound to yours," Carrick continues, fucking her as tears fall from her eyes. "You were there every second of every day. In every breath, in every kiss, in every stroke of our fists, every lick of our tongues. You were never a curse, Cyn. You were always the cure to our brokenness. I will love you forever, my beautiful witch."

"And I you," Cyn cries out, and with those words she comes, tears pouring from her eyes as her legs shake and her body trembles.

Not long after cum spills from our heavy, twitching cocks, Carrick fills her up with his love, coming too.

24

C^{yn}

"Thank you, Christy. I appreciate your call. Speak soon, okay?" I say, placing the phone back on the cradle and sighing heavily.

Carrick looks over at me from his seat beside the fire in the corner of the office, watching me intently. His mouth is pursed in a hard line, the orange flecks in his black eyes reflecting the flames flickering in the hearth.

"Your father?" he asks, brows furrowed.

I nod, my throat tight. "He's dying."

The words falling from my lips seem so unreal. How is my father dying? How does something like that happen and only now I find out about it? I feel strangely disengaged from emotion. The man who barely paid me any attention growing up, the man my mother loved, is dying.

I don't know how to feel about that.

"Cyn, shit. I'm sorry," he says, getting to his feet and pulling me into a hug, his hand cupping the back of my head, stroking my hair.

"But you hate him. Why are you sorry?" I say, unable to look him in the eye.

"It doesn't matter what I think about him. You care for him, and he's dying."

A sudden rush of pain fills my heart and I'm not sure that I understand it. "He's my father, but he's never been a dad. I don't know how to feel right now."

Carrick holds me tighter, and I sink into his touch, drawing strength from his arms as I try and make sense of the hurricane of emotions swirling inside my chest.

"Did Christy have a vision?" Carrick asks. "Is that why she called?"

"No. My uncle Jack contacted The Masks. He thought I was still there." I laugh a little bitterly at that. "He wanted to speak with me. Jakub made up an excuse so he wouldn't know I'm here with you..."

I pull out of Carrick's arms looking up at him, knowing in my heart what I have to do. He reads my expression and shakes his head. "Absolutely not."

"I have to, Carrick. I have to say goodbye."

"Say goodbye? To whom?" Arden asks as he steps into the office, looking between us both. He's wearing a pinafore, his sleeves rolled up to his elbows, the scent of chamomile and honey following him into the room. We were making a lotion together in the kitchen when I left him to take the call from Christy.

"My father's dying. I have to go home."

"*This* is your home," is his immediate response, a mixture of worry, concern and a dose of fear cutting across his face.

"Of course it is. I'm not leaving you, but there are things I need to say before–" I begin, but he shakes his head, cutting me off.

"Then you call him."

"Arden, I can't do that."

"And I can't risk losing you to them."

"They're my family," I argue.

"And you think that makes a difference? I will not lose you again."

"I agree with Arden," Carrick adds. "It's too risky."

"This isn't your decision. It's mine. I *have* to go."

"For a man who doesn't love you?" Carrick says, his words hurting me even though he's right.

"I know he doesn't love me, but my mother loved him. She loved him and she never got to say goodbye, Carrick," I say, my eyes brewing with tears my father doesn't deserve as I fold my arms around my chest, hugging myself. "I can do that for her. I can do that for her memory."

Arden crosses the room, cupping my face in his hands. "We can't lose you. It would destroy us, Cyn."

"Arden, we've got a problem," Lorcan says, striding into the room.

"We know, Niall O'Farrell," Carrick says, cutting him a look.

Lorcan frowns with confusion, looking from his phone back up to us. "No. Connall and Tom are almost here. Beast couldn't hold them off any longer. He's with them now."

"How long do we have?" Arden asks, dropping his hands from my face and drawing me into his side.

"About twenty minutes, they're crossing from the mainland now."

"Fuck! Nice of Beast to give us a head's up!" Carrick exclaims testily. "I'll grab the guns."

"Guns?!" I shake my head. "No. No guns."

"Cyn, it's just for protection," Arden says as I step out of his arms, scowling at him.

"They're not here to hurt me," I say. "And I will not stand any more bloodshed. Do you understand?"

"Of course they're not here to hurt you, but I'm pretty sure Tom won't have any problems loading a bullet into our heads," he retorts with a wry smile.

"They're with Beast, he won't let that happen. I won't let that happen," I argue. "No. Guns."

"Fine. No guns. But you bet your arse we're serving them some of your calming tea. Tom has a temper on him and it might chill him out enough not to do something stupid," Lorcan says, trying to lighten the mood.

"I'll get it prepared," I say tersely, chewing on my lip as worry churns my stomach. It's been so peaceful these last couple of days since we made love. Why now? Why couldn't we have a little more time with each other before danger found us again?

As I move to walk away, Arden reaches for me, his fingers

curling around my wrist as he says, "Family or not, I will load a bullet in Tom's skull if he tries to take you from us."

"Then I'll just have to convince him not to," I reply, before slipping past Lorcan and into the hallway beyond.

◆

"I t's been a while," Tom says as he steps into the parlour with Connall, surveying Arden, Lorcan and Carrick with caution before resting his gaze on me. His dark blue eyes, that are so like my mother's, soften in recognition before he clears his throat. "You're the image of Aoife."

"Thank you–"

My reply is cut short as Beast strides into the room looking more than a little green.

"Fuck that crossing. I think I lost half my guts on the way over. At one point I thought it was gonna come out the other end too," he says, flopping onto the sofa opposite. "Remind me to never step on a boat again."

"That'll be problematic given that's the only way back to the mainland," Lorcan says, pouring everyone a cup of my tea with a grin as though the tension isn't palpable.

"Ah fuck," Beast groans.

"Have a seat," Arden offers, placing his hand on my thigh and giving it a slight squeeze. Tom notices but doesn't show any reaction as he sits beside Beast, and Connall settles down onto the sofa on the other side of him.

I push the teacups towards my uncles then Beast. "It'll warm you up *and* settle your stomach," I add, smiling at Beast.

"Thanks, sweetheart," he says, taking a tentative sip, eying me over the rim of the cup. I see the exact moment when the taste hits him. "Damn, that's good. Has it got honey in it?" Beast asks, smacking his lips together.

I nod. "It does, amongst other things."

"This ain't gonna make me shit, is it?" he asks, drawing the cup away from his lips. "I've seen what you can do. Impressive, by the way."

I can't help it, I laugh. His lightheartedness is a breath of fresh air. "I'm not in the business of poisoning friends."

"Thank fuck for that. You're looking well. It's good to see you smiling after the hell you went through," he adds, looking pointedly at Tom. "Got to count for something, right Tom?"

Tom doesn't respond, he keeps his assessing gaze fixed on the four of us instead. My gaze flits back and forth between Beast and Tom. Beast is trying to lighten the mood, but Tom's not having it. I'm beginning to feel uncomfortable under his scrutiny when Connall reaches for his tea cup, lifting it to his lips, his eyes widening a little as he takes a sip.

"This tastes like..."

"The tea my mother used to make?" I suggest.

He nods. "Tom, you've got to taste it. It's exactly how I remember it. Aoife always used to brew us this tea. Especially after we got into fights."

Tom meets my gaze, picking up his own cup and taking a sip too. "So it does," he says, a hint of sadness in his eyes as he looks at me. "You make healing remedies like Aoife did?"

"Yes. She taught me about the benefits of herbs and plants from an early age, and then my grandmother continued after she died because she knew how important it was to my mother that I learn her craft."

"And your father allowed that?"

"He didn't know."

"I see," his voice trails off as he places his cup back on the saucer. "You'll have to forgive me. I'm not normally this–" He swipes a hand through his salt and pepper hair, trying to find the words.

"This much of an awkward bastard?" Beast finishes with a snort.

Tom raises his brow. "I was going to say this impolite. It really is a pleasure to meet you, Cynthia."

There's a warmth in his eyes as he regards me. A kindness beneath the controlled authority that can't be faked. I look down at my hands in my lap, feeling a mix of emotions coursing through me: from relief that Tom is loosening up, to uncertainty of what he might do next.

"Cynthia, I'm a reasonable man, but I am very protective of the people I care about. The only reason I didn't come here earlier demanding to see you is because Beast, for all his faults– of which there are many–persuaded me not to."

Beast rolls his eyes. "Thanks, mate. *I think.*"

"I appreciate you giving us space, and for not shooting the men I love before we've even had a chance to talk," I reply, garnering a smirk from Beast.

"Don't count on anything yet, there's still time," he says with a reassuring wink so that I know he's joking.

Carrick snorts. "Not happening."

"By all rights, I *should've* shot you dead the second I found out you'd known Cynthia as a child and failed to tell me," Tom says, levelling his gaze at Carrick.

"That was our history. It had nothing to do with you," he replies evenly.

"But I'm willing to let that go," Tom continues, giving him a warning glare, "Given what you did to save her from those bastard Skulls."

"What Carrick meant to say," Lorcan cuts in, "Is that we apologise."

Tom nods. "I do, however, want you to explain to me why you thought it was okay to call in a debt on my niece, keep her here under your roof for six months, and then not tell me she was in trouble."

"We're the Deana-dhe, we don't have to explain a thing to you," Arden replies coolly.

"Cut the shit!" Tom snaps, narrowing his eyes at Arden. "Haven't I been a good friend to you all? Haven't I welcomed you into my home countless times? I know exactly who you are, and out of respect I've stayed away this long. I did that for you, now I'd appreciate a fucking explanation. Cynthia is *my* blood, and she has a family who love her and who are waiting to meet her properly. I have every right to be angry, so don't give me that *'we're the Deana-dhe'* bullshit. It won't cut it this time."

"We did what we did *because* we love her," Arden responds unapologetically.

"And you think that alone gives you the right to keep her from us? Feck, boy. That isn't love, that's ownership. There's a big difference."

Arden's teeth grind together and Carrick stiffens beside me, but it's Lorcan who speaks with a calm resolve, and I couldn't love him any more for it.

"Cyn needed time to heal, and she needed us to help her to do that. Think of it from her point of view, Tom. She'd never met you before, and she'd been through something traumatic. She needed familiar faces. We were never going to keep you from her forever. We were just waiting for the moment when she was ready to take that step."

Tom considers Lorcan's words, taking a sip of his tea before focusing his attention back on me. "And have they taken care of you, Cynthia?"

"Yes."

"But not always?" he asks knowingly, a gleam of anger in his eyes.

Beast shrugs. "You *were* little shits to her."

"We all make mistakes," I say, cutting a look to Connall who shifts uncomfortably in his seat. "What I can tell you is that I am here with Arden, Lorcan and Carrick not just because they own me, but because I own them too. The past is in the past. We can't change what happened, but we can make sure we don't make the same mistakes again. I'm happy. I love them. There's no question that I want to be here with them. Will you respect that?"

"Aoife loved your father, and look where that got her," Tom counters. "Love isn't always enough."

"Love is more than enough," I argue.

"Yet your father's actions, out of so called *love,* killed her."

Connall clears his throat, opening his mouth to speak, but I shake my head. What's the point of him admitting what he did?

Killing my mother has hurt us all so much already, what good would it do telling Tom the truth now?

"You know sometimes when I close my eyes and try to picture my mother, all I get is this grainy image, like a photograph that's faded in the sun. It hurts me that one day I might not remember what she looked like at all. That I won't see her smile as clearly as when my father made her laugh at something seemingly insignificant. That I won't remember how her eyes lit up when he entered the room and pressed a kiss against her forehead, not letting go for the longest time." I meet Tom's gaze. "He loved her, and she loved him, and whether you want to believe it or not, she was happy."

"You were a child, Cynthia. She died when you were four. How could you possibly know that what you saw was love?" Tom argues.

"Because when my father found her dead, he lost himself to a grief that he never recovered from. He loved her deeply, fiercely, and all the light she grew inside of him was snuffed out the minute her heart stopped beating."

"Your father is not a good man, Cyn," Tom adds, as if I don't already know that.

"You're right, he isn't," I reply, heaving out a deep breath. "But he was a good man to her."

"He stole her from us," Connall says this time. "If he hadn't, she would still be alive today."

"If he hadn't, *I* wouldn't be alive today. Everything happens for a reason, the good and the bad. We may not like it, but it's the truth. I guess *you* just have to uncover the reason why things happened the way they did, to better understand the part you played in it," I say, hoping he understands my point without having to spell it out.

"So you believe in fate?" Tom asks.

"I believe that there are forces bigger than all of us. I believe that we're either here to learn a lesson or to teach one, even if we don't like it."

Connall turns his face away, but not before I see the weight of his guilt. I understand the burden of it and can sympathise. In my mother's death there is a lesson for him, he's just got to figure out what that is, just like I had to do.

"That's an interesting view of the world," Tom replies, thoughtful.

"I don't know if Beast or Connall told you everything that happened recently," I say, curling my fingers around Arden's hand, "But I lost a friend. Her name was Faith and she died in the most horrific way at the hands of Soren and his cruelty. I promised to keep her safe, I promised she'd have a life beyond that horrible place she survived for three years. But she died, and because of that I lost myself."

"So you're saying your friend died to learn a lesson? It seems impossibly cruel."

"It *is* impossibly cruel, and I hate that it happened to her. Do I wish every day that it hadn't? Of course. I believed so much that she would live. *I* learnt a hard lesson when she died. I learnt that I can't save everyone no matter how much I want to. I couldn't save my mother from dying any more than I could save Faith from bleeding out on that floor."

"So the lesson you learned was that bad things happen to good people?" he asks me.

"Yes. I learnt that at a very young age, and was reminded of it." I reply. "But more importantly, I learnt that in order to honour the people I've loved and lost, I have to *live*."

"And you want to do that with these men?"

I smile at each of them in turn, my heart swelling with love. "Yes. I do. Arden, Lorcan and Carrick found a way to reach me when I was lost to grief and guilt. Without them, I wouldn't have survived Faith's death. Their love saved me, and for a little while my mother's love saved my father."

"His love was a curse," Tom argues.

"No. *Their* love was the cure. It just never got the chance to fully bloom into its full potential."

"He had her for five years. How long does it take?"

"There's no time limit on healing, or how fast someone should fall in love. My father was a complicated man. I never understood him. But my mother saw something in him that no one else did. She loved him, and her love was enough. It *was*."

Tom thinks for a moment, mulling over everything I've said. "So you're asking me to forgive and forget what the O'Farrell's have done to the O'Brien's over the years? Is that it?"

"No, I'm not asking you to forgive my father."

"Then what are you asking?"

"I'm asking you to understand that *nothing* is straightforward, not the road we walk, not the hand fate plays us, and especially not what we do for love. You're entitled to be angry, but you're not entitled to make a decision for me. That is my right alone."

Tom releases a long breath. "If you want to stay with the

Deana-dhe, I won't stand in your way. This is your life, Cynthia. I respect your decision."

"Thank you."

"But what about your father? He might not be so accepting."

"He's dying."

"Fuck," Beast exclaims, blowing out a breath. "Sorry, Cyn."

"I think he's been dying a little bit everyday since my mother was killed."

"What are you going to do?" Tom asks me.

"I'm going to ask some old friends to accompany me home this one last time."

25

C^{yn}

"I promise to be careful," I say into my phone two days later, Arden's worried voice throbbing in my ear. "But you don't need to worry, I'm with The Masks, they'll take care of me. You know they will."

"Cyn, if you don't call me within the hour then we're coming for you. This helicopter will get us to you in twenty minutes," Arden replies, putting the phone on loudspeaker so Carrick and Lorcan can hear.

"It's going to be okay. You shouldn't have wasted a debt on a fancy helicopter. It's very *Mission Impossible* of you," I joke, trying to ease the tension.

"This isn't a joke, Cyn," Carrick adds, grit in his voice. I can just imagine the scowl on his face too, and something about that makes me feel so *loved*. He cares enough to worry about my well-being. I've never felt more loved than I have with these three men.

"I know it isn't. But we know it's going to work out, right? We have the drawing," I remind them. "There's a point in our future where we're safe, happy. I have to trust in that."

"If you feel threatened at any point, you leave with Jakub. Let Leon and Konrad deal with your family like we discussed, okay?" Lorcan adds, reminding me of our plan.

"Okay. I promise," I reply. "Now I've really got to go. I love you."

"Love you too," the three reply in unison before I click off the phone.

Already out of the car Jakub, Leon and Konrad wait for me to join them. Sliding the phone into my coat pocket, I step onto the gravel drive in front of my family home. It's a huge sprawling mansion perched on the hill overlooking the rolling fields of Kells, a village thirty minutes drive from Kilkenny City.

The house is a glorious relic, built to look like a castle with grey stone walls and turrets at each corner. It has a long driveway with well-tended gardens that sit beyond rows of perfectly manicured trees. It's been almost two years since I've been back, and I'd forgotten just how grand my childhood home is. With its imposing facade and weathered brickwork covered in moss and ivy that creeps along the face of the building and worms its way around the windows, Kells Manor is as magnificent as ever.

"Are you okay?" Leon asks me, drawing my attention away from the gargoyles glaring out from the corner of each turret.

"No, I'm not."

Leon nods. "You say what you need to say, then we leave, okay?"

"That's the plan," I reply, forcing steel into my spine.

"If we don't report back to Arden within the hour, there'll be more bloodshed," Konrad adds, watching me carefully. "He made it very clear to me that he will have no issue razing this place to the ground."

"I'm fully aware of what's at stake here. I just want to say goodbye. To draw a line through this part of my life for good. Once I'm done, I will walk away and never look back."

"Are you certain?" Jakub asks me.

"There's nothing here for me anymore. I don't want any part of this life."

"Then we should get this done," Jakub comments.

I hesitate. It would have been so easy to stay away and never come back, to turn my back on the man who turned his back on me his whole life, but my mother loved my father and if I can do one thing for her it's to say goodbye to him for her.

Jakub rests his hand on my lower back. "Shall we?"

"Thank you for coming with me. Thank you for everything you've done," I say, my voice thick with emotion.

Jakub dips his head, whilst Leon and Konrad reward me with a tight smile. If you were an outsider looking in with only their reputation as reference, you would see three incredibly dark, troubled men standing beside me. But I know differently. I know they've become more than the product of their abusive pasts. That they've learned how to be human, how to have empathy, how to be compassionate, to live in kindness, and to love. It's partly because of them that I'm here today, but it's a hell of a lot more to do with Christy that they've become the good, kind, empathetic men they are now.

"It's us who should be thanking you, Cynthia. This is the least we could do," Jakub says. He reaches for my hand, briefly squeezing my fingers. "Ready?"

Taking a deep breath, I follow Jakub as he walks up the steps towards the huge oak door, my heart pounding as I ponder what awaits me inside. As soon as I step over the threshold, a wave of warmth washes over me and I find myself standing in the grand entrance hall with its marble floors, crystal chandeliers and art deco furniture. In spite of the grandeur, there's an overwhelming feeling of sorrow that hangs heavy in this place like an invisible fog.

"I wasn't aware that you'd be accompanying Cynthia," a familiar voice says, as my uncle Jack appears from the study to the left of the entrance hall.

He's similar in height to my father, but that's where the physical similarity ends. Where my father has jet black hair and deep blue eyes, Jack has a mousy brown mop of curls and brown eyes that hold no depth. He has the same O'Farrell coldness though. He has that in spades.

"We called ahead and left a message," Jakub says, moving to stand by my side, whilst Leon and Konrad flank the other. I'm struck by the sense of protection they provide, grateful for their presence. "I'm assuming you didn't receive it?" he adds.

"I did not," Jack replies, casting a cautious gaze between us before resting his eyes on me. "Cynthia, it's good to see you."

"Hello, Uncle Jack," I reply, not returning the compliment.

Whilst Jack has been more present in my life than my father, he's still an O'Farrell. There's a bitterness that runs through their veins, a cold-heartedness, and honestly, I can't understand why the men of the family are so distant and emotionless given their mother was so warm and kind.

"Where is he?" I ask, wanting to get this over with.

Jack looks between me and The Masks. "You can wait in the parlour," he clips.

"We will accompany, Cynthia," Jakub counters with firm authority.

Jack shakes his head. "He's dying. He doesn't need a room full of people he barely knows."

"Then Jakub will accompany Cynthia for moral support and Leon and I will wait in the parlour until she's ready to leave," Konrad says, eyeing Jakub who nods in agreement.

"As you wish. Cynthia, Jakub. Follow me," Jack replies without wasting another second before twisting on his heel and striding towards the stairs that lead up to my father's wing of the house.

Instead of immediately following, I remain glued to the spot, seized by a sudden rash of fear until Jakub reaches out to me and gently grips my elbow.

"I'm here," he says quietly, reminding me that no matter what happens here today, I'm not alone.

Taking strength from his presence, I make my way slowly

up the stairs behind my uncle Jack, towards my father's bedroom suite at the far end of the corridor of the west wing.

When we enter his bedroom, my father is lying in the centre of his huge, four poster bed looking gaunt and pale beneath the eiderdown. To say I'm shocked is an understatement, he's barely someone I recognise. Cancer has taken hold of him and reduced him to a shell of what he once was. There's no peace in his sleep, his body displaying for all to see how he's suffered. His lips are dry and cracked, parted on rattling breaths, his eyes are sunken in their sockets, his cheeks hollowed out, and his once muscular arms reduced to bones draped in sagging skin. I resist the urge to cry, not because I don't feel empathy for his situation but because I need to remain strong to do what I must.

"How long does he have left?" I ask, my gaze shifting, taking in every detail of this room which hasn't changed since my mother died many years ago.

Her portrait still hangs above the antique dresser, her favourite armchair still positioned near the window beside my father's reading chair. Even her favourite vase is filled with fresh flowers on top of the bedside table. It seems strange that I feel so much of her in this room, when there's so little of my father left.

"Days, if that. He's been holding on for you," Jack says, motioning me to get closer to the bed.

"For me? If that's the case why not contact me before now?"

"Niall is a stubborn man, proud, and pigheaded. They're traits us O'Farrell men carry like a ball and chain. I made the call because I knew he was close to leaving us, and I wanted to give you the opportunity to say your goodbyes."

"Thank you," I reply, feeling a swell of something painful inside my chest.

"I shall wait outside. If you need me, just call," Jack replies, before leaving the room, gently shutting the door behind him.

"Are you sure you want to do this?" Jakub asks me, pity in his gaze.

I nod, forcing myself to step closer to the bed, dreading what might happen next.

"Father?" I say tentatively, my steps faltering when, for one brief moment, I'm not sure if he's still with us or not. Then I hear him drag in another laboured breath and know that he is.

"Father?"

Reaching out, I touch his arm gently, feeling the brittle bones beneath his paper thin skin. He stirs in response to my touch, and I lower myself on the edge of his bed, allowing him to wake up before saying anything further. When his eyes flutter open and focus on me, it takes him a moment to register who I am. Then recognition sparks in his tired gaze and he smiles weakly.

"You came," he croaks before reaching out a shaky hand towards me.

His palm is cold and clammy, but his grip is surprisingly strong when he takes hold of my hand. "I've missed you."

I wish I could say that I missed him too, but the lie is caught in my throat and I can't seem to form the words. My father has been absent for the better part of my life. Yes, we might've lived in the same house together, but he was never present unless there was something he wanted from me. I recall a couple dozen conversations with him over the course of my entire life and they were always perfunctory at best, and stilted at worst.

"Are you in pain?" I ask him, knowing that in my bag I have a tonic that will help ease his suffering should he need it.

"Not now that you're here, my sweet girl."

Sweet girl?

In all my life, my father has never referred to me as his sweet girl.

"You always did take the pain away," he continues, lips wobbling as he tries to smile.

I stare at him, confusion and disbelief warring within me. Is this the same father that had ignored me my entire life? Where did this sudden tenderness come from?

Is this what death does? Does it strip a man of the darkness of his soul as well as all the life from his body? They say that your life flashes before your eyes right before death comes to take you. Does my father regret how he treated me? Is this his way of apologising for not loving me? I'm not sure that a few minutes of tenderness can make up for all the time he barely registered my existence.

"Your smile lit up a room," he continues, a tremulous smile pulling up his lips as he looks at me.

I stare at my father, unable to fully comprehend the change in him. He has never been this affectionate with me before, not once in my life.

"Why now?" I ask him, my voice trembling despite my best efforts to stay strong.

"I've missed you so," he replies, lips wobbling as tears glisten in his eyes. "I've missed you so much, my sweet girl."

"Cynthia," Jakub says, resting his hand on my shoulder.

Something in his voice makes me look up at him, and when I see the sorrow in his eyes, the truth suddenly hits me.

My father doesn't see me.

He sees my mother.

He thinks I'm her.

Jack was wrong. He hasn't been waiting for me. He's been waiting for her.

"Oh Aoife, my sweet girl, my love. I've missed you so," my father says, a single tear sliding down his cheek as he looks at me and sees the only woman he ever loved.

I drop my head, tears filling my eyes knowing that even in his last moments I was never on his mind. For years I've wished that he would be different towards me. Had a small part of me hoped that in his last moments we could make peace? Of course I had.

But I'm not cruel enough to correct him. I am my mother's daughter after all. All I can do is offer him some small measure of comfort during this last moment that we have together.

"I've missed you too," I say, my voice cracking.

It's not a lie. I've missed the father he was supposed to be. I've missed the laughter we should've shared. I've missed the companionship of a man who was supposed to teach me things, and provide me with knowledge. I've missed the arms of a father who cared whether I laughed or cried. I've missed a dad.

"Is it time to go home now?" he asks, the light slipping from his eyes with every word that passes through his lips.

"If you're ready, then yes, it's time to come home to me," I say softly.

Jakub's fingers tighten on my shoulders and I almost break at the tenderness and love I feel emanating from him. But I don't break.

I remind myself why I'm here.

To say goodbye to my father, to my past, to the family I never felt I belonged to.

After this moment I'm ready to move forward and make a family of my own with Arden, Lorcan and Carrick.

I'm ready to meet my mother's family and form a bond with them.

I'm ready to find happiness, to surround myself with laughter and friends, love and happiness. I'm ready to *live*.

"I'm ready," my father whispers, echoing my thoughts as his strength fades with every rasping breath.

"Take my hand. Come home to me, Niall," I say, being my mother for him, giving him peace in his last moments as I move closer to him on the bed.

He takes hold of my hand and pulls it onto his chest where I can feel the unsteady thump of his heart beneath my palm, each beat getting further and further apart.

"You were always my beating heart," he mutters, and then with one last shuddering breath his hand slips from mine, and he's gone.

26

Carrick

Two weeks later

"The dining room's that way," Cyn says with a smile as I grab the tray of drinks from her hand and settle it on the side table in the hallway, before snatching her against my chest in a rough kiss.

"I know that," I reply, smiling against her lips and reaching down to grab her arse, the silky material of her knee length dress sliding over her skin. "I've been hard all night, Cyn. Watching you give your attention to all those men."

"All those men?" she replies, amusement in her voice. "Grim and Christy are here too. And those men you're referring to are my family and *our* friends."

"I don't like sharing you," I mutter against her mouth, before sliding my tongue between her lips and kissing her laughter away.

"We both know that isn't true," she replies, her hands reaching up and cupping my cheeks as she pulls back, smiling at me.

"Lorcan and Arden don't count. We're basically the same soul divided into three bodies."

"Is that so?"

"Uh huh," I say, my fingers pulling up her skirt as I search for the warmth of her pussy.

"Carrick, stop it!" she warns, but there's no heat behind it, unless you count the warmth leaking from between her legs.

"You're wet for me," I say, dragging her back into a darkened alcove along the hallway, just deep enough to hide what we're doing should Tom, Connall, Beast or any number of our guests walk out.

"And you're hard for me," she replies, her hand stroking over my erection. "But we really *should* be getting back."

"Can a man not seek out his woman for some alone time?"

"See that's the thing, Carrick O'Shea, we're not alone. We have a home full of guests."

"I'm over it already," I say, as I glide my finger over her clit and press warm kisses to her neck. "I think we should call Donovan and get him to come and pick them all up now. I don't think I can wait another minute to sink my cock inside of you."

"It's almost midnight. We can't send them home now," she protests, her words catching in her throat as I tease her nub with expert fingers.

"Well, if you insist on allowing them to stay whilst I go insane with wanting you, the least you can do is give me ten minutes of your time," I reply, slipping my middle finger inside of her as she drops her head against my shoulder and moans.

"Just ten minutes?" she jokes, meeting my gaze as she bites down on her lip again, trying to hold in the gasp as I slide another finger inside of her.

"Pretty sure I'll get you to explode in under five," I reply, my words strained.

"Make it three and you have a deal," she says with a wicked gleam in her eye.

"Challenge accepted," I say, withdrawing my fingers. I then take her hand and practically drag her along the corridor in my haste to get her somewhere private.

She giggles as I hustle her into the office where Arden and Lorcan are waiting.

"I thought you wanted to be alone with me?" she teases.

"I told you, we're basically the same person, so this counts as being alone," I reply, kicking the door shut behind me and flicking the lock.

"And you two are supposed to be keeping our guests company," Cyn exclaims, narrowing her eyes at the three of us, a smile playing about her lips.

"They're fine chatting amongst themselves for ten minutes. When I snuck out they were playing Gin Rummy, and Grim was wiping the floor with them all," Arden replies, licking his lips as his gaze slowly peruses over every inch of our woman. She looks beautiful tonight in an emerald dress that skims over her curves and shows off her shapely legs, its thin straps begging to be rolled off her shoulders.

"Three minutes actually," Cyn says, arching her brow, a pretty pink glow rising up her chest.

"What?" Lorcan asks, pulling a face that makes me laugh.

"We have *three* minutes to make our woman come," I explain.

"I don't think you're going to be able to do it," she teases, lifting her brows in challenge.

"And if we do? What do we get in return?" Arden asks, climbing to his feet as he stalks towards her.

"The taste of my come on your lips?" she suggests with a smirk that has my dick twitching.

"I mean, I'll happily accept that reward," Lorcan says, undoing the top button of his shirt and licking his lips.

"As much as that *is* a great reward, that's not what I want," Arden says, flicking his gaze to me, and winking.

I know that look, and if I know Arden as well as I think I do, I'm pretty certain of what he's going to ask for.

"Okay then, if you're able to make me come in just three minutes, what do you want in return?" Cyn asks, taking a step back towards the door as Arden stalks towards her.

"At some point in the future, you're going to run and we're going to chase you," he says, his voice a dark rumble of need that spills into the air between us.

"And what will happen when you catch me?" Cyn asks, her

lips parting on a ragged breath as Arden pins her against the door with his body.

"We're going to fuck you until you see stars, and whilst we do that we're going to put a baby in your belly."

"Fuck, yes," Lorcan and I agree in unison.

"A baby?" she whispers.

"I want us to make a family of our own, Cyn," Arden says, cupping her face. "Do you want that?"

"Yes," she replies without hesitation, the biggest most beautiful smile on her face. "I want you to put a baby in me. I want us to be a family more than anything."

I look at Lorcan and fucking smile so hard my cheeks ache. He returns my smile, laughter bubbling up his throat.

"If only Tom and Connall knew what we were discussing, they might change their minds and shoot us dead for having a baby out of wedlock," I say.

"Who said anything about not being married first?" Arden asks.

"Wait, what? *How*?" Cyn asks, looking between the three of us, a mixture of joy and confusion on her face. "It's against the law to marry more than one man, and I'm sorry I won't choose. I can't. I love you all equally."

"You *can* admit that you love me more," Lorcan says with a naughty grin.

"Stop it," Cyn replies, laughter in her voice. "I love all of you and I wish I could marry all of you, but that's just not possible."

"I've already thought about that," Arden replies. "There's nothing to stop us making our own vows in front of the people we care about the most. I don't need an official piece of paper to know that what we have is a true, everlasting love. All I want is a commitment from each of us. This will be a marriage of four souls that are perfect for each other." Arden looks between us. "We can do it tomorrow, before our friends go home. What do you say?"

"I say hell to the fucking yes," I reply, my heart damn near bursting out of my ribcage.

"Lorcan?" Arden asks.

"Absolutely. I'm in. I love you. All of you, so fucking much."

Arden nods, smiling, his gaze falling to Cyn. "Cyn?"

She shakes her head in disbelief, her smile so wide it's like the sun has fallen from the sky and lit up her face in a beautiful golden light. "Yes. Yes. Yes," she laughs.

"Oh thank fuck," Arden replies, pressing a lingering kiss against her mouth. "But first we've got a challenge to win." He takes her hand and walks with her to the desk, patting it. "Up you get, future wife. Spread those legs for me," he says.

"Whatever you say, future *husband*," Cyn replies, sliding her arse onto the table and resting her palms against the wood as she slowly parts her thighs.

"Good girl," Arden whispers, pressing a kiss against her bare shoulder as he smooths his palms slowly up her thighs, dragging the dress upwards until it gathers around her hips and reveals a thin strip of white cotton covering her pussy. "So fucking beautiful."

My dick throbs as he lowers his head between her thighs and runs the tip of his nose up her crease, breathing in. "You smell like heaven," he says, drawing upright and cupping the back of her head, kissing her deeply. "It fucking makes me so happy that I'll get to call you mine every day for the rest of my life."

"Ours," Lorcan adds.

"Ours," I agree.

"Yours," Cyn says, heat creeping up her chest as love seeps into her eyes. "You know it's already been longer than three minutes." She chews on her lip, holding in a smile as Arden rounds the desk and reaches into the top drawer.

"The three minutes doesn't start until I say so," he replies lightheartedly as he pulls out a tube of lube, locking eyes with me. This time it's my fucking cheeks heating.

"Bossy," Cyn laughs, unaware of what Arden has in mind.

"Lorcan get over here!" Arden demands and we all laugh.

Lorcan jumps to his feet, smirking. "Are you not up for the challenge, then Arden?"

"Oh, I'm up for it," he replies. "And I know exactly what will get Cyn off in under three minutes."

"Yeah, and that's my tongue on her pussy," Lorcan replies, as he lowers himself in front of Cyn, and pulls her knickers off placing them on the table. She chews on her lip as she stares down at him, her gaze heated. I don't know about Lorcan, but when she looks at me like that I damn near combust.

"That, *and* her watching me fuck Carrick," Arden replies, cocking a finger to me as more heat rushes to my dick. This isn't exactly what I planned, but fuck, I'll take it.

"You don't play fair," Cyn gasps, her nipples beading beneath her dress as I lock eyes with her. The heat in them makes my dick impossibly hard. She's turned on at the thought, and I couldn't love her any more for it. There's no jealousy in her eyes, only love, pure and undiluted.

She loves us. We love her. We love each other. In the end that's all that matters.

"Let the challenge begin," Lorcan says, grasping Cyn's hips and pulling her to the edge of the table. He swipes at her once with the length of his tongue, pulling a low moan deep from her chest before casting a look at us over his shoulder. "I've got this covered, just make sure you live up to your part, yes?"

"Don't worry, in a couple of minutes Cyn will be coming so hard the whole of Ireland will hear her screams not just our guests," Arden promises, unbuckling his jeans and flicking off the cap of his lube.

"Oh God, *yes*," Cyn hisses, her eyes wide, her pussy already wet with arousal as she fixes her gaze on Arden and me.

Reaching inside my trousers, I free my cock, allowing my trousers and boxers to fall past my knees. Fisting myself, I watch Lorcan lower his mouth back to Cyn's pussy and begin eating her the fuck out.

Cyn groans, her eyes billowing with lust as Arden presses a kiss against my neck and slides a lube covered finger gently inside my arse.

"Fuck," I hiss." My dick jerks in my hands as he presses two thick fingers inside of me, slicking me up, scissoring them, getting me ready.

"Time starts now," he says over my shoulder, before grasping me around the back of my neck and urging me to rest my hands on the table right next to where Lorcan is busy eating Cyn out.

God the sounds she makes, and the way she lets out these little pants of pleasure as she watches Arden line his cock up against my hole, is such a fucking turn on. My dick swells in my hand, becoming an aching, pulsing, throbbing organ that's just begging for release. My balls tighten up inside of me, fizzing with fucking sensation.

"Keep making those noises, Cyn, and I'll come before Arden can even get his dick inside of me."

"Don't you dare," Arden snarls, swirling the puckered hole with his finger, making sure it's nice and lubed up. "You'll come when I say you come," he adds, before pressing the tip of his dick inside my arse, his swollen tip edging past the tight ring of muscle. It's a searingly painful sensation that quickly becomes ecstasy as my body accommodates his girth and pleasure builds in the base of my spine.

"Fuuuuuuck," I heave out, by heart banging almost out of my chest as I lock eyes with Cyn and she whimpers, her cheeks flush, her chest heaving.

"Use her panties, Carrick. Wrap the drenched material around your cock and when I fuck your arse think about how tight her pussy is going to be when she comes for Lorcan. I know I will be," Arden says, sliding inside of me inch by toe-curling inch.

He seats himself there, pressing up inside of me. I can feel the ridges of his cock hit my prostate and my dick fucking leaks come just from the pressure.

"Damn it, Arden," I pant as he rolls his hips just a little and I fist my cock tightly with her knickers.

"Oh God, please," Cyn chokes out as she flicks her gaze

from my face to my dick.

"Don't beg Him, He doesn't listen to sinners. If you want to come, beg me for it, Cyn. Beg Carrick and Lorcan. We want to hear you say it," Arden commands.

Lorcan chuckles against Cyn's core, the wet, sloppy sound of his tongue fucking her pussy heaven to my ears as Arden pulls back out of me, and I let out an undistinguishable sound as Cyn chokes out her order.

"Fuck, Carrick. Make him come," she says with a moan, her legs beginning to shake.

"Your wish is my command," Arden replies, then rails me against the fucking desk.

Hard and fast, he fucks me, one strong arm helping me to stay semi-upright whilst he pounds into me over and over again. His pelvis hits my arse, his balls smacking against my skin as he pushes me forward. The sound of our hips meeting and the wetness of Cyn's pleasure as Lorcan eats her out is something I will treasure forever.

"Fuck that feels good," I rasp, so fucking close to coming, my cock almost as full as my heart.

I love them all so fucking much. My family. My best friends, my lovers. My Cyn, my heart.

"Yes, oh please, yes, Lorcan, like that," Cyn whimpers, her gaze flicking between the three of us.

"You want me to lick you like this?" Lorcan asks, his mouth suctioning over her clit, as he flicks her with his tongue.

"Yes, like that. Like that," she mewls, as Lorcan ups his pace, sliding a finger into Cyn's pussy.

I watch them with heavy lidded eyes as he crooks his finger

inside of her, reaching that tender spot. She gasps, then moans, her arms collapsing as she falls back onto the table.

She's so close. I am too. So fucking close.

Arden keeps up the pace, his dick hitting my prostate over and over until I can't think straight. My mind fucking tumbles into a whirl of feeling and sensation. Goddamn this feels good. So fucking good.

"Oh please. Yes. Please make me come," she begs between ragged breaths.

My beautiful witch is writhing on the desk now, her fingers wrapped in Lorcan's hair. I know how good he is with his mouth and tongue. I've felt them wrapped around my cock countless times over the years. He's a fucking expert at oral sex.

And Arden? He's an expert at knowing what we need at any given moment. He knew Cyn would be turned on by us fucking, he knew Lorcan would be the best person to eat her out, and he knew I would take his cock without hesitation.

"I'm close," Arden cries out, his control slipping now too as he thickens impossibly inside of me.

The ridges and grooves of his beautiful cock spearing me open as he fucks me with abandon.

"This is how our life will be. Fucking. Loving. Laughing. Living," Arden grinds out, slamming into me. He fucks me how I need to be fucked, how we all want to fuck Cyn: without restraint.

"Yes!" Cyn wails, almost sobbing at the pleasure building between us.

"There will be no boundaries, no walls, no rules. We'll be free to love each other in any way we choose," he continues, his arm tightening around my chest as my legs begin to fucking shake.

"Yes!" I roar, this surge of sensation centering at the base of my spine.

"I fucking love you all," Arden says, reaching up to grasps my throat, his hot breath feathering over my neck, and I know what he's about to do right before he does it.

The second his teeth sink into my skin, I'm seeing fucking stars. They explode behind my eyes in a blaze of light. "Fuck, I'm coming!" I yell as warm, thready cum fires out of my cock into Cyn's balled up knickers.

"Mhmmmm, mhmmmm, ahhhhh!" Cyn cries out as she jerks and shakes, her body practically wrapped around Lorcan's head as he laps up her come, gorging on her release.

"That's it. Fuck his face, Cyn!" I demand, and seconds later Arden's orgasm crests, his teeth digging deeper into my skin as he pumps his warmth into me, pulsing and rocking against my arse until eventually he stills, breathing hard, laughing against my back.

"Don't think I've ever come as quickly," he says after a while, kissing the bite mark, his arm loosening from around my chest as he pulls out of me slowly.

"Me either," I admit, blowing out a shaky breath as Arden swipes his silk handkerchief between my arse cheeks, cleaning me up.

"We might need to do this again, only next time I'm fucking Cyn's pussy with my tongue," Arden says, as I pull up my trousers and tuck my dick away.

"We'll have to toss a coin, because this has made me thirsty,"

I reply, still holding Cyn's knickers that are ruined now with my cum.

She slowly blinks up at us, a satisfied smile on her face. "That was... *intense*," she says, shifting into a seated position, her dress falling back over her thighs as she looks between us.

"You're telling me," Lorcan rasps out, swiping at Cyn's juices around his mouth and chin, a pained look on his face.

"You okay?" she asks, a tiny giggle releasing from her lips.

"I'm not sure. I think my dick is about to fall off," he replies with another pained laugh.

"You're gonna have to deal with that, mate," I say, handing him Cyn's ruined knickers as I glance at the bulge in his pants. "We've kept our guests waiting long enough."

He takes them from me, mouth dropping open as Arden barks out a laugh. "Hey, don't look at us like that, you got to feast on the tastiest pussy on this planet."

"But I–" he begins, his mouth slamming shut as Cyn reaches for him, cupping his dick over his trousers. She snatches the rest of his sentence from his lips as she squeezes him, pressing a kiss against his lips.

"Double or nothing?" I suggest, my dick already getting hard again at the thought of easing inside her swollen pussy.

"You've had your fun. Now go make our excuses whilst I give Lorcan his reward," she replies, arching a brow when we don't immediately leave. "Go on."

Arden chuckles, gripping my arm and dragging me from the room. The last thing I hear before I close the door behind me is the sound of a zipper being pulled down and Lorcan swearing under his breath.

27

C^{yn}

"You look beautiful," Christy says, as she looks over my shoulder and into the mirror before us. "This dress is stunning."

"Thank you. I'm still so surprised that Arden organised all of this," I reply, studying my reflection. "I had no idea."

The dress *is* stunning. Made of chiffon and silk in a pale yellow that compliments my skin tone, it has embroidered wildflowers climbing up from the bottom of the skirt. I recognise all of them, the tiny pink-white flowers of the valerian, the nodding, pale blue bell-shaped harebells, the spotted throats of the pink foxgloves, yellow buttercups and violet periwinkles to name a few. The skirt swirls around my legs as I walk, drifting over the floor in soft caress, yet the top half is as fitted as the skirt is loose. The corset is the same pale yellow silk with a plunging neckline, hugging the curve of my breasts beautifully.

"Sexy yet demure. He's completely nailed it. This dress is so you, Cyn," Christy admires, grinning.

"He did good," I reply, chewing on a smile as I look at myself, really look at myself.

I've never felt truly beautiful. As a child without a voice I'd faded into the background. I was barely seen and definitely not heard. But now? Now I feel like the centre of their universe. I feel seen, heard, and understood in a way that I never was before.

"Arden was incredibly detailed about what he wanted," Grim adds, pushing off from the wall as she strides towards me. "From the softness of the fabric to the wildflowers he chose to be embroidered on the skirt. He said those flowers blossomed in the fields near their childhood home, and now that you're their home, he wanted you to feel like you were walking through the memories they cherished as much as they cherish you."

"He said that?" I whisper, my fingers touching the delicate flowers that rise all the way up to my waist.

"He's a lot more romantic than I ever thought he could be," Grim says with a wry smile. "I've got to hand it to him, I'm impressed."

"I can't believe he's planned this whole thing. When he said he wanted to invite my family and friends to the island for the weekend, I thought it was because he wanted to appease the

O'Briens, not that he was planning a wedding, albeit an unusual one."

"Hey, a marriage is a marriage. It doesn't matter who officiates it," Grim says.

"I know that," I say with a warm smile that spreads out from my middle and wraps me up in its joyous embrace. "It's real to us, that's all that matters."

"Did Carrick and Lorcan know?" Christy asks me.

"Not until yesterday when we..." My voice trails off and my skin heats at the memory of what happened in the office between us. God, I was loud. My cheeks heat to unbearable levels. "About that–"

Grim and Christy exchange looks and laugh.

"Hey, don't worry about it," Grim says, waving away my concerns. "We've all been there. I've had loads of people walking in on Beast and me shagging over the years, the most memorable was when Cleveland walked in on me spread across my office desk with Beast's head between my legs."

I gasp, covering the laugh bursting out of my mouth. "Who's Cleveland?"

"A member of my security detail," Grim replies, adding a little blush to her cheeks. Not that she needs any makeup, she's naturally beautiful just like her sister Christy.

"Oh my God. What did you do?"

"I told him to get the fuck out."

Christy bursts out laughing, and I follow suit. That warmth I feel inside growing in the presence of these women. It feels good to be happy. To have friends like this. People I can trust.

"What about Tom and Connall? Not sure they'd be as okay with it as the rest of you."

Christy giggles. "Connall was already half-cut and Tom kept his fingers in his ears for the most part."

"The Masks, however, had a smirk on their faces the whole time. I'm pretty sure it's the first time I've seen them actually crack a smile," Grim adds, teasing Christy.

"They smile all the time," she retorts with a roll of her eyes.

Grim snorts. "Yeah when they're balls deep in your–"

"Whoa!" Christy shouts, holding up her hands and waving them at her sister. "That's enough of that talk, thank you very much."

"The point is," Grim continues as she glides on some deep red lipstick to finish her look, "Is that we're all adults. We all fuck, and we enjoy it, loudly. There's nothing wrong with that."

"Loudly?" I question, my cheeks burning.

"*Loudly*," she replies with a grin.

"Oh God," I reply, wincing.

"There's that name again. You know us fellas might get a complex if you women keep shouting out his name whenever you're feeling emotional," Beast says as he steps into the room looking very suave in a pair of black trousers, shiny black dress shoes and a crisp white shirt.

"Would you prefer if we cried out to Jesus?" Grim asks, striding over to him and straightening his tie.

He gives her a wide grin then plants a kiss on her newly painted lips, that gets hot and heavy in less than two seconds flat. "Babe, given the choice I'd have you crying out *my* name at every damn moment," Beast replies, smirking, his lips stained red.

Grim swipes her thumb over his mouth. "Well if you're lucky, I'll be hollering your name all night long later. We've got to do *something* to drown out this lot because I have a feeling it's gonna get noisy."

"Just remember to close the door whilst you're getting down and dirty, I don't need to see Beast's hairy arse again," Christy adds with a smirk.

"You've seen Beast's arse?" I whisper, eyes wide.

"It was in a vision, so it doesn't bloody count," Beast says, pointing a finger at Christy. "Not to mention the fact that I do *not* have a hairy arse. This beauty is fuzz free." He slaps his arse to make a point.

Christy giggles, cutting a look at Grim who bursts out laughing. It's so contagious that I can't help but join in until we're all laughing at Beast, who is scowling with his thick arms crossed against his chest.

"Oh love, we're just joking around. Come here... *Gorilla*," Grim whispers loudly enough for us to hear. We all burst out laughing again.

"I'll give you bloody *Gorillas in the Mist* in a minute when you see the back of me and my hairy arse as I head out to the jetty and bugger off to the mainland if you lot carry on the way you are," Beast replies with a surly expression, which only makes us laugh even more.

It feels good to laugh. To joke around with friends who are fast becoming family.

"What's so funny?" Lorcan says as he steps into the room,

then gasps as his gaze lands on me. "Cyn, you're... Fuck me, you're *stunning*."

"Get out!" Christy shrieks, "You're not supposed to see Cyn before the wedding. It's bad luck!"

"Bad luck my arse," Lorcan replies, striding over to me. He stops short, just a step away looking breathtaking in a tailored suit the colour of the deepest ocean. His hair is styled in a curtain that flops over his right eye in a way that makes me want to tug on the strands and kiss him stupid.

"You don't believe in bad luck?" I whisper, completely oblivious to anyone else in the room now that he's here and looking at me like I'm the life sustaining oxygen that he needs to breathe.

"I believe in *us* more than anything," he replies, lifting his hand to cup my cheek. "Look at you."

His thumb caresses my cheek before he lowers his mouth to mine and brushes a tender kiss over my lips. I can't help it, my fingers find the lapel of his jacket and I pull him closer, kissing him back deeply. As we kiss, the love I feel blossoms inside my chest, the petals of our friendship have already grown into something everlasting, now the roots take hold spreading through the very heart of me, forming unbreakable foundations.

We kiss for an eternity, yet not long enough, until Christy clears her throat, and we pull apart reluctantly.

"Sorry to interrupt," she says, looking between us. "But I think it's probably time we head down to the chapel."

"To get *married*," Lorcan adds in wonder, wrapping his

fingers around mine and giving me the sweetest, most goofiest grin ever.

"That's right, lover boy," Beast says with a laugh. "Look at you all love-drunk on that kiss."

"Don't forget, I've got my gun with me."

"Your gun?" I frown.

"Tattoo gun," Beast replies with a wink. "A little dickybird tells me you need three tiny butterflies tattooed onto your wedding ring finger."

I gasp. "So it's *you* who tattoos my finger? I always wondered."

"I guess so." He smiles broadly.

"When?"

"After the ceremony. Don't worry, I'll be gentle. I promise."

I beam at him. Happiness blooming inside my chest.

"Can I have a minute alone with Cyn?" Lorcan asks.

"Like you all wanted a minute last night, yeah?" Beast asks with a wink.

"*Of course*, we'll be waiting for you in the chapel," Christy says, giving me a quick peck on the cheek before ushering Grim and Beast out of the room. We can hear the three of them laughing all the way downstairs.

"So," I say, my voice trailing off, as Lorcan looks down at me with an unreadable expression.

"So," he replies, chewing on his lip.

"Was there something you wanted to say?" I ask gently.

"Arden did an amazing job with this dress and this whole surprise ceremony. He's sneaky."

"He sure is," I agree. "I'm so happy... Aren't you?"

"So fucking happy, Cyn," Lorcan is quick to reply.

"Then why do I get the sense something's bothering you?"

"Arden has organised all of this, and Carrick has his own surprise," Lorcan says, raking his hand through his hair.

"He does?" I ask. "What?"

"I won't spoil it for him. You'll have to wait and see."

"Is that what's bothering you?" I ask, pressing my hand against the centre of his chest as I look up at him. "As much as I love this dress, I would've married you all naked. I don't need gifts. I just need you. All three of you."

Lorcan laughs. "Naked might've been fun, but I'm not sure Tom or Connall would've gone for a nudist wedding."

I can't help but smile at that. "You know what I mean."

"I do," he replies, his warm hands resting on my shoulders as he looks at me intently. "But I still wanted to give you something too."

Reaching into his jacket pocket he withdraws a red velvet box and opens the lid revealing a stunning brooch of a butterfly with wings made of amber, the deep orange and red of the stone resembling flames.

"Oh wow," I exclaim, reaching out to touch the delicate wings

"You like it?"

"I do, it's beautiful."

"I wanted you to have this as a reminder, not just of my love for you, but also what this butterfly symbolises."

"What does it symbolise? I've always wondered."

"We're called the Deana-dhe not just because the fields where we grew up were filled with butterflies as beautiful as this one and the name reminded us of home, but because Deana-dhe literally translates to butterfly and fire. The butterfly symbolises the soul, and fire is transformation. You witnessed us becoming the Deana-dhe. You knew us before we stepped into that role, and you know us as the men we are today. You survived the chaotic fire of our transformation, and look at you now—stronger and more courageous than ever, as beautiful as this butterfly," he says, pinning the broach carefully over my heart.

My breath catches in my throat as I take in its beauty, and I feel my heart swell with love. "I don't know what to say."

"You don't need to say a thing, because I've always under-stood you without words," he whispers, tracing his finger along my jawline before cupping my face in his hands and kissing me tenderly on the forehead. "Every time you wear this brooch remember, that no matter what happens or wherever life takes us, our love is always here, as strong and as beautiful as this butterfly. You are mine forever, Cyn... *Ours*. Always have been... Always will be."

I blink back tears as Lorcan takes a step back from me letting out a deep sigh before taking my hand in his. "Are you ready to become Mrs Deana-dhe?" he asks me.

"Never more ready," I reply.

When we reach the chapel, Connall is waiting outside for us. He has his hands tucked into his trouser pockets with a troubled look on his face.

"Can I have a minute with Cyn?" he asks Lorcan. "This won't take long, I promise."

Lorcan nods his head. "Of course." Giving my hand a

squeeze, he presses another soft kiss to my cheek. "See you soon, okay?"

"Nothing will stop me," I reply, watching him step inside the chapel and gently close the door behind him.

"You look beautiful," Connall says, a heavy sigh drifting from his lips.

"You're sad," I reply. "Don't be. This is a happy day for me."

"I've taken from you, Cynthia. Aoife would've loved to be here today."

"And she is. In here," I reply, pressing a hand over his heart.

"I don't deserve your forgiveness."

"I've never blamed you for her death."

He places his hand over mine, curling his fingers around my palm. "Why not?"

"You made a mistake. You were a child, Connall."

"Doesn't make it any better. I took her from you, from us all."

"You have to forgive yourself. My mother wouldn't want you to punish yourself like this. That wasn't how she lived her life. She was kind, understanding. She loved my father after all."

Connall nods, his eyes glazing with tears. "You're a gift, you know that?"

"I didn't. I wasn't seen or heard for a long, long time, but I know that now. Thanks to you all."

"You'll always have a home, a family with the O'Briens. You ever need us, you call and we'll come. No questions."

"I know that, and I intend on calling, a lot. I like you. I like Tom, and I'm looking forward to meeting the rest of my family."

Connall grins, but then the smile falls and I know the guilt he feels is back. "I should tell them, shouldn't I?"

"I've thought about this a lot, and I'm not sure that on this occasion that telling the truth is the right thing to do." I sigh. "What good would it do, you telling them now? It doesn't change anything. She's gone. The truth won't bring her back, but it could put a wedge between you all and I don't want it to. Do you know what I do want?"

"What's that?" Connall asks.

"For you to be happy. Let it go, Connall. Let your guilt go and find happiness."

"You're too good for any of us, just like Aoife," he replies, drawing me into a hug.

I rest my head against his chest, only pulling apart when Tom steps out into the hallway. He frowns as he looks between us, but he doesn't question what we've been talking about or why Connall looks close to tears, he simply smiles and says, "Are you ready to get married?"

I nod. "Absolutely."

Letting me go, Connall steps back and looks over my head to his brother before dropping his gaze to me. "I know Tom won't ask, but I will. As the head of our family, and Aoife's favourite brother, will you let him walk you down the aisle?"

I smile up at Connall, looking over my shoulder at Tom who grins, bright spots of red colouring his cheeks.

"Are you blushing Uncle Tom?" I ask, smiling so wide, my cheeks hurt.

"I do believe I am," he replies with a chuckle. Then his

smile drops, and he holds his arm out for me to take, serious now. "Will you do me the honour, Cynthia?"

"Absolutely," I reply, sliding my arm through his.

Connall grins, and pushes open the doors to the tiny chapel where my friends, family, and the men I love await.

The chapel is filled with the scent of flowers and sunlight, streaming in through the windows behind the altar. I pause at the entrance, taking in the beauty before me, my breath catching in my throat. The pews are draped with white lace and lined with ivory candles, their light bouncing off every surface and creating a soft glow that has me spellbound. My gaze falls to the altar where Carrick stands singing *Fields of Gold* by Sting, his beautiful voice ringing out in harmony and filling me with so much emotion.

He smiles at me as he sings, and there's no pain in his eyes, no trauma. Just love.

Pure, undiluted, love.

My heart lurches as Tom guides me down the aisle towards Lorcan, Arden and Carrick, the soft swish of my skirt wrapping around my legs, my bare feet warm against the cool stone.

Our guests smile broadly as I pass them by. Leon and Konrad are standing either side of Christy, beaming. True, heartfelt smiles pouring over me with their love.

Grim and Beast have their arms wrapped around each other, Connall standing to their left. All of them are grinning. Beast winks as I pass by. "Stunning," he mouths.

Ahead of me Jakub waits at the altar, acting as our officiant. He grins, and his smile has the power to warm even the coldest of hearts. The power of Christy's love shines right out of him as I approach.

But even his smile can't outshine the love I feel from my men as Carrick sings the last line of the song, declaring his love for me with every word and every note. They stare at me intently, tears glistening in their eyes, companions to the ones sliding down my cheeks.

"Take care of her," Tom says, patting my hand and kissing me on the cheek before he steps to the side and takes a seat.

"Every day for the rest of our lives," Arden answers, taking my hand in his.

I can't help but smile through my tears as I look between the three of them, my gaze landing on Carrick. "That was so beautiful. Thank you for the gift of your voice."

"It was always your voice that was the gift," he replies, taking my other hand and kissing my knuckles.

"I love you all so much," I murmur, overwhelmed with emotion.

Lorcan presses a kiss against my cheek, his hand lowering to my chest as he rests it over my heart. Arden lifts my hand to his lips, as Carrick runs his thumb over the back of mine. We stand like that for a long moment, each of us silently basking in the connection we share.

The heat emanating from Lorcan's palm is electric and I can't help but smile up at him when he finally pulls away and takes Arden and Carrick's hand in his, joining us all in an unbreakable connection as we hold hands.

"We're gathered here today to celebrate the joining of these four souls, bound together by history and heartbreak, healing and patience, passion and love," Jakub begins.

"Here, here!" Beast calls out, wolf-whistling and making us all laugh.

Jakub clears his throat then continues. "Love can give us the strength to persevere through difficult times. It enables us to open up our hearts when otherwise we might not have. It is, ultimately, what brings us together and what makes us human." His gaze lifts over our heads and I know he's looking at Christy, at his brothers, the loves of his life, before he returns his gaze to us. "It's time to say your vows."

Arden lets out a shaky breath, speaking first. "I was never supposed to fall in love with an O'Farrell," he laughs, shaking his head, his amber eyes shining like liquid gold. "I pushed you away. I ran from the connection I felt the second you walked into your bedroom at Silver Oaks. I was a kid in pain, who hurt, but thanks to you, I'm a man who can love, and fuck, Cyn, I love you so damn much. I can't wait to build a home here with you. To grow a family so that when we're gone, our love will live on in them."

I give him a watery smile, unable to respond because I'm so filled to the brim with emotion. So utterly in love. Then Lorcan begins to speak, and that love just grows and grows.

"I wasn't strong enough to face my feelings, instead I hid behind Arden's and Carrick's. I let you down, Cyn. I stayed quiet when I should've spoken up," he says, fixing his gaze on mine. "Never again. I love you immeasurably. I love us. We were always meant to be. Soul mates, soul ties, or not. What we feel for each other is real and true and everlasting. I will love you in this life and the next."

A sob rises up my throat, but I'm not sad. I'm so so happy.

"Cyn," Carrick says, his thumb circling my knuckles. I meet his gaze, waiting with trembling lips and a heart bursting with joy. "When I was a kid I wanted to steal your voice. I needed to hear it by any means possible. I believed that in your voice I would find peace because I couldn't find it in mine. The truth is, I *never* hated you. I was afraid of you. Afraid of the power you held over me, over us. You didn't need to scream, or shout to get our attention. You held it with your silence, and you keep it now with your love and affection, your strength and courage. You helped me to love my voice again, and I will sing to you every day until my very last breath."

I blink back tears of joy as Jakub nods in approval before finally turning towards me expectantly. Swallowing deeply, I take a deep breath before speaking; the words pouring out of my mouth like an indelible tattoo upon our hearts.

"My loves," I begin, looking between them all in turn, "The three of you are my family, my lovers, my best friends. We're forever tied together, not by a spell cast by a witch," I say, laughing a little, "But by love, loyalty and friendship. My heart belongs to each of you completely because it knows no bounds when it comes to loving all that is you."

I pause briefly to collect my thoughts before continuing in a low whisper: "My life has been forever changed because of you—for the better–and so today I make this vow. I promise to keep loving and learning the depths of your hearts. I promise to always trust in our love, to be loyal and faithful to what we have. I will water it daily, feed it and nurture it until it grows into a field of wildflowers as beautiful as the flowers embroidered onto this dress I'm wearing now. And when our bodies return to the soil, it will sustain that field of wildflowers so that every year our love will bloom, living for all eternity. That is my solemn vow."

"Cras es noster..." they reply in unison.

Tomorrow is ours.

And so it was.

EPILOGUE

C^{yn}

T hree months later.

"W hat?" I ask softly, looking up from the delicate butterflies Beast's skilled hands inked into my skin to Arden who's standing in the doorway of the kitchen, leaning against the frame.

"You look deep in thought, what is it?" Arden asks me, his gaze flicking from my face to my brand new notebook sitting open on the kitchen table. It's already a quarter filled with new recipes, alongside drawings of the plants I've used, and a diary recording our love story since we got married three months ago.

"Just happy, that's all," I reply as the summer sun pours through the window behind me, warming the bare skin of my shoulders. It's probably the hottest day I've experienced here on the island and I love how vibrant and alive it makes me feel.

He nods, leaning against the door frame, watching me closely. "I could make you happier," he says, pushing off the door and striding towards me.

"I doubt that," I reply, twisting on the stool, turning to face him.

He grins, drawing his thumb across my bottom lip as he looks down at me. He's caught the sun working outdoors, and the slight tan of his skin suits him.

"She of little faith," he says, sliding his thumb between my lips when I smile up at him. "How about I remind you of a little bet we made not so long ago, hmm?"

"Hmmm," I reply, suctioning his thumb into my mouth, swirling it around the tip. His pupils widen, lust billowing in his eyes as I taste his skin.

He groans softly as I stand, pressing my body against his, already feeling warmth pooling between my legs, my braless breasts rubbing against his firm chest, nothing but thin cotton of my sundress and his t-shirt separating us. Withdrawing his thumb, he gently pulls at my lower lip, capturing it with his mouth, before kissing me.

I wrap one arm around his neck, my hand slipping down to the growing bulge between us. My fingers trail lightly up and down his length as I pull back, looking into his eyes, a playful glint in mine.

"It's time, Cyn," he murmurs, licking his lips, his erection growing under my gentle hand.

"Time for what?" I ask him sweetly, knowing full well what he's getting at. Excitement thrums in my veins, my blood pumping with a restless energy as I wait for him to spell it out to me.

Seconds later he does.

"It's time for you to *run*."

My breath catches as he steps aside, his expression changing to an animalistic need that seems so contrary to the happy laughter that bubbles out of my chest as I pick up the long skirt of my dress, and take off.

My first instinct is to hit a left and head outside just like I always used to do at Silver Oaks when we were kids. I run past Lorcan as he steps out of the office, a screech parting my lips as realisation dawns on his face and he lunges for me.

"You've got a one minute head start and then I'm coming for you!" he yells, his hooting laughter following me out.

Shoving open the front door, I step onto the stone pathway and make a split second decision, running towards the outhouse. I pass Carrick who's digging out a new flower bed, he looks up and I dance on the spot, my cheeks flush, excitement zipping through my body.

He drops the trowel and climbs to his feet reading my expression easily.

"Oh, fuck yes," he exclaims, flicking his gaze over his shoulder as Arden and Lorcan step out of the house.

Another squeal of happiness releases from my lips as I turn on my feet and run. My feet pounding against the grass, the salt-scented breeze rippling over my skin as I head towards the bluff and the remains of an old lookout that sits there.

I can hear them chasing me, their feet pounding the grass, their laughter growing louder as they gain on me. I know it won't be much longer before one of them catches me so I run faster, my lungs burning as adrenaline pumps through my veins.

The bluff looms closer and closer and with each step I take, the anticipation builds. I know when they catch me there will be more than just laughter; there will be lips, hands and bodies tangling together in raw desire. I can almost feel Arden's arm around my waist as he kisses my neck, Lorcan's mouth feasting on my pussy and Carrick's tongue dancing with mine in a passionate kiss.

I skid to a stop just at the top of the bluff, hiding amongst the ruins of the old lookout, shading me from the heat of the summer sun. Knowing there is no place to go, I spin around to face them with a wide grin on my face, breathless but exhila-rated by the thrill of being caught. Knowing what comes next makes me quiver with pleasure.

Arden is the first to reach me, pulling me into his arms tightly as he wraps his hand around my waist and slams his mouth against mine in an urgent kiss that leaves us both panting for more. He slowly steps back with a mischievous smirk on his face only to have Lorcan take his place. His lips find mine hungrily and without hesitation, while Carrick steps up behind us both placing hot kisses along my shoulder blade as his body presses against mine. My breath hitches as Lorcan's voice pierces through the lust-filled haze clouding my mind.

"Let's get rid of these clothes," he says urgently, tugging off his shirt and throwing it to the ground, his trainers, shorts and socks quickly following suit. Gripping his erection, he moves into the shade, eyeing me with a heavy dose of desire as he says; "My dick needs the shade of your pussy, *wife.*"

A roar of laughter fills the air as Carrick and Arden follow suit, eagerly undressing themselves before turning their attention towards me. Smiles spread across their faces as they circle around me like hungry lions ready to devour their prey.

"Off," Carrick says, tearing at my clothing with eager fingers until I'm left standing in a pile of shredded fabric at my feet.

"I liked that dress," I pout.

"We'll buy you ten more," Lorcan says, his finger trailing down the centre of my chest, swirling around my belly button before hooking under the waistband of my knickers, peeling them slowly down my legs. "Or maybe we won't. I like the thought of you walking around naked," he mutters, dropping to his knees before me and burying his nose in my pussy, breathing me in.

"Lorcan," I gasp, grasping the back of his head and shamelessly spreading my legs, needing what he so clearly wants to give.

"I agree. You naked all the time would be fucking delicious," Arden says, circling behind me as he wraps his arm around my waist, kissing and nibbling my neck whilst Lorcan eats me out.

"Fuck yes," Lorcan mumbles against my pussy, his hand

reaching up as he squeezes my breast, rolling my nipple between his finger and thumb.

I gasp, sensation building, heat pooling between my legs as my pussy pulsates around Lorcan's skilled tongue.

"Ohhhh, this is it, isn't it?" Carrick asks, fisting his engorged cock as he steps towards us.

"This is it," Arden agrees as Carrick presses his mouth against mine and fucks me with his tongue.

It's only then I realise what they mean.

This is the picture Arden drew all those years ago when we were kids. He'd seen our future, had known what was coming, and here we are playing it out in the shade of these ruins on the island we call home.

It doesn't take long for them to drag me down onto the grass, our laughter and hungry moans of desire lifted into the air only to be lost beneath the gentle crash of waves fifty feet below us. We stay there like that for hours; touching and tasting each other until there's nothing left but sensation radiating from every fibre of our being, until all that remains are four bodies entwined beneath the stars above us.

That night we sowed the seeds of our love with another kind of magic, the kind that formed a life deep within my belly.

Nine months later our little girl was born, a little girl we called Faith, and as I held her in my arms we made a promise that her life will be blessed with happiness, joy and most of all unconditional love. The same kind of eternal love that we will feel for each other in this life and beyond.

The End.

ACKNOWLEDGMENTS

Thank you so much for reading Cyn and the Deana-dhe's love story! I have to admit, this story ended up being a lot darker than I'd anticipated, particularly when it came to the traumatic experience that Cyn, Faith and the other women experienced at the hands of the Skull Brotherhood.

Truthfully, it surprised me.

How? I hear you ask. I'm the author, I should know what's going to happen in my books, right?

Well, yes and no.

I am what is called a 'panster' writer. This literally means I do not plot my books. I have a vague idea of where I want a story to go, and then the characters take me on a journey and their story unfolds. Because of this I actually struggled a great deal with Faith's storyline. Ask my PA Courtney who I went back and forth with over the fate of Faith. I STRUGGLED.

When I met her character I desperately wanted her to live. Then I got to the night of the 'celebration', and she didn't. I wrote that scene and sobbed.

That was *hard*.

Probably one of the hardest scenes I've ever written.

And like some movies, I actually wrote her an alternate

ending where both she and her baby survived. I kept writing that story, but no matter how many times I tried to give Faith a happily ever after it just didn't feel honest. In the version where Faith and her baby survived I felt like I was being safe, avoiding difficult subjects. It's scary to write something that could negatively impact a reader, but I never write something just for the shock factor.

I write honestly, and with intention.

As cliche as it might be, sometimes bad things do happen to good people, and it's horrible and heart wrenching and so fucking hard to digest, but as I kept writing this version, that was a theme that bubbled to the surface. For better or worse, I knew it was important not to sugarcoat it.

Life *is* fucking unfair, but on the flip side it's also beautiful and worth living for.

Cyn struggled coming to terms with the loss of her friend and her unborn child, as much as I did writing this book.

Yes, this story is about loss, grief, trauma and tragedy, but ultimately it's about the healing power of love, friendship and found family.

I hope that shines through.

Thank you for reading.

Much love

Bea Paige.

ABOUT THE AUTHOR

Bea Paige lives a very secretive life in London.

She likes red wine and Haribo sweets (preferably together) and occasionally swings around poles when the mood takes her.

Bea loves to write about love and all the different facets of such a powerful emotion. When she's not writing about love and passion, you'll find her reading about it and ugly crying.

Bea is always writing, and new ideas seem to appear at the most unlikely time, like in the shower or when driving her car.

ALSO BY BEA PAIGE

The Deana-dhe Duet (dark reverse harem)

1 Debts & Diamonds

2 Curses & Cures

Grim & Beast's Duet (M/F second-chance, bodyguard romance)

#1 Tales You Win

#2 Heads You Lose

Their Obsession Duet (dark reverse harem)

#1 The Dancer and The Masks

#2 The Masks and The Dancer

Academy of Stardom

(friends-to-enemies-lovers reverse harem)

#1 Freestyle

#2 Lyrical

3 Breakers

4 Finale

Academy of Misfits

(bully/academy reverse harem)

#1 Delinquent

#2 Reject

#3 Family

#4 Academy of Misfits box set

Finding Their Muse

(dark contemporary reverse harem)

#1 Steps

#2 Strokes

#3 Strings

#4 Symphony

#5 Finding Their Muse box set

The Brothers Freed Trilogy

(contemporary reverse harem)

#1 Avalanche of Desire

#2 Storm of Seduction

#3 Dawn of Love

#4 Brothers Freed box set

Contemporary Standalone

Beyond the Horizon

For all up to date book releases please visit

www.beapaige.co.uk